The New Number One

Titles from Geoffrey Lewis:

Flashback
ISBN 978-0-9545624-0-3

Strangers
ISBN 978-0-9545624-1-0

Winter's Tale
ISBN 978-0-9545624-2-7

Cycle
ISBN 978-0-9545624-3-4

Starlight
ISBN 978-0-9545624-5-8

A Boy Off The Bank
ISBN 978-0-9545624-6-5

A Girl At The Tiller
ISBN 978-0-9545624-7-2

The New Number One
ISBN 978-0-9545624-8-9

The New Number One

Geoffrey Lewis

SGM
Publishing

ISBN 978-0-9545624-8-9

Printed and bound in the UK by
CPI Antony Rowe, Chippenham SN14 6LH

First published in Great Britain in 2009 by

SGM Publishing
35 Stacey Avenue, Wolverton, Milton Keynes, Bucks MK12 5DN
info@sgmpublishing.co.uk
www.sgmpublishing.co.uk

About The Author

Geoffrey Lewis was born in Oxford, in 1947. Educated at the City's High School, and Hatfield University (then a polytechnic), he has since followed a varied career, including spells as a research chemist, security guard, and professional photographer. After many years in the motor trade, and eight years as the owner and captain of a canal-based passenger boat, he is now semi-retired and concentrating upon writing.

The author, Geoffrey Lewis, on the *Nutfield*

After a childhood spent close to the Oxford Canal, his love of the waterways led him to live aboard a narrowboat on the Grand Union Canal for sixteen years. Now back on dry land, he lives in Wolverton, a stones-throw from the towpath, and recently took on the duties of Captain on the historic pair – *Nutfield* and *Raymond* – which are to be seen at many waterways events throughout the year.

Photographer, bell-ringer, real ale drinker, and American car enthusiast, he is currently engaged upon a number of new writing projects including more stories set in the working days of England's canals.

Acknowledgements

Rather than try to pick out some names from the plethora of people who have, knowingly or otherwise, helped me with this trilogy of stories, I think now it might be more honest of me to offer a broad thank-you to the people of the waterways, both ancient and modern!

To those of today who, like myself, have developed a love of England's canals which has led them to delve into their history and then to dispense that accumulated knowledge to others, whether by written or spoken means. I have enjoyed the fruit of their labours, sitting at home and reading their words, or listening to them talk of their wisdom, frequently over a welcome glass of ale in some waterside bar.

And especially to those of yesterday, the generations of working boat men and women who lived for real the life I have tried so poorly to describe in these pages. Men, women and children who were for so long despised and derided by those who made their lives 'on the bank', whose working lives contributed so much to England's life and industry over two hundred years. Late in the day it may be now that their way of life has vanished forever, but it is good now to see those who remain being at last treated with the respect they have long deserved. It has been my privilege to meet a good number of them, and I am proud to have been privy to some of their tales, and to have been allowed to pick their brains from time to time.

And so it seems only fitting that for this final volume of my story, I dedicate this book:
To the People of the Boats.
We will never see their like again; let us never forget them.

Introduction

The Inland Waterways Association was inaugurated in February, 1946, at a meeting in Gower Street, in London. It was the inspiration of two like-minded men, Robert Aickman and Tom Rolt, canal enthusiasts who were distressed at the state our waterways were being allowed to fall into after six years of war; two men who first met on a narrowboat at the top of Tardebigge Locks in August 1945, while the war in the Pacific was still raging.

Over the sixty-two years since then, it has grown to become not only a huge, democratically-run organisation of people who love Britain's waterways, but an influential force in their preservation and restoration – many of the canals we can enjoy today, whether it is as boaters, anglers, walkers, naturalists, cyclists, or just casual visitors, are there to be enjoyed because of the efforts of the Inland Waterways Association.

The spark of an idea, which was to become the story of *The Boy Off The Bank*, had been with me for some years before it began to germinate, and it was during that process that it occurred to me that 2006, the year when I planned to have it ready for publication, would be the I.W.A.'s diamond jubilee. So it seemed only fitting that a book which tells of the canals in the years immediately before the founding of the Association should commemorate that significant anniversary.

This was followed by *A Girl At The Tiller*, which covers the end of the war and the start of nationalisation, and now – the last of the trilogy – *The New Number One*.

Geoffrey Lewis
January 2009

Chapter One

Mabel Oldroyd creaked to her feet in the private parlour at the back of the house, and made her way through in response to the ring of the doorbell. Norman would be in the kitchen, washing up after dinner – not too onerous a task, on this Sunday in September 1948, as they had only two couples staying over the weekend. Maybe Annie, three doors down, was right, and they should permit children again; but they weren't getting any younger, and the thought of youngsters clattering around the place, buckets and spades in the hallway (not to mention sand everywhere...) was more than Mabel wanted to face at her time of life.

Most of these old houses by the waterfront, once proud Victorian homes, had now become boarding-houses – those that hadn't been turned into flats. She and Norman had run the Seaview Guest House since way before the War, taking it over from her parents when they had retired to the little cottage along the coast. They'd both passed away now, of course – and one day, she and Norman would move to the cottage, when they decided to sell up. No children to pass it on to – a flicker of sadness crossed Mabel's homely face, at the memory of Ruth, their only daughter, who'd died in a Nazi attack on Felixstowe where she'd been stationed with the Wrens, as she walked along the hall.

She opened the front door:

'Good afternoon?' The couple standing there both smiled at her; the young man, his arm around the girl's waist, replied:

'Good afternoon – Mrs Oldroyd?'

'That's me – you'll be Mr Baker, will you?' His smile grew warmer as he nodded; she beckoned them inside, ushered them into the guests' parlour, with its big bay window and views of the sea. The couple looked around them, a gentle smile on the man's face, while his girl looked almost nervous; Mabel waved them to the comfortable old armchairs and sat down herself:

'Welcome to Seaview, Mr Baker, Mrs Baker.' At this, the girl blushed and glanced up at her husband who chuckled:

'We're still getting used ter that, Mrs Oldroyd! Oi'm Moichael, 'n this is 'Arriet. We only got wed yesterday, yeh see.' Mabel nodded:

'Yes – Mr Vickers told me when he booked you in. He and his wife and children used to come here regularly, before the war, but we've only seen Ben and Olive once since. I suppose the girls are all grown up now.' Harriet, her nervousness eased by their hostess' chatty manner, relaxed and smiled as she went on: 'You two actually work on the boats, do you?'

'That's roight. We roon a pair o' boats on the Loonon ter Birnigum roon.' Mabel smiled at them:

'It must be a fascinating life! We get a number of boaters here, thanks to Ben Vickers. Now – let me show you to your room.' She stood up and led them out into the hall again: 'I've put you in the front room, on the top floor – it's got a lovely view out over the sea. I hope you don't mind the stairs?' Michael chuckled again:

'We'll manage! Oi used ter live in a house, when Oi was small, boot Oi 'aven't slept oopstairs since Oi was ten – 'Arriet's lived in the boats all 'er loife!'

'This must seem very strange to you, my dear?' Mabel turned to address Harriet as she led them up the stairs; Harriet smiled back:

'Oi've been in 'ouses, oonce or twoice before – it's all a bit of an adventure, fer me! Yeh've got so mooch room!' It was Mabel's turn to laugh:

'Yes – Norman and I have visited Mr Vickers, once, and he showed us the boats. I'll never know how you manage in those tiny cabins!'

In the front upstairs room, they assured Mabel that they would be quite comfortable, thank you; she left them to settle in, unpacking their few things from the battered old attaché case borrowed from Henry Caplin, Harriet's father.

Michael slipped off his heavy jacket, dropped it on the bed which seemed to them to occupy at least half an acre, and went to gaze out at the view. Harriet, in the same pretty blue flowered frock she had worn for her wedding, slipped her arm around his waist:

'It's so beautiful, Moikey! The sea goes on fer ever, doosn' it?' He laughed: 'Not quoite, loove! Boot it is pretty spectac'lar, ain' it?'

''Ave yeh been ter the seasoide before, Moikey?'

'A coopl'a toimes, when Oi was little, 'fore Oi left 'ome.'

'Before yeh coom on the boats?'

'Yeah. With moy Mum 'n Dad...' She looked up at his face:

'Yeh miss 'em, Moikey?' He hesitated:

'Not really. Oh, Oi'd 'ave loiked moy Mum ter know yew, 'n yew 'er. Boot she's gone, 'n nothin' can 'elp that. 'Im – 'e joost used ter swear 'n shout, 'n knock oos about, me 'n 'er both. Oi ain't sorry 'e's dead.' He looked down at her, smiled gently: 'Boot that's all a long toime ago. Things are diff'rent, now, eh?' She smiled back:

'Mm-hm.' He raised his eyes to the view again, spoke contemplatively:

'Oi've got a new Dad, 'n a loife Oi loove. Moy sister's with me, 'n little Carrie – 'n now Oi've got yew: Moy woife!'

'Are yeh 'appy, Moikey?'

'Oh, yes!' His voice betrayed his certainty; he smiled down at her again: ''Ow 'bout yew?' Her arm tightened about his waist:

'Couldn' be 'appier!'

Chapter Two

'Yeh'll do no sooch thing, Albert Baker!' Fourteen-year-old Ginny stood beside the boat, in the dungarees she favoured while they were working, hands on her hips. The old boatman, her unofficially-adoptive father of six years, smiled ruefully and subsided into the hatches of the Sycamore as she went on: 'Las' toime yeh went lock-wheelin' yeh ended oop in the 'ospital!' Her forceful tones couldn't quite disguise the hitch in her voice at her last words.

'H'okay, Oi give in!' Alby threw up his hands in submission. And, he had to admit, she was right – back in the spring, he'd suffered a heart attack at the Three Locks, near the village of Soulbury, which had resulted in the two girls making a spectacular dash for help, all the way to Sister Mary at Stoke Bruerne, on their own – Mikey had been in hospital himself, with appendicitis. Now, with the boy away on his honeymoon, they were down to three again, which was why Alby had intended to take some of the heavier work off of the girls' shoulders. But Carrie, standing beside Ginny with a big grin on her face, backed up the older girl:

'Tha's roight, Dad – yew leave the lockin' ter oos, we can manage!'

'All roight – get goin' then or oos'll be 'ere all day!'

The Sycamore and the Antrim, Alby's pair of boats, stood by the towpath above the top lock of Long Buckby flight. Loaded with cases of HP Sauce, destined for Fellows, Morton & Clayton's warehouses at City Road Basin in the centre of London, the boats were resplendent in their red and green livery, brasses gleaming, the cloths spotless. As proud of their turn-out as any boaters, Alby's crew had made extra-sure of their smartness the day before, in honour of Michael's wedding in Braunston's parish church. Now, they were continuing with the trip – Michael and Harriet would join them in London after their few days break, in time to load for the return journey.

An uphill British Waterways pair emerged from the lock, their captain waving a greeting with a cheery ''Ow d'yer do' as he passed. Alby threw the clutch rod in as Ginny pushed the fore-end of the ready-breasted boats out and steered them into the lock; the girls pushed the gates shut as he stepped off onto the lockside and hurried to the bottom gate to wind up the paddles. As the boats descended to the roar of water running through the open paddles, Ginny hopped onto their old bicycle and set off to prepare the next lock of the seven; as the weight of the water came off the bottom gates, Alby and Carrie, leaning on the balance beams, felt them give and swung them open. Alby jumped nimbly down onto the cabin-top and drove the boats out; Carrie stepped onto the butty as it passed under the Watling Street bridge.

The process was repeated at the next lock, and the next, until at last they emerged from the bottom lock, under the gaze of the railway embankment, and set off along the sixteen-mile pound to Blisworth Tunnel and Stoke Bruerne.

It had been a late start, that Sunday. Most of the other boaters, Harriet's family, the Wardens, the Hanneys, and all who had stopped in Braunston to wish the newly-wed couple well, had got away at first light, but Alby and the girls had waited to see Michael and Harriet off on the train to Great Yarmouth. Now, eager to make up lost time, they flew along the pound as fast as the silted channel would allow. Twenty minutes in the pitch dark of Blisworth Tunnel; half an hour down the seven locks of Stoke Bruerne; ninety minutes to Cosgrove Lock; they tied, tired but happy, by

Great Linford wharf, not long after darkness had descended. Dinner, one of Ginny's usual excellent stews, had been taken on the pound above Cosgrove; now, they strolled over to the Nags Head for a quick drink before retiring.

'We'll not stop long – Oi want ter get away sharp in the mornin'.' Alby was feeling slightly fretful about the lost time still. Carrie smiled at him over her lemonade:

'We can be in City Road day after termorrer, can' we, Gin?' Ginny grinned at the ten-year-old she now thought of as her younger sister:

''Course we can! Boot not if Dad knocks 'imself oop agen.' She looked pointedly at Albert, who chuckled:

'All roight, point teken! Oi'll do as Oi'm told!' He looked from one to the other of them, and felt the familiar swell of pride in his heart; to change the subject, he said: 'Oi wonder 'ow Moikey 'n 'Arriet are getting on?'

'Oi bet they're 'avin' a grand toime,' Carrie said enviously, 'Oi mean, off boy the seasoide, no work teh do – 'n the weather's grand fer 'em, ain't it?'

* * *

The subjects of their thoughts were enjoying a last stroll along the seafront after supper. The night was not cold; arm-in-arm, they paused to gaze out over the gentle swell, listening to the soft rustle of the waves, savouring the ozone in the air; Michael looked down at his young bride, love shining in his eyes:

''Arrie?' She raised her face to him, and he saw that love reflected: 'What are yeh thinkin'?' She looked back at the ocean:

'It's so lovely, isn' it? So diff'rent from the cut.'

'Aye. Oi'd forgotten 'ow noice it is.' He hesitated: 'D'yeh wish we could stay?' She looked at him, considering:

'No – not really. It is noice 'ere – boot it isn' 'ome, is it? 'N what would we do?' He laughed softly:

'Per'aps Oi could be a fisherman!' She laughed with him:

'No yeh couldn'! Yeh'd miss the cut, 'n yer Dad, 'n the girls!'

'Yeh're roight, Oi couldn' leave the boats. Oi wonder 'ow they're getting on?' Harriet gave his arm a gentle shake:

'They're doin' quoite well without oos, Oi'm sure!'

'Yeah, Oi s'pose yeh're roight. Boot Oi can' 'elp woorryin' 'bout Dad, with 'is bad 'eart.'

''E'll be foine – Ginny'll mek sure as 'e don' do too mooch, yeh know what she's loike with 'im!' Michael laughed:

'Tha's true!'

'Moikey...' Harriet sounded thoughtful: ''Ow old is yer Dad?' Her question gave him pause for thought, as well:

'Oi don' roightly know – never thought ter ask. 'N 'e's your Dad 'n all, now yeh're moy Missus!' It was Harriet's turn to laugh, her joy echoing in her voice:

'Oi s'pose 'e is, at that! Now stop woorryin', Moikey – Let's h'enjoy ar 'oliday!' A sparkle rose in her eyes which was not entirely due to the street-lamps: 'Let's get back – we should be workin' on the next generation o' Bakers!'

He slipped an arm around her waist, drew her close and kissed her cheek: 'Aye, mebbe yeh're roight – wouldn' do ter be neglectin' our duty...'

Chapter Three

When the gathered boating clans had scattered from Braunston in the dawn after Michael's wedding, two other pairs of Fellows, Morton & Clayton boats had set away northward. As smart, as spotless as Alby Baker's pair, they worked together, running butty as the boaters would have it, despite carrying different cargoes to different destinations. Bill Hanney, with Vi, his wife, and eighteen-year-old Stevie, had a load of tinned goods for New Warwick Wharf, part of the FMC depot at Birmingham's Fazeley Street; his oldest son, Billy, whose crew consisted of his young wife Sylvie and the sixteen-year-old Kim Warden, were carrying aluminium ingots for a foundry on the Soho Loop of the Birmingham Canal Navigations.

They made good time – along the stretch of canal shared with the Oxford route, then north from Wigrams Turn; down Wigrams three, Stockton flight, then the more spread-out locks which dropped the Grand Union into the valley. Uphill again, through The Cape, then Hatton Twenty-One; they tied for the night outside The Black Boy, close to the town of Knowle and just short of the five locks.

Inevitably, conversation in the bar turned upon thoughts of Michael and Harriet. All of the Hanney family retained a kind of proprietary interest in Michael – it had been Billy and his father who had rescued him from the freezing water of the winter canal as a ten-year-old kid, and Stevie had ever since been his closest friend. They drank to his health; they drank to his good fortune – as if they and others had not done so in sufficient volume over the last two days – and they drank to the prospect of a new little Baker, in due course:

'It'll be good fer Alby, teh 'ave grand-kids,' Vi opined.

'Ar, it will 'n all!' her husband agreed: ''E moost 'ave about given oop that oidea when Alex was killed.'

'Yeah – Oo'd 'ave thought it, when we buried 'is missus, eh?'

''E said ter me a whoile ago, it's loike 'e'd been given a whole new chance. Furst Moikey, then Ginny 'n now little Carrie! Yeh woonder if he's gonna pick oop any more kiddies!'

'Oh, Oi 'ope not, Bill – 'e ain't gettin' any younger, 'n with 'is bad 'eart...'

'Oi s'pose yeh're roight. Boot if 'Arriet can give 'im a few grand-kids, 'e'll be over the moon, eh?'

''Course 'e will! 'N ther's Ginny, yet – she'll be gettin' in tow one day.' Bill looked at his youngest son:

'Is that roight, Stevie?' The boy blushed:

''Ow should Oi know?' This raised a laugh around the table – it was common knowledge that he and Michael's sister were sweet on each other.

'Oh, give 'em anoother coopl'a years, Mr 'Anney – she's only fourteen!' Kim's remark raised another chuckle; Vi gave him a thoughtful look, but all she said was: 'They'll all sort 'emselves out in toime, Bill.'

'Where's little Josh, Mum?' Sylvie asked; Vi chuckled:

''E's sound asleep! Wore out after yestiday, 'e is!'

'It was good to see him and Carrie together at the wedding, wasn't it?'

'Ar – they've both of 'em coom on since after their folks doied,' Bill agreed.

'They drowned in that accident in Regent's Canal Dock, didn't they?' He nodded, as she went on: 'It's a shame they can't be together all the time, don't you think?' Vi looked at her thoughtfully:

'Aye, it is, girl. Boot, at the toime, it seemed loike the best thing fer 'em. Oi mean, she 'ad a thing about Moikey – yer know as 'e saved 'er loife, a coopl'a years before?' Sylvie smiled:

'Yes – he gets all grumpy if you even mention it!' That got a laugh around the table – they all knew how sensitive Michael was about what they thought of as his heroics.

'So, yeh see, it was best fer 'er ter stay with 'im, with Alby 'n Ginny. Boot they'd never 'a coped with 'im 'n all. Oh, Ginny'd 'aye med a fooss of 'im, boot 'e needed more'n that...'

'Soomeoone ter moother 'im!' Billy interrupted, getting another laugh.

'Did the trick, though, din't it?' His mother asked; she turned to Sylvie again: ''E's roight, loove, that's what the kiddie needed, soomeoone ter loove 'im. So we took 'im on – 'n joost look at 'im now!' she finished proudly. Sylvie asked, hesitantly:

'Would you... could you see them back together, sometime, now that they've got over it all?' Vi smiled, a little sadly:

'Oi don' know, loove. Mebbe. Carrie's well settled, even calls 'erself Baker now, yeh know? She'll never leave Moikey – so it'd be a case of 'im goin' ter join 'er. 'N Oi ain't sure as 'e'd want teh, 'e's h'enjoyin' 'imself with oos, Oi reckon. Boot – if Kim's Dad's roight, 'n Fellers's do pack it in soometoime, Oi can see oos leavin' the boats, mebbe...' Bill was gawping at her, his mouth open:

''Ow did yeh know? Oi've bin thinkin' about what we'd do, 'n 'bout a job on the bank, wi' the coomp'ny, per'aps – boot Oi ain't said nothin' ter no-oone!' It was Vi's turn to chuckle:

'Oi know yew better'n yeh think, Bill 'Anney! Any'ow, if that 'appened, we'd mebbe suggest 'e goes wi' them, if 'e wants. If Alby agreed, o' course.'

'You'd miss him, though, Mum?'

''Course Oi would, girl! It's been...'

'Loike 'avin' Jack back agen, eh Ma?' Billy asked, quietly. Vi nodded, swallowing her feelings; she smiled at Kim.

'Ar Jack would 'ave been your age, now, Kim.' He replied, gently:

'Oi know, Mrs 'Anney. Oi remember playin' with 'im, when we was little.' Billy reached over and put a hand on her arm:

'That was a long toime ago, moother.' Vi nodded, her smile sadly self-conscious: 'Oi know – boot Oi can still miss 'im, can' Oi?'

''Course yeh moost, loove.' Bill agreed: 'Boot think – we got two lovely grand-kids, thanks teh ar Gracie, and anoother on the way.'

Sylvie had sat back, to listen to their talk; now, she leant forward again: 'Maybe I can cheer you up a bit more, Mum?' Vi looked up:

'Oh? 'Ow's that, loove?'

'I think you've got another grandchild on the way.' Vi's eyes lit up; Bill turned to his daughter-in-law, a huge grin on his face:

'Yeh mean...?' Sylvie nodded:

'I can't be absolutely sure, yet – but yes, I think I'm pregnant!' Billy had been staring at her, his mouth hanging open:

'Yew... Yeh're...?' Sylvie laughed, took his jaw in her hand and eased it closed; she leant to him and kissed him quickly on the lips:

'Like I said, Billy, I'm not certain – but I reckon you're going to be a Daddy.' He stared at her a moment longer, then threw his arms around her and kissed her back:

'Oh, Sylv! What shall we call 'im?' She chuckled:

'It might be a her, you know!'

'Oh – Ah, yeah, so it moight... Coom on, let's 'ave anoother drink!'

His father insisted on buying the round – it had occurred to Bill that this grandchild would be a Hanney, whereas little Jack, Rosie and 'number three' were all Caplins. While he and his two sons were at the bar, Vi reached across, took Sylvie's hands in both of hers:

'Are yeh pleased, girl?' Sylvie nodded, beaming:

'Oh, yes! I'm so glad I decided to come back to the boats – I'd be bored stiff in that typing pool. And I'd never have met my Billy...'

Vi just squeezed her hands, her own happiness gleaming in her eyes. Her oldest son and Sylvie had been married little more than a year – to some of the boaters, they seemed an odd couple, he a born-and-bred illiterate boatman, she an educated girl 'off the bank'. But they had fallen for each other at their first meeting when Sylvie, one of the 'Idle Women' of the wartime years, had found life in an office too staid for her and had returned to the boats, looking for a place in a crew. And found a husband instead.

Bill and his elder son returned to the table where they were all seated, passing around the drinks. Vi looked around for her youngest, spotted him leaning on the bar, pint glass in hand, talking to a young barmaid; he caught her eye, gave her an almost nervous smile and turned back to his conversation. Vi took a sip from her glass of stout, her eyebrows raised; she nudged her husband, who followed her gaze for a moment before shrugging his shoulders. He turned to young Kim Warden:

'D'yeh reckon ther's anythin' in what yer Dad was sayin' th'oother day?'

'Oi don' know, Mr 'Anney. 'E ain't said anythin' ter me.' Kim's father, Jack, had overheard something on the dock in Birmingham which suggested their employers might be going out of business, and the unsettling rumour had been circulating at the wedding. The boy went on: 'If y'arsk me, it's loike Billy says – Fellers's is too big a coomp'ny ter joost pack oop loike that.'

'Oi 'ope yeh're roight, boy! Boot it's true ter say that loads are gettin' 'arder ter coom boy. 'Fore the war, yeh'd no sooner be empt than they'd be chasin' yer ter load agen – boot now yeh can be a whoile sittin' around 'n waitin'.'

'Boot even if they did sell out ter the gov'mint, Dad,' Billy joined in, 'the work'd still be ther', wouldn' it?'

'Ar – boot if it ain't enooff ter go 'round? 'Oo are they goin' ter lay off, eh? Won' be the Grand Union men 'oo've been with 'em a whoile, will it? It'll be oos Fellers's men, yeh can bet yer loife!'

'H'okay – boot Fellers's 'ave been around a long toime, ain't they? They ain't goin' ter give oop joost like that, are they?'

'Look at all the things they got, Mr 'Anney – all the boats, the wharves 'n the ware'ouses, the lorries! They'll never give oop that easy!' Kim lent his support to Billy's argument; Bill looked at the pair of them for a moment, then shook his head:

'Nah! Oi reckon yeh're roight, they'll keep goin', Oi'm sure, even if things are a bit sticky fer a whoile. Once the gov'mint gets that drudgin' doone, fix things oop proper-loike, we'll be busier 'n ever.'

Chapter Four

Also among the mass exodus from Braunston that Sunday morning
had been another two pairs captained by a father and a son: The
Towcester and the Bodmin, under Harriet's father, Henry Caplin,
and the Birmingham and the Andromeda, in the hands of her
older brother Joe, were all part of the newly-nationalised fleet of
British Waterways. Formerly run by the carrying arm of the Grand
Union Canal Company, they had, along with the entire fleet and
its traffics, been absorbed by the British Transport Commission
when the government took over the previous January.

Away at the break of day, heading south, they were a long
way ahead of Alby Baker's boats by the time they tied up for the
night; it was well after dark that Henry, his crew now depleted to
himself and his wife, and fourteen-year-old Sam, led the way into
the little pub near Old Linslade. Close on their heels came Joe,
and his younger brother Ernie, seventeen now, who, with his wife
Grace, made up his crew until his own children would be old
enough to lend a hand. Grace, Bill and Vi Hanney's daughter,
had stayed on the boats with little Jack and Rosie; six months
pregnant with 'number three', she was anyway glad to rest after
their long day.

'Wher're yeh for, Dad?' They were propped, drinks in hand,
in a corner of the tiny bar of The Globe. Son had only caught up
with father at Braunston, and they hadn't had time, among the
festivities, to talk shop:

'Coal, fer Apsley, Joe. 'Ow 'bout yew?'

'Coal 'n all – fer Nestle's.'

'Yeh'll be straight ter Bulls Bridge then, off-loadin' ther'?'

'Yeah. We'll see yeh ther', later – oonless we get a back-load roight off.'

'Ah. Ther's too mooch 'angin' about nowadays, fer moy loikin'.'

'Ther's talk of 'em goin' after new loads, more work, Dad.'

'Oi know, boy. Boot they'll be loocky ter mek oop fer what they lost in the freeze. 'N if they don' get about that drudgin', fix the cut oop, it'll do no good any'ow.'

'Oh, they'll get on it, Dad, they ain't stoopid!' Henry gave his son a cynical smile:

'Oi ain't so sure! Look at the state o' things: Stratford Cut's gorn, 'n yeh strooggle ter get ter Cadb'ry's down the Worcester. 'N yeh'll be loocky ter get more'n a 'alf-load down the bottom road out o' Birnigum now, it's got so silted oop.' Joe shrugged:

'They'll 'ave ter do it, won' they? If they want ter keep the cut goin'. Give 'em toime, Dad!'

''Ow's Gracie, Joe?' Suey Caplin stepped in to change the subject; her son gave her a happy smile:

'She's foine, Ma! She gets toired, now, of an evenin', usually stays on the boats with the kiddies.'

'When's she due?'

''Bout Christmas!'

'What're yeh gonna call the babby, 'ave yeh thought?'

'Dunno...' Joe paused: 'Jack was after Gracie's little brother...'

'The oone as drownded?'

'Yes, Dad. 'N Rose was after grannie Caplin. Mebbe we'll call this'n after yew or Mum.'

'Hnh! That'll be noice, boy.' Henry's non-committal words couldn't disguise the pleased sparkle in his eye.

'Oi woonder 'ow Moikey 'n 'Arriet are gettin' on,' his wife speculated. 'They'll be at the seasoide boy now.'

23

''Ow long are they stoppin'?' Joe asked.

'Coopl'a days – they're gettin' the train ter Loonon ter meet the boats at City Road, Alby said.'

'Oh, roight...'

''Ow long'll it be 'fore she's got a babby on the way?' Suey wondered.

'Oh Mam!' Sam raised his eyes to the heavens; Joe laughed:

'Yew wait, yoong Sam! Yer turn'll coom!'

'They did mek a loovely coople yestiday, din't they? It'd be good ter see 'em with a kiddie or two...'

'Give 'em toime, Ma!' Henry led the amusement at his wife's ambitions.

'What about yew, Ernie? Any girls tek yer fancy yet?' his mother asked; Joe chuckled at his brother's sudden discomfiture:

''E's got a fancy fer yoong Katie Nixon, Mam,' he said, as Ernie tried to hide his embarrassment.

'That roight, boy?' Henry asked.

'Well, yeah, Oi s'pose so,' Ernie reluctantly admitted; he turned to his brother, appealed for his support; 'She's a pretty girl, ain't she, Joe?'

'Aye, she is!' Joe accepted.

'Ken's a good man; 'n 'er Mam was Jennie Whitlock 'fore she married 'im.' Henry put in a good word for the family: 'Good loock teh yeh, boy, if she's the girl yeh want!'

'Ginny's getting' ter be a real beauty, as well, ain't she?' Joe commented.

'Moikey's sister? She's a lot loike 'im, ain't she?' Henry concurred.

'Ah – real pretty girl, she is, now. So tall, fer 'er age!' Suey agreed.

'She's got loovely eyes...' They all turned to Sam at his dreamy comment: 'What're yeh lookin' at me fer? Oi joost said...'

'We 'eard, boy!' Henry was grinning; Joe chuckled:

'Fancy 'er, do yeh?'

'No! Oi mean – well – she is pretty, ain't she?' He looked around their faces: 'Any'ow – Stevie 'Anney's sweet on 'er, ain't 'e?' Suey took pity on her youngest:

'She's only yoong, loike yew Sam. Things can change, 'fore either of yeh's old ennooff ter be thinkin' o' that.'

* * *

The hour was late: Michael lay stretched out in the huge double bed, feeling peaceful, warm and tired. Harriet, curled in the crook of his arm, her head on his chest, stirred languorously:

'Oi moost be the loockiest girl in the world...'

'Mm-m?' He looked down at her in the dim glow of lights through the curtains; she raised her head, and a mischievous twinkle lit her eyes:

'Mmm Two more whole days, 'ere boy the seasoide – no work, no chores...'

'And?' She feigned ignorance:

'And what?'

''Ow about the coompany?'

'Oh – well...' she pretended to consider the matter: 'It's noice ter 'aye yeh along, Moikey.'

'Hnh! Oi could alwes go back, leave yeh 'ere alone!' She raised a hand, punched him gently under the chin:

'Don' yew dare, Moichael Baker!' He bent his head, kissed her on the forehead: 'Then it's about toime yeh started treatin' yer 'usband with a bit o' respect, Missus Baker!' Harriet wriggled comfortably in his arms:

'That sounds so good, Moikey – Oi still can' get used teh it. Oi'm so 'appy, ter be with yew.'

'Me too, 'Arrie. Oi'm so glad we're tergether, now.'

''N goin' ter be, fer alwes, ain't we?'

''Course we are.'

Chapter Five

Wednesday afternoon, and City Road Basin was its usual hive of activity. In the London terminus of much of Fellows, Morton & Clayton's business, surrounded by warehouses, numerous pairs of boats in their bright red and green livery were tied apparently at random, some loading, some unloading, a few just moored awaiting fresh orders.

At the side of one of the bigger warehouses, the Sycamore and the Antrim lay, the holds uncovered, while men heaved two-hundredweight sacks of sugar from handcarts over the gunwales and stacked them, under Albert Baker's stern direction. He turned to Carrie, sitting on the cabintop:

'Go put the kettle on, girl!'

'Yes, Dad!' She jumped down and disappeared into the butty cabin; he turned back and looked down upon Ginny, helping to manoeuvre the sacks in the hold of the motor boat, with a feeling of guilt – she had forcibly banned him from helping, himself, afraid that his weak heart would let him down. He lifted his flat cap, scratched his head, with that familiar mixture of pride and amused vexation as he watched her for a moment; she glanced up, smiled at him before turning for the next sack.

''Ey oop, what's goin' on 'ere then?' Alby turned, a delighted grin splitting his weathered face at the sound of the voice behind him.

'Moikey! 'Arriet! It's grand ter see yeh back!'

'It's good ter be back, Dad.' Michael echoed his grin; Ginny looked up and waved, a welcoming smile on her own face as he called out a hello to her. Carrie appeared like a jack-in-the-box from the cabin, and jumped onto the wharf to throw her arms around him:

'Moikey! Oi've missed yeh!'

''N Oi've missed yew, Carrie.' He hugged her back, as Alby stepped forward to embrace his daughter-in-law:

'Welcome back, 'Arriet. Did yeh h'enjoy yerselves?'

'Oh, yes, Dad! It was loovely, 'n the sun shone all the toime – boot it is good ter be back!'

'Carrie's joost got a brew on – boy the toime we've 'ad a coopa, they'll be about doone 'ere, 'n we can get clothed oop.'

'Back ter the groindstone, eh Dad?' She laughed as she turned to give the little girl a quick hug; Carrie scampered back down into the cabin, to emerge moments later with a handful of steaming mugs. Michael took his, had a quick pull from it before peeling off his jacket and jumping down into the hold to help the men; Ginny gave him a quick grin as she hefted one end of a sack onto a waiting pile near the mast.

'Moichael! Yeh've got yer steppin'-out trousers on – don' yew dare ruin 'em!' He looked up, a grin on his face, at Harriet's shout:

'Turnin' into a proper woife, ain't she, Dad!'

Late afternoon, and the pair were tied near the entrance to the basin, making room for other boats to load on the wharf. Michael, now in his heavy moleskin work trousers and an old shirt, was clambering around the gunwales with Alby, roping down the cloths in their traditional fashion over the stands and top-planks, covering and protecting the cargo beneath. Harriet, her frock now replaced by a black skirt and simple blouse, was in the cabin preparing a meal, while Ginny and Carrie mopped down the cabinsides, making the paintwork gleam in the sunlight ready for their trip to Birmingham.

The last strings tightened to Alby's satisfaction, the two men sat on the gunwale to rest after their exertions. Harriet handed out fresh mugs of tea; Ginny passed theirs around to Michael and Alby, then went down inside to help with the dinner.

'Can Oi go 'n play, Dad?' Carrie had spotted some other children she knew, along the dock.

'Ten minutes, loove. We'll be away then.'

''H'okay!' She scurried off.

''Ave yeh 'eard any more about what's 'appenin', Dad?' Both had been disturbed by the rumours going around at the wedding. Albert shook his head:

'Nothin' h'official, loike. Boot Oi've kep' me ears open since we got 'ere las' noight – 'n soome o' the men are sayin' the same as Jack, that the coomp'ny's losin' mooney, 'n they moight sell oop.'

'What'd it mean fer oos, Dad?'

'Oi dunno, boy. 'Oi s'pose, if they sold the 'ole lot ter the goverm'nt, we'd joost carry on, same as usual. Oi mean, work'd still 'ave ter be doone, wouldn' it?'

'Boot we'd be workin' fer British Waterways, loike 'Arriet's Dad?'

'Reckon so.'

A brief silence fell, while Michael drained his mug:

'What d'yeh think o' that, Dad?' Alby thought for a moment:

'Oi ain't quoite sure, boy. Yeh listen ter 'Enry, or Joey, any o' the old Grand Union men, 'n they don' seem too 'appy wi' things. Oh, a lot of it's 'bout the new colours 'n that...'

'That blue 'n yeller don' look anythin', doos it?'

'Nah – real drab. 'Ow can yer 'ave any proide in yer boats when they look loike that?'

'S'roight.'

''N they're sayin' same as ar fellers – they're losin' too mooch toime, every trip, waitin' fer orders. Oh, we're h'okay, wi' the sauce roon, boot a lot o' men are toied oop a day or more, 'tween loads.'

'Yeah. Yeh wouldn' think ther'd be that mooch trade in bottles o' sauce, would yeh?' Alby laughed:

'Oi don' moind, boy, if it keeps oos working!'

''N yew loike a dollop o' sauce on yer sausages, 'n all, Moikey!' Ginny had emerged from the cabin to listen in to their conversation. He turned to grin at her:

'Well, yeh need soomat ter give 'em a bit o' flavour! Ther' ain't mooch pig or cow in 'em, that's fer sure!' Ginny sighed:

''Alf a book o' the meat ration, 'n they taste loike cardboard!'

'Yew remember the sausages we 'ad 'fore the war?' Alby sounded reminiscent: 'Real meat in em, 'n some 'erbs…' Michael looked at Ginny, whose eyes turned skyward in resignation…

Nine o'clock, and the boats were tied just West of Black Horse Bridge, in Greenford. A good, quick run around the Regent's Canal, and now they were well along the Paddington Arm, towards Bulls Bridge and the main line.

In the bar of the pub, Michael stood arm-in-arm with his wife. A tired Ginny leant against Alby, whose spare arm encircled her shoulders, and Carrie sat at an adjacent table with a glass of lemonade and a packet of crisps, carelessly listening to their conversation. Her ears pricked up, however, as Michael said:

'Can Oi ask yeh soomat, Dad?' Alby laughed:

'Yeh can ask, boy, boot Oi moight not 'ave the answer!' Michael chuckled, but it was Harriet who spoke up:

'We were woonderin', Dad – 'ow old are yeh? If yeh don' moind me askin'.' Alby looked surprised – but he paused, his brow wrinkled in thought:

'Well now – Oi ain't too sure! We never took too mooch notice o' things loike that, birthdays 'n all, when Oi was a kid.'

'Yeh moost 'aye soome oidea, Dad?' Michael prompted.

'Oh, well – Oi remember the old Queen's do, 'er jubilee – Oi'd 'ave been about your age, when Bill 'Anney furst found yeh, Oi s'pose. That were no sooner over than she was gone, 'n we 'ad the King, Edward that was...' He paused, lifted his cap to scratch his head: 'Oi married moy Rita joost 'fore the war – the furst war, that was. The war to end all wars, they called it – got that bloody wrong, din' they?'

'Did yew go ter the war, Dad?' Ginny asked.

'No, loove. Fellers's got oos all listed as bein' needed 'ere – a preserved h'occupation, they called it. Ar Alex coom along joost at the end o' the war...'

'Yeh didn' 'ave no more kiddies, Dad?' Harriet asked; he shook his head:

'No – we troied 'n troied, boot it joost din't 'appen. Rita was so oopset...' He looked around at them, a smile spreading over his features: 'So was Oi, o' course – boot it don' matter now, look – Oi've got all yew lot!'

Michael had been doing some mental arithmetic:

'So yeh moost be 'round sixty, now, Dad?' Alby stopped to think:

'Yeah – Oi s'pose that'd be soomwher' near.' Carrie's voice joined the discussion:

'Let's mek this yer birthday, Dad!' Alby laughed:

'Whoy not? 'Ave yeh got me a present, then?'

'Oh! No, Oi ain't...' The little girl sounded crestfallen; he took pity on her:

'It don' matter – Oi'm too old fer presents, any'ow! Coom 'ere!' She got up and went to him; he put his beer glass down on the bar, gathered her into his arm and kissed her forehead. She grinned up at him:

''Appy birthday, Dad!' The others joined in, and a chorus of 'happy birthday's rang around the bar, to the amusement of the other customers.

'What's the date?' Ginny asked the world at large: 'We'll 'ave ter remember it!' The landlord turned to the calendar on his wall, grinning hugely:

'The twenty-second of September,' he informed her.

Chapter Six

Ben Vickers' breath misted in front of his face as he stood on the towpath outside the old Stop House. *If we get another freeze like '47...* In his position as dock manager at Braunston, Vickers was much more aware than the boatmen of the fragility of their trade. The big freeze of early 1947 had cost Fellows, Morton & Clayton dear, as it had all the carriers, big and small alike – not just in lost trade while the boats were immovable, but in lost contracts, work shifted onto the roads which had never returned to the canal. And this cold snap in mid-November didn't auger well...

A contemporary of Albert Baker, and, like Albert, born in a narrowboat's back cabin, Vickers had returned from voluntary service in the Royal Navy in 1919 to a job on the dock. Largely self-educated, he had risen during the twenties and thirties to eventual management of the entire stores and maintenance operation of FMC's Braunston facility. Now, he was looking forward to approaching retirement; and this latest upheaval didn't please him at all. A conscientious man, however, he was making the effort to talk to all of 'his' crews as they passed, to let them know what was going to happen over the coming months and years. And today, he was waiting for the Sycamore and his old friend.

They had, he knew, been at Stoke Bruerne the night before; if they'd got away as promptly as was Alby's habit they'd be by here anytime: *Lunchtime – and it's still bloody freezing!* He was impatient to get back to his warm office, and the flask of hot soup Olive had made up for him, but now the distant tonk...tonk...tonk, tonk...tonk…tonk of a Bolinder engine could be heard coming from the direction of the locks. He walked towards the old iron bridge which spanned the entrance to FMC's boatyard, in what had once been a part of the Oxford Canal but remained now only as a truncated arm, and peered towards Butcher's Bridge, further along the Grand Union's main line. And there they were, the fore-ends of the pair with the distinctive company colours on the top bends emerging through the bridge, pushing aside the thin mist which rose from the chilled waters. The boats were still breasted from the locks – Vickers knew it was their habit to stop briefly as they passed through, in the hope of a letter from Michael and Ginny's grandfather.

Approaching the old junction and its iron bridge, Michael saw Vickers standing there, watching them. He knocked the clutch rod out, letting the boats drift, losing speed as they turned slowly towards the bank; Ginny, on the butty's fore-end, threw the rope to the dock manager – Vickers walked with the boat, holding the bows in close as Alby stepped off the stern and dropped the strapping line around a bollard, easing the laden pair to a halt. He tied the fore-ends to a handy ring as Ginny asked:

'Any letters fer oos, Mr Vickuss?' He shook his head:

'Not today, Ginny. I wanted a word with you all, though.'

'Oh? What's amiss, Ben?' Alby asked as he walked up. Michael followed him, having stepped across from the motor, his arm around his wife's waist after helping her jump down from the butty's gunwale.

'Hello Mikey, Harriet – how are you both? And you, Alby?'

'We're foine thanks, Mr Vickuss,' Harriet answered for them all; Alby laughed:

'Oi'm gettin' fat 'n flabby, 'cause they won' let me do no work!'

'We're not 'avin' yew strain yer 'eart again, Dad – it's fer yer own good!' Ginny, still stood on the fore-end, chipped in.

'Rules me worse'n a flippin' woife, this girl doos!' Vickers laughed with them: 'Where's Carrie? Is she all right?'

'She's foine 'n all – Oi've got 'er watching the pot,' Harriet told him; as if on cue, the little girl poked her head out of the butty's hatches with a big smile and a wave:

''Ow do, Mr Vickuss!'

'Hello, Carrie!' He called back; she disappeared again, returning to her chore.

'To answer your question, Alby: Nothing's amiss, exactly. But I wanted to tell you, as I'm telling everyone, about the board's decision. So that you don't get any half-baked tales from the towpath telegraph.'

'So what's doin', Ben?'

'As you may have heard, the company's been losing money. We only got through the war because the government guaranteed our losses, and now, even with the increased rates we've been allowed to charge, things are no better. So they've decided to wind the company up. Oh, there's no need for you to worry.' He'd seen their immediate reaction. 'The Transport Commission have said they'll take everything over, the boats and the trade and so on. So you should be able to carry on, pretty much as usual.'

'When's this all 'appen, then?'

'I don't know for sure, Alby. It'll take quite a while to sort everything out, after all, Fellows's is a pretty big company. Next year some time, I'd imagine. For now, it's business as usual!'

'Oh... What about yew, Ben? Will we still be coomin' 'ere fer ar dockin' 'n the loike?'

'I don't know yet. The DIWE have already got all the old Grand Union docks and yards, and I doubt if they'll want all of ours as well. We'll have to wait and see.'

'Ah...' Alby suddenly grinned: 'Well, yeh can alwes join oos! We could do wi' a grease-moonkey fer that ol' Bolinder, eh, Moikey?' Vickers laughed:

'I might be taking you up on that yet, Alby!'

* * *

'What d'yer reckon, Dad?'

''Bout the coomp'ny?'

'Aye.'

Pressing on after their conversation with Vickers, they'd reached their regular stopping-place at the Cape of Good Hope, in Warwick. The girls were sitting around a table, chatting cheerily with a number of boatwomen, wives and daughters of men in the national fleet; Alby and Michael stood by the bar, pints of mild to hand:

'Oi still ain't sure, boy.' Alby took a long draw from his pint, put the glass down again: 'Loike Ben says, we oughtta joost be able to go on loike alwes – work'll still be ther' ter be done, won' it?'

''Ev'ryoone's sayin' loads are gettin' 'arder ter get, Dad.'

'Oi know – boot wi' Fellers's, they get the jobs, 'n we joost 'ave ter do 'em. 'N we ain't gone short o' work yet, 'ave we?'

'No, boot – suppose things got 'arder? We can only do what jobs the coomp'ny finds. If we 'ad ar own boats, was ar own boss...' Alby was staring at him, incredulous:

'Yeh're jokin', Moikey?'

'No, Dad! Think about it – we could go wher' the work was, 'round Birnigum, even down the North; we wouldn' be toied ter what the coomp'ny 'ad fer oos.' Alby was still staring at him; he shook his head:

'No, Moikey! Oh, Oi can see what yeh're getting' at, 'n if things got that 'ard, yeh might be roight. Boot as we are, we've got steady trips, no 'old-oops wi' loadin', no woorries at all, 'ave we?'

'No, Oi s'pose not, Dad. 'N any'ow – 'ow'd we afford ter buy a pair, eh?' He laughed at his own over-stretched ambition. Alby put a match to his pipe, drew on it until a cloud of smoke drifted around his head:

'There moight be ways, if we 'ad teh, boy...'

Michael raised his eyebrows, but before he could pursue the matter, a blast of cold air swept over them as the door opened, and a voice spoke:

''Ey oop, Alby, Moikey – 'ow're yeh doin'?' He looked around:

''Ello, Bill! Joost stopped, 'ave yeh?'

'What're yeh 'avin', Bill? Stevie?' Alby asked the new arrivals as the youngest Hanney closed the door behind himself.

'Two points o' moild?' Bill looked at his son; Stevie nodded.

'Two points o' yer moild, landlord!' Alby passed on to the waiting publican. 'Wher's Vi?' Michael asked.

'Littl'un's feelin' a bit poorly, Mum's stayed on the boat with 'im,' Stevie replied; Carrie had looked up as they entered:

'Can Oi go 'n see 'im?'

''Course yeh can!' Bill told her; she jumped up and dashed out, pulling her coat around her against the cold night air. Ginny got up from her seat and came over; Stevie slipped an arm around her shoulders with a grin as she smiled at him; Michael asked about their trip. Albert turned to his old friend:

'Yeh've 'eard 'bout the coomp'ny closin'?' Bill nodded:

'Aye. Mr Vickuss tol' oos the oother day.'

'What'll yeh do?' He shrugged:

'Stay as we are, Oi s'pose. Fer now, any road.'

'Yeh ain't goin' ter look fer that job on the bank?'

'Nah – not yet. Nothin'll change 'til nex' year, 'e reckons. Whoile ther's plenty o' loads fer oos, we'll carry on – if things get 'ard, mebbe we'll 'ave ter think agen. 'Ow 'bout yew?'

'Yeah, no reason ter look fer trouble, is ther'? Ben reckons it won' bother oos, we'll joost be doin' the same work fer a new boss. So whoy rock the boat, eh?' He decided against mentioning Michael's crazy idea of running their own boats.

Chapter Seven

'O-oh – Star of wonder, star of light, Star of royal beauty bright...'

Michael's voice joined the final chorus of 'We Three Kings', added to the round of cheers as it finished. Christmas had, for him, long been a high point of the year; even the mean Christmases spent in the house in Wolverton, when his mother had scrimped to give him and his brother and sister the smallest gifts to mark the occasion, had been special to the growing child. And now, when, in the depths of the winter, the boaters would for once take the time to rest from their labours, to pause in the unremitting round of their lives, it had an even greater significance for the young man; the first Christmas to be spent with his new wife.

The bar of the The Boat Inn, at Stoke Bruene, was crowded to bursting, hot and smoky, a fire blazing in the grate. He was propped in a corner by the door, Harriet snuggled happily in the crook of his arm; he grinned across at his Dad, leaning on the bar, his old pipe clutched in his hand, Ginny and Carrie both squeezed into a seat beside him. The night of Christmas Eve had barely begun; Harriet wriggled comfortably against him, and he looked down to meet the gleam in her eyes, bent his head to kiss her forehead. Joey Caplin, the other side of the door, reached for his melodeon and began a jaunty tune, and Michael's mind drifted back over the years:

He had spent the first Christmas Eve of his life on the boats with Albert and Gracie, at Marsworth, quite quietly, in the Red

Lion – but the next morning had brought surprises: His own windlass from his captain, a carved wooden toy warship from the 'big brother' he'd only met once before he was killed at sea, and the spider-work belt, now much too small for him even if it still languished with his other clothes in the cabin, from Gracie. The memory brought a smile to his lips, which grew as his mind moved on:

The next year, they'd been here, in this bar. The gathered boaters then, always eager for 'the music', had quickly realised that the skinny kid of twelve had a fine, clear voice and an ear for a tune, a good memory for the words of the carols he'd learnt in school – they'd cajoled him into singing for them, over and again until his throat had felt dry and scratchy, joining in with gusto for the choruses. He'd felt their attitude to him change, that night – early on, he'd still been the subject of their scrutiny, their curiosity, the strange 'boy off the bank' who'd appeared in their midst almost two years before. But, by that final rendition of 'Silent Night' which had brought tears to a few eyes, he had felt himself to be, at last, one of them, a boatee boy in his own right.

'N we 'aven't looked back since! Looking around, he wondered if it was possible to be happier – surrounded by the people he loved most, his thoughts strayed beyond the barroom to the others who meant so much to him: Bill and Vi Hanney, and his best mate Stevie, somewhere south of them loaded with barrels of Mitchell and Butler's best; Billy, and his now-definitely pregnant wife, probably still in Birmingham after loading that day at Coombeswood; Henry and Suey Caplin, his in-laws, with young Sam, he knew not where. And Grandad Morris, of course, his Mum's father, in his little house in Buckingham.

Joey finished his tune, and a hubbub of conversation rose into the silence. Michael grinned across at him, called over:

''Ow's Gracie?' Joe smiled:

'Oi'm goin' ter check oop on 'er, in a mo when Oi've fmished me beer!' Michael nodded:

'Give 'er moy loove – we'll see 'er in the mornin'.'

'Roight! Yew two ain't got a littl'un on the way yet?' Michael laughed:

'Nah – we're still practicin'!' That raised a bellow of laughter all around them, as Harriet blushed pink and hid her face in his jacket; someone clapped him on the shoulder.

From near the bar, a voice started a rendition of 'Hark the Herald Angels', but a sudden hammering on the door brought a hush to the noise, made everyone look around. Michael snatched it open, wondering what was wrong, knowing that something had to be from the urgency of the sound:

'Daddy! Daddy! It's Ma – coom quick!' Jack Caplin threw himself upon his father. Joe gathered him into his arms, wrapped his coat around himself and the little boy and dashed out:

'Get Sister, will yeh, Moikey?' he flung over his shoulder. Michael gave Harriet a quick squeeze, told her to stay there, and hurried out himself. Over the lock, he knocked on Sister Mary Ward's door; it was quickly flung open, and the Sister gave him a beaming smile:

'Gracie, is it?'

'Yes, Sister. Little Jack joost coom fer 'is Dad.'

'I'm on my way, Mikey – go and say I'll be right there.'

A small crowd was gathered around the Andromeda's stern, a couple of other boatwomen inside with Gracie while Joe sat on the gunwale, his face creased with concern for his wife and the unborn baby. Harriet stood on the bank, shivering in the cold night air, feeling ineffectual; Michael came up, put his arm around her:

'Sister's on 'er way,' he told Joe, who looked around gratefully. A face looked out of the cabin, round and cheerful, under a traditional bonnet:

'Yew tek Jack'n Rosie inter the motor, Joe, keep 'em out o' the way, eh? We're 'ere teh 'elp the Sister if she needs oos.'

'Yeah – roight, h'okay.' He sounded distracted, but he called to his son: 'Coom 'ere, Jackie, coom in the warm wi' me.' The little boy scrambled into his aims. 'Wher's Rosie?'

''Sleep, Daddy.'

'H'okay – let's go see if she's all roight, shall we?' He took the child down into the motor boat's cabin, leaving the doors open in order to be able to know what was happening.

'Shall Oi coom wi' yeh, Joe?' A woman's voice asked, he sounded relieved as he replied:

'Would yeh, Rene?' A buxom figure stepped down to join him, as the Sister hurried up and let herself into the butty.

'Coom on, Loove – nothin' we can do 'ere, let's get back in the warm, eh?' Michael suggested; Harriet nodded gratefully.

Alby had fresh drinks waiting for them in the bar:

'H'ev'rythin' h'okay, is it?'

'Seems loike it, Dad. Sister's ther', 'n soom o' the oother women.'

'Ah, she'll be foine then! Let's drink ter the new kiddie!' Voices were raised from the crowd:

'Teh 'im!'

'Or 'er!'

'Christmas babby, eh?'

'Aye – special, en't it?'

'Good loock ter 'em all!' Michael called over the hubbub; glasses were raised all around.

* * *

Christmas morning dawned bright and still; an even greater air of festivity hung over the boats at Stoke Bruerne than would be usual for the time of year. The boatwomen, wrapped in bonnets and shawls, formed a constant crowd whose composition changed as time passed around the blue-and-yellow pair tied on the old wharf; their men, each calling to pay their respects to the new arrival but less inclined to hang about in the chill air, coming by on their way to the pub. Michael and Albert, leaving their own boats tied near the old mill basin, made their way across the lock; Harriet and the two girls were already there, talking to Gracie who sat in the stern well, cradling the baby, as they strolled up. Joe leant against the cabinside, an early pint of mild in his hand, looking proud but slightly bemused; Rosie, well wrapped up against the cold, sat on the roof by the watercans, while Jack was playing with a couple of other children nearby.

'Mornin' Joe, Gracie – 'ow's the littl'un?' Alby greeted them; Joe grinned:

'Mornin', Alby – 'e's foine!'

''Ow 'bout yew, Gracie?' Michael asked; she smiled up at him:

'Oi'm grand, Moikey! Tek a look at yer new nephew!' She eased the blanket away from the baby's face as he bent to see:

''E looks woonderful, Gracie – yeh moost be so pleased?'

'We are that, Moikey,' Joe replied; he chuckled: 'Yer turn next, eh?'

Harriet smiled eagerly as Michael said:

'Would be great, wouldn' it? We'll 'ave ter keep troyin'!' He laughed as Harriet turned pink again, put his arm around her and kissed her cheek. Recovering her composure, Harriet asked:

'What're yeh gonna call 'im?' Gracie looked around:

'We were gonna call 'im 'Enry, after Joe's Dad...' Joe himself took up the tale:

'Boot as 'e coom las' night, joost as we was about ter sing ''Ark the 'Erald', we thought as we'd mebbe call 'im after an angel. What d'yeh think ter Gabriel?'

Ginny looked up, surprised but smiling, and Carrie clapped her hands, as Harriet said:

'That's loovely, Joey! Couldn' be noicer.' Joe laughed:

'Oi joost 'ope Dad won' be oopset!'

'Oh, 'ow could 'e be, with a new grandson ter fooss over? 'N Ma'll be oover the moon, won' she?'

'Wher' are yer folks, Joe?' Alby asked.

'Down Bulls Bridge, Oi reckon. 'Opefully, we'll meet 'em in the nex' day or so. We got coal on, fer Apsley. Boot they'll 'ave 'eard boy then, no doubt!'

They all laughed: The unerring if unfathomable towpath telegraph was a fact of life on the canals, carrying news farther and more quickly than logic suggested was possible.

'Yeh'll 'ave ter troy 'n mek it an evenin' meetin', so's they can wet the babby's 'ead wi' yeh!'

'Aye, we'll troy 'n do that, Alby!'

And that same lunchtime, even in the absence of his grandparents, the baby's head was indeed well and truly wetted in the bar of the Boat Inn.

Chapter Eight

Springtime: Hedges were a mass of buds, their soft greens taking over slowly from the bare grey of winter, and the trees in the fields were covered in blossoms. It had been a beautiful day, the countryside of England putting on its best show to welcome the longer days of the approaching summer. Evening sunshine slanted across the open landscape, laying an almost fiery glow on the treetops, striking low over the towpath hedge to light the cabinsides and cloths of the boats, reflecting warmly off of the polished brasswork of chimneys, chains and tillerpins. Three pairs ran in turn behind the shade of each clump of trees, to emerge again moments later into the light; each as smartly turned out as the last, paintwork spotless, ropes scrubbed white, brasses gleaming.

Billy Hanney stood at the tiller of the Skate, gazing forward in the wake of the other two pairs: Away in front of him, his mother leant in the hatches of the Kerry, her relaxed bulk speaking of her contentment with her lot even at that distance; the length of her boat and eighty feet of towline beyond her, his brother Stevie looked equally at ease, sat on the cabintop of the Acorn, leaning over slightly to hold the tiller with his left hand. And beyond them again, he could see Alby Baker at the 'ellum of his butty, the Antrim, and young Carrie steering the Sycamore under the watchful eye of Mikey. He glanced back, watching his wife as she steered their butty, the Middlesex, trailing on its long line behind him. Sylvie caught his eye and gave him a loving smile, and his heart swelled with pride: *'Ow can a man be 'appier than me? Oi've got a lovely missus, 'n ar furst babby due any toime...*

He looked around, the beauty of his surroundings lifting his feelings even more, if that were possible: To his left, sunlight poured across the open fields, the fresh-sprung crops sparkling under its caress; to the right, below the shade of the high canal bank, the village of Rowington looked sleepily idyllic, an occasional chimney-pot catching the rays of the fading day.

The three pairs had come together at Brentford, ordered to load for the same job; all were carrying ingots of aluminium destined for a foundry in Birmingham. All loaded in one day, they had, by mutual agreement, stopped by the gauging locks overnight and set away at first light the following morning. Running butty, each crew helping the other, had seen them stop the first night in Berkhamsted, the next at Fenny Stratford; last night had been spent in Braunston, and tonight would see them tie along the pound from Hatton to Knowle ready for a last day's journey onto the Birmingham Canal Navigations and into the Soho Loop where lay their destination.

Beneath his outward happiness, Billy was aware of a feeling of vague uneasiness. The same feeling was affecting all the captains he knew, all of the boatmen employed by Fellows, Morton and Clayton; with the impending winding-up of the business, they all had the same impression of the ground beneath their feet being slowly shifted, the balance of their working round slowly changing. All of the old FMC wharves and docks had been handed over to the national operations of the Docks and Inland Waterways Executive, except for a few which had been sold off separately — until this trip, Alby Baker's boats had still been carrying bagged sugar from London for HP Sauce, even though the City Road warehouses had been sold to one of the tenant companies, and the old Fazeley Street premises were now owned by the sauce people themselves. Their return load of cases of sauce had also continued up to now, but they all felt that the future held a disturbing level of uncertainty. And soon, they had been told, the boats themselves would become the property of British Waterways, the carrying arm of the national company – what further changes would that bring?

He felt a tap on his leg, and moved aside to let the third member of his crew emerge into the evening light. Kim Warden, just past his seventeenth birthday, gave him a grin as he handed over a fresh mug of tea:

'All roight, Billy?' He edged around to stand on the gunwale, his legs braced against the cabinside as he took a long draught of his own tea.

'Foine, mate.' Billy put his mug down after taking a swig: 'Yeh got a spare fag?' Kim reached into the pocket of his jacket, extracted a ready-made roll-up from his tobacco tin and gave it to Billy, took another for himself; he struck a match, lit Billy's as he leant over and then his own. They puffed contentedly in silence for a while, before he asked:

'Stoppin' at the Black Boy ternoight, yeh reckon?'

'Probly. 'S oop teh Alby, 'e's in froont.'

'Aye.' Kim chuckled: 'Your broother seemed quoite keen on the oidea, when 'e suggested it this mornin'!'

'Yeah... What's 'e oop teh?'

'No oidea.'

The two young men sank into a companionable silence once more as their boats swept on, gazing down on the roof of Ivy House Farm, its timber-framed structure nestling below the towpath, and under the arch of Turner's Green Bridge.

Minutes later, a quarter of a mile in front of the Skate, Michael watched the battered, neglected arch of the brick towpath bridge of Kingswood Junction slide past. A hundred yards away to the west, along the short linking cut, lay the disused Stratford-on-Avon Canal, the waters of the Lapworth lock flight now weed-grown and abandoned. *Meks yeh woonder if they ever will sort the cut out!* More than a year after the government had taken over the canals, and still hardly any of the desperately-needed maintenance work had actually been done. They had, to be fair, attracted some new trade, new contracts – but it was all on the still-usable routes like the Grand Union; it seemed as if the other parts of the system, like the Stratford cut, were to be left to their fate, to fall derelict and become no more than weed-filled ditches meandering across the countryside.

Carrie, still at the tiller, suddenly looked down and stood aside from the hatches.

'Tea oop!' Harriet emerged, carrying three steaming mugs; she set them down, and gathered up the empty dinner plates. They had eaten on the pound after leaving Shrewley Tunnel; now, a last mug of tea before they would tie for the night. Then, a round or two of drinks, maybe in the Black Boy or the Kings Arms...

A distant thud sounded over the steady beat of the Bolinder; Michael looked around, a frown on his face:

'Looks loike trooble!' Carrie and Harriet both looked behind them; Alby was peering over his shoulder too, and they could see Ginny's head in the butty hatches as well. A cloud of heavy black smoke hung over the Acorn, drifting slowly in the gentle breeze, and even at that distance the boat seemed to be slowing, turning towards the bank.

'Pull 'em oover, Carrie, Oi'd best see what's oop.' The girl slowed the engine, turned the boats towards the towpath; behind them, Alby was heading for the bank as well, anticipating Michael's decision. The pair both settled against the towpath edge; Harriet took the back-end line from the motor as, behind them, Ginny did likewise on the butty. They held the boats in place as Michael stepped off and began to run back towards the spot where Bill Hanney was now peering disconsolately into his engine-hole.

'What's the trooble, Bill?' Michael asked as he reached them. Stevie, holding his own back-end string, told him:

'Cylinder-'ead. Blown a bloody great 'ole in it.'

'That roight, Bill?' The older boatman straightened up reluctantly:

'Moost 'ave bin cracked fer ages. Boogger! We ain't goin' nowher' loike this.' By now, Billy too had brought his boats to a halt and came running up:

'What's oop, Dad?'

'Bloody 'ead's blown, boy. Noothin' ter be doon 'ere.'

'Oh shit! Tha's booggered it.'

'Aye.' Bill looked around: 'Can yeh tow oos ter the Black Boy, lad?'

'Yeah – t'ain't far, is it.'

'Coopl' a moile, mebbe.'

'Oi'll drop back 'n pick oop yer butty, then Billy won' 'ave so mooch ter pull.'

'Yeh sure, Moikey?'

''Course! We'll leave the Antrim wher' it is fer the moment – Oi'll back oop wi' the motor.'

''Roight, Moikey – Oi'll 'ang Dad's motor on be'ind ourn, then Sylvie can keep 'im straight with our butty.'

They separated, Michael running back to the Sycamore, Billy to the Skate. In minutes, the six boats had been rearranged into two sets of three: Michael's motor had the two butties, Bill's Kerry and his own Antrim, on long lines one behind the other; similarly, Billy had the disabled Acorn on an eighty-foot line with the Middlesex another eighty feet beyond, the butty acting to keep the dead motor in line as they travelled – any motor boat relies mostly on its prop-wash for steering control.

Thus slowed by the extra weight behind them, it took Michael and Billy almost an hour to reach the bridge by the Black Boy pub, on the Warwick Road. Tired and disconsolate, they tied the boats on the towpath. Half an hour later, washed and brushed up, they were all sitting in the public bar trying to raise their spirits while Bill used the landlord's telephone to report his troubles.

Chapter Nine

'Yer ale's 'ere, Dad!'

Bill Hanney sank into a vacant seat and took a long pull at the pint of mild his elder son indicated. He set it down again with a satisfied sigh:

'Boogger, that's better!'

'D'yer get through ter the coomp'ny, Bill?' Alby asked; Bill chuckled:

'Yeah, in the end! Fergot, din't Oi, troyed ter call Mr Vickuss at Braunston – loine don' work no more. Boot Oi got Mr Noob'ry at Bull's Bridge – 'e's sendin' soomoone out termorrer teh 'ave a look at oos.'

'Mr Noob'ry's h'okay – 'e always looked after oos when Oi was wi' Dad,' Harriet said. Bill nodded:

''E seems loike a decent feller, roight enooff.'

'Yeh tol' 'im it was the 'ead, did yeh?' Stevie asked.

'Yeah – boot 'e wants teh see fer 'imself. Said 'e'll mek sure the fitter's got a noo 'ead with 'im, any'ow, so mebbe it'll get fixed roight off.'

''Ow long a job is it, Bill?' Michael asked.

'Don' roightly know. Got ter tek a few hours, though.'

'We'd best get goin' then, in the mornin'?'

'Yeah – no need fer yew teh 'ang about, yeh moight as well get yer loads ter James's. We'll coom on as soon as we can.'

'Roight-o Bill.'

'Oi woonder 'ow Ben's gettin' on?' Vi speculated.

'Yeah – Oi 'ope 'e's h'enjoyin' 'is retoirement!' Alby said.

'It seems a shame to see him stuck on the shelf like that, after all the years he's given to the canal. I mean, he's too young to retire, surely?' Sylvie asked.

'Oi don' know, 'e's about moy age,' Alby told her: ''N 'e's 'ad that little cottage in the village fer a good whoile, so they've a place ter be. 'N the coomp'ny's give 'im a decent pension, so they'll be h'okay.'

'Seems odd, don' it, not ter 'ave the dock at Braunston,' Billy observed.

''S'roight. Moind yew, Nurser's 'ad been in their part o' the old yard since way 'fore the war, so Oi s'pose it was sense fer Fellers's ter let 'em 'ave the rest of it.'

'Oi 'ope those two kiddies're all roight out ther' in the dark.' Carrie and Josh, obviously happy to be in each other's company, had stayed out to play on the towpath – on their own, as there were no other boats tied there that night. Now, though, Vi sounded concerned.

'Oi'll go 'n see, shall Oi,' Ginny volunteered.

'Please, loove. Call 'em in, will yeh?'

'H'okay.'

Ginny got up from where she had been sitting, inevitably, next to Stevie; she disappeared out of the door. Vi turned to Sylvie, asked how she was feeling, and as the three women fell to talking about the imminent arrival of the baby, Stevie slipped out of his seat.

'Wher' are yew goin', boy?' His father asked; the youngster gave him a slightly guilty look:

'Won' be a minute, Dad.' Billy watched his younger brother stroll across the bar-room; he caught Kim's eye, and they exchanged a significant glance. Bill, Albert and Michael had begun to speculate on what orders they would get for the return trip, and Billy was brought back to the conversation as his father asked him:

'What d' yer reckon, Billy?'

'Eh – what? Sorry, Dad, Oi weren' listenin'.'

'Oi said, what's the odds they'll 'ave oos ter Coombeswood?'

'Dunno, Dad – Oi 'ope not!' Nobody liked the heavy, dirty job of handling the steel tubes from Stewarts and Lloyds.

So only Kim was looking as Stevie leant against the bar; the young barmaid, a pretty brunette in her teens, gave him a smile and wandered over, and the two began to chat.

The door swung open, and the two children scurried in. Kim got to his feet as he saw Ginny follow them; he called to her:

'Would yeh loike anoother drink, Gin?' But he was too late, she'd noticed Stevie, leaning eagerly on the bar, the girl laughing at something he'd said. She stood rooted to the spot; he went up to her and took her by the elbow:

'Let me get yeh a drink, Gin.' She turned to him and looked at him for a moment as if he was a total stranger. Then she visibly shook herself and gave him a smile: 'H'okay, Kim, thank yeh. 'Alf o' shandy, please.'

''Ow about yew, Carrie? Josh?' he asked the children.

'Lemonade, please Kim.'

''Ave they got that Coca Cola?' He smiled at the boy:

'Oi'll ask for yeh, Josh.' He guided Ginny to her seat, smiled her into it like a high-class maitre d', and then walked over to the bar.

Minutes later he was back, four glasses in hand – he passed the lemonade and Coca Cola to the children as Vi told them to 'drink oop quick, then get yerselves 'ome ter bed', and the half-pint glass to Ginny. She was sitting stiffly upright, looking upset and angry at the same time; he sat next to her:

''Ow's yer granddad gettin' on, Gin?' She looked around and smiled at him again:

''E's foine, thank yeh! We 'ad a letter from 'im las' week...' She slowly relaxed as she told him all about Fred Morris's pretty garden, and how he had a cleaning woman come in now to help him, twice a week; Kim sat and listened, being as eagerly attentive to her as he knew how.

Stevie returned to the table after about half an hour. Halfway across the floor, he stopped in his tracks as he realised that Kim had taken his seat; a frown flickered over his face for a moment, but then he walked on, casually taking the empty chair between Sylvie and his father.

'All roight, Stevie?' Billy asked; his younger brother gave him a quick smile:

'Yeah, foine. Oi joost stopped ter arsk fer the bogs, 'n got chattin' wi' the barmaid.'

'Ar, so we saw. Wher' are they then?'

'What?' Stevie looked puzzled.

'The bogs, o' course.'

'Oh – er...'

'Roun' ther', be'ind the bar,' Vi pointed. She gave her younger son a steely look, and he dropped his eyes. The awkward silence held for a moment, to be broken by Harriet asking:

'Ladies 'n all, Vi?'

'Yes, loove.' Harriet got up and walked off. Ginny had been watching Stevie from beneath lowered eyelids; now she put a hand on Kim's arm and turned to him with a beaming smile:

''Ow's yer mum 'n dad gettin' on, Kim?' He returned her smile:

'Oh, pretty fair, Oi reckon. 'Aven't seen 'em fer a whoile, but they was foine las' toime we passed 'em. Down Batch'eth, that was.'

'Yeh don' know wher' they are now?'

'Nah. Last Oi 'eard they'd orders teh load at Loime'ouse, timber fer Olton.'

'Oh...'

As the two chatted, both Vi and Sylvie had been looking at them. Now their eyes met, and Vi shook her head, looked Heavenward for a moment. Sylvie gave her a smile, shrugged her shoulders. Billy, meanwhile, had returned to the men's conversation, discussing a recent hold-up following a collapsed culvert near Weedon.

A little later, as they all rose to go back to the boats, Stevie edged around towards Ginny. She looked up at him, and he wilted at the fire in her eyes, turned away and walked off with his head hung low. Kim took her arm; she smiled at him and allowed him to walk her back to the Antrim. Vi and Sylvie exchanged glances again, both aware of the evening's undercurrents.

Remembering his breakdown, Bill grumbled all the way back out onto the towpath, Billy commiserating with him while Alby clapped him on the shoulder with a cheery:

'Don' woorry, mate, they'll soon 'ave yeh fixed oop! We'll see yeh at James's, Oi 'spect.'

Michael and Harriet trailed along behind, arm in arm as always, her head resting against his shoulder. Suddenly, she raised her head, asked him:

'Yeh still loove me, Moikey?'

''Course Oi do!' He stopped, turned her to face him. 'Whatever meks yeh arsk that?'

'Oh – noothin'. Joost wanted ter be sure.'

'Oi'll alwes loove yeh, yeh know that, 'Arrie.' He needed no reply except for the look on her face; her arm went around his waist as they started walking again:

'Oi think Ginny 'n Stevie 'ave fell out, though.' He looked down at her:

'Oh? What gives yeh that oidea?' She laughed:

'Yew men! Yeh don' see what's 'fore yer oiyes, too busy jawin'! She caught 'im chattin' oop that barmaid, that's what.'

'The good-lookin' oone wi' the brown 'air?' She stopped walking, made him look at her:

'Moichael Baker, yeh're a married man, yeh ain't s'posed ter notice oother girls!' It was his turn to laugh:

'Ol' Ben Vickuss was roight, yeh are very pretty when yeh're angry!' She gave him a wry smile, reached up to punch his jaw gently with her fist; then she drew him with her as she walked on again:

'That oone, yes.'

'She angry?'

'Oh, ah! Din't yeh see, she's let Kim walk 'er back ter the boat.'

'Oh! Oh... Oi thought they'd... yeh know – oone day, 'er 'n Stevie...'

'Din' we all. Mebbe they still will, p'rhaps it'll blow oover.'

'Yeah... Oi 'ope they ain't gonna be daggers drawn – she's moy sister, 'n 'e's moy best mate.' Harriet gave his waist a squeeze:

'Don' woorry, Moikey. Whatever 'appens, they'll get oover it.'

Chapter Ten

Early the next day, two pairs set off for Birmingham. Their overnight stop had not been far from the locks at Knowle, so Michael took the bike to set them ahead, leaving Carrie to steer the motor while Harriet made some breakfast; on the butty, Alby steered whilst Ginny got herself ready to work the locks. The big modern locks are easy and fast to work, so both pairs were clear and travelling the ten-mile pound to Camp Hill within the hour.

On the second pair, Billy had left Kim in charge of the Skate while he joined his wife on their butty. He had caught a little of his father's disgruntled mood, talking to him before they'd started; and now he grumbled over his bowl of porridge about the delay of having to go 'long way 'round' into Birmingham.

'What do you mean?' Sylvie asked him. 'We always came this way.'

'In the war, yeh mean? Well, yeh would 'a doon. Boot 'fore the war, when Oi was a little kid, we used ter go top road – turn back ther' at Kingswood 'n go on the Stratford Cut, oop ter Kings Norton 'n then ter Worcester Bar. Puts yeh on the Birnigum canals straight on, yeh see? Ther's joost the eighteen locks o' Lap'erth, then its level goin' all the way ter the Old Main Loine. This way, we've 'ad the foive at Knowle – then cooms down'ill six o' Camp 'Ill, six back oop at Ashted, 'n the Ol' Thirteen. 'N all o' them's narrer, so yeh're dooble-workin' fer the butty. Meks 'ard work of it.'

'I see what you mean. The other way's blocked, is it?'

'All silted oop, 'n soom o' the gates are 'angin' off, yeh can' go that way at all now.' Sylvie nodded:

'If we had a load for Birmingham, we'd go this way; then usually it was bottom road to Coventry and load coal for somewhere around London.'

'Yeah – we din' get that way mooch, wi' Fellers's. Mostly this way, from Fazeley Street or soomwher' straight back ter City Road.'

Whilst his captain was relaxing on the butty, Kim leant casually in the hatches of the motor boat. His face wore a wide smile, his brown eyes with an unaccustomed twinkle as he dwelt at length on the events of the previous evening: *She's a crackin' girl! 'N if Stevie's lost h'int'rest...* He gazed ahead, his eyes on the girl standing in the stern well of the Antrim, her tall slim figure emphasised by her habitual dungarees, her long blond hair cascading from under her flat cap: *She even let me kiss 'er...* That the kiss had been a quick peck on the cheek, knowingly under the surreptitious watch of Stevie Hanney, he conveniently ignored in his elation.

Left behind outside the Black Boy, Bill Hanney stood and fretted in the hatches of his cabin, drinking the endless cups of tea passed to him by his wife when he remembered, and letting others grow cold. It was a pleasant, bright morning; Stevie was out on the towpath, keeping young Josh amused by kicking an old ball around, a practice which required one or the other of them to retrieve it from the water at regular intervals.

Around ten o'clock, an old Morris van drew up outside the pub, and two men made their way through the garden to the immobilised boats. The one in the suit knocked on the cabinside after giving a cheerful 'hello' to the young man; Bill had ducked inside for a cigarette; now he stuck his head out:

''Mornin'.'

'Good morning – Mr Hanney?'

'My name is Lionel Bartram, from British Waterways. This is our fitter, Dave King. We've come from Bulls Bridge – what's the problem?' Bill eyed them dubiously:

'Loike Oi tol' Mr Noob'ry las' night, me 'ead's boost. Bloody great 'ole in it.'

'Oh – right. Can we repair it?' Bill snorted:

'If yeh got a noo 'ead wi' yeh, yeh can. Ain't no fixin' this'n.'

'Oh... Take a look will you, Dave?'

'With your leave, Mr 'Anney?' the fitter asked; Bill gave him a nod, and he climbed down into the engine room. Moments later, his head appeared in the side hatch:

'He's right, Mr Bartram. Cylinder Head's split, part of it's blown out completely, it'll have to be replaced.'

'What did Oi tell yeh?' Bill growled.

'Yes – very good, Mr Hanney. We'll have to get you one...'

'Yeh ain't got a spare wi' yeh?' The suit shook his head:

'We had to find out what was needed, first...'

'Oi bloody tol' yeh on the tellyphone! 'Ow long's it gonna tek ter get oone?' Bartram looked at his overalled companion, who gave a sympathetic grimace in Bill's direction:

'Saltley'll probably have one – they were the main dock for Fellows's boats. Maybe they could bring one over?'

'Oh – yes. Okay; I'll go and call them.'

'Tellyphone's in the poob – yeh'll 'ave ter knock soomoone oop.'

'Oh. Right – I'll be back right away, Mr Hanney. Don't go away, will you?' he accompanied this attempt at humour with a weak smile, which elicited a black frown from the boatman, and a wide grin from the fitter:

'Sorry, mate! It's all bloody managers now, 'n none of 'em know anythin' about anythin'. Mr Newbury – he's the boss down there...'

'Yeah, we know Mr Noob'ry.'

'He told me you'd be needing a replacement head, but smart-arse there said we'd better check first. If Saltley can send one over, I'll get it swapped as quickly as I can — I've got me tools with me.' Bill heaved a sigh:

'Thanks, mate. We've got h'ingots on fer James's, on the So'o, 'n they don' loike ter be kep' waitin'.'

* * *

It was getting dark when Dave King finally emerged from Bill's engine room. Bartram had returned from the pub with the news that Saltley did indeed have a spare head for Bill's engine, but that they didn't have anyone free to bring it over; he then partly redeemed himself in Bill's eyes by offering, rather sheepishly, to go and fetch it, when the boatman pointed out that they were all losing money as long as he was stuck where he was. And Bill's mood improved even further after a lunchtime session in the pub with King, financed by the ten-bob note Bartram left with the fitter.

By the time the suit returned, the new cylinder head and gasket in the back of the van, King had stripped off the old one. He quickly fitted the new one, then remounted the blowlamp and other fittings; another half-hour then to start up and run the engine, to be sure all was well, and he climbed out onto the bank beside Bill's relieved grin:

'Sounds okay now, Mr 'Anney?'

'Aye, pretty good, Dave. Thanks, mate.'

'Will you make a start now, or leave it until the morning?' Bartram asked.

'We could stay 'ere ternoight, Dad, mek a quick start in the mornin', don' yeh think?' Stevie suggested; but Bill shook his head:

'Oi want ter get ahead, boy. We can mek it ter Katie de Barnes ternoight, no trooble. Then we moight get unloaded at James's termorrer.'

'Oh – yeah, h'okay.' The boy sounded disappointed, but he went to untie the fore-ends. Bill shook the fitter's hand.

'Thanks agen, Dave. See yeh down Bull's Bridge soomtoime.'

'Yeah – take it easy, Bill.'

'Good luck, Mr Hanney.' Bartram held out his hand; Bill took it after a momentary pause:

'Thank yeh, Mr Bartram.'

Two hours later, they tied outside the Boat Inn in Catherine de Barnes, near Solihull. Stevie had been plotting along the way, leaning on the gunwale while his father steered the Acorn around the pound above Knowle; now he asked:

'Can Oi use the boike, Dad?'

'Whatever fer?'

''E wants ter go back 'n chat oop that barmaid at the Black Boy,' Vi told her husband; Bill stared at his son:

'Boot – what about yew 'n Ginny?' The boy shrugged:

'T'ain't gonna work out, Dad. Oi...'

'Let 'im go, Bill. They'll 'ave ter sort 'emselves out.' Bill held his son's gaze until he dropped his eyes and shrugged again, then he reached out and put a hand on his shoulder:

'Go on then, boy. Don' mek a fool o' yerself, will yeh?'

'Oi won', Dad.'

* * *

A vague air of annoyance hung over the two crews sat around a table in the Windmill, in Winson Green. They'd arrived at James's foundry in mid-afternoon, only to be told that there was no-one free to handle the ingots they were carrying, and they would have to wait and unload the next day. When pressed, the foreman had told them casually that a shipment had just arrived by lorry, and had to take precedence over their loads.

Harriet and Sylvie had taken the opportunity to get out their dolly tubs and do a load of washing, which had then been strung up in the evening sunshine over the open holds to dry, while Ginny set about preparing a communal meal, eagerly assisted by the

Skate's young crewman. Michael and Billy had looked at each other and laughed when Albert had commented that his daughter and the Warden lad seemed to be getting on very well all of a sudden:

'Yeh missed it too, did yeh, Dad?' Michael asked.

'Missed what?'

'Las' night, in the Black Boy – Gin saw Stevie chattin' oop the barmaid, 'n give 'im the cold shoulder. Kim saw 'is chance, 'n started mekin' a fooss of 'er!'

'Oh, bloody 'Ell! Oi 'ope we ain't gonna 'ave any trooble 'tween 'em. Any'ow, she's too yoong ter be gettin' serious 'bout any boy.'

'Yeah – boot she's gettin' ter be real pretty. 'N so tall fer 'er age, she looks older'n she is,' Billy pointed out.

'Oi s'pose yeh're roight, Billy. We'll 'ave ter keep an oiye on 'er...'

'Don' woorry, Dad, no-one's gonna 'urt moy little sister!' There was a glint in Michael's eye.

Over their drinks in the pub, discussion turned to Sylvie's condition:

'Any day now, ain't it, Sylv?' Harriet asked; Sylvie nodded happily, patting the bulge below her waist:

'Any toime at all!'

'Are yeh gonna look fer a load, or wait fer the babby ter coom?' Alby asked Billy.

'Oi ain't sure what ter do fer the best, Alby.' Harriet studied the other woman's posture, the flush on her cheeks:

'Oi think yeh should 'old on, Billy. Get ter Warwick Bar, or Sam'son Road, wher' yeh're near the 'orspital. Sam'son Road'd be best – ther's a midwoife 'andy 'oo'll coom if she's needed.'

'Aye, per'aps yeh're roight. What d'yer think, Sylv?'

'It might be best, Billy. He could come any time now.'

'Or she!' her husband chuckled. Ginny looked up from her conversation with Kim, in the corner seats:

'D'yeh want a boy or a girl?' Billy replied:

'We don' moind oither way, Gin. We'll be joost as 'appy if it's a 'im or a 'er.'

''Ave yeh thought about names yet?'

'Oh yes!' Sylvie smiled: 'Billy says we should call him after my parents, so it'll be George if he's a boy, and Emily if she's a girl.'

'That's noice, Billy,' Michael commented; the other man coloured slightly: 'Seemed roight, with Sylv losin' 'er folks in the war.' He looked up with a smile as Harriet leant over to give him a kiss on the cheek:

'Yeh're a big softie, Billy 'Anney!'

Chapter Eleven

Their annoyance of the day before was somewhat assuaged when the boats were called into James's dock first thing the next morning. Alby gave his turn to Billy, letting him unload first, so that they could get away as early as possible; the young man swung his deep-loaded boats in under the brick arch which opened on the foundry's internal wharf with a studied panache. As they were lifting out the heavy ingots of aluminium, which were then taken and stacked by the foundry's workmen, the foreman came over:

'I've got Waterways on the 'phone, askin' ow yeh're doin.'

''Ave they got h'orders fer oos?' Billy asked.

'They want one o' yeh ter go ter Noo Warwick Wharf fer a load o' beer, ter tek ter Park Royal. But yer missus looks like she's about ter pop.' Billy laughed:

'Aye, she's doo any toime! Oi'm goin' ter Sam'son Road, gonna loy they 'til the babby cooms. It's ar first, 'n Oi ain't tekin' no chances.'

'Fair enough, mate. I 'ope it all goes well fer yeh.'

'We'll tek the beer roon,' Michael offered – he had been lending a hand unloading Billy's boats.

'Right-oh, I'll tell 'em that. You're Mr Baker, right?'

'Moy Dad's captain, boot yeh, that's oos. The Sycamore and the Antrim.'

'Right-o mate. Third pair's comin', are they?'

'Yeah. They 'ad a breakdown, day 'fore yestiday, boot they should be 'ere anytoime.'

* * *

A jubilant Bill Hanney arrived just as the foundry's workforce returned after lunch. The Sycamore was already empty, and only about half of the load remained in the Antrim; Alby looked around as Bill and Stevie walked into the warehouse, their boats tied in the arm outside:

'Ey oop, Bill – yeh made it then!'

'Yeah – fitter from Bull's Bridge 'ad oos a noo 'ead on 'fore the day was out. We stopped at Katie de Barnes las' noight.'

'D'yer see Billy on yer way?'

'Oh, ah! Met 'im in the Ol' Thirteen – goin' ter loy at Sam'son Road fer the babby ter coom, 'e says.'

'Looks real h'excoited, doosn' 'e?' Michael paused in dropping an ingot onto the dockside. Bill chuckled:

'Yeah, not 'alf! 'N Sylvie's lookin' grand, ain't she?'

'Radiant!' Harriet called up from within the hold.

'Aye, that's the word fer it!' Bill agreed.

Ginny had seen Bill and his son approach; she had watched them for a moment, but then turned back to her task before Stevie could speak to her. He'd stood listening to the exchange about his brother; now he walked along the dock to where Ginny was heaving out ingot after ingot. He bent and took one out of her hands as she hefted it:

'Ginny?' She glared at him.

'What?'

'Can Oi talk teh yeh?'

'Oi'm busy – we've got work ter do.'

'Later, then?'

'Oi 'spect we'll be away then – we've h'orders ter Fazeley Street ter load.'

Geoffrey Lewis

'Please?' She hesitated, then relented:

'Well – mebbe. If ther's toime.'

'H'okay... ' She turned back to the remaining ingots in the hold behind her; Stevie watched her for a moment but then turned away, reluctantly.

An hour later the Antrim too was empty, and Michael ran the boats out to make way for Bill's pair. They tied outside, to tidy and sweep out the holds; Carrie and Josh, happy as always to see each other, mopped off the cabinsides and polished the brasses between them.

'Oi wish 'e'd put as mooch inter keepin' ar boats smart as 'e doos your'n!' Vi commented with a laugh.

As soon as Alby was satisfied with the boats' appearance, they were away, heading back around the Soho loop to Old Turn Junction and the thirteen locks of Farmer's Bridge. Stevie, hard at work humping aluminium out of the Kerry, looked up to watch them go – he hadn't got that word with Ginny, even then.

Back down the Old Thirteen, turn right at Aston Junction and down the six tired and unkempt locks of Ashted on the Digbeth Branch; left turn out of Typhoo Basin and they were at Warwick Bar and the now-nationally run facility of New Warwick Wharf. Seven o'clock in the evening, and the Sycamore and the Antrim were tied just outside the loading canopy ready for their cargo of barrelled beer to go aboard the next morning.

Harriet had managed to get a mutton stew cooked while they were slogging down the locks – she and Ginny would loosely take turn and turn about to do the cooking, day by day – and now they all ate together, sitting around the butty's well under overcast skies.

'Gonna rain ternoight?' Alby speculated.

'Reckon so, Dad.' Michael agreed; he changed the subject: 'D'yeh think we'll get the sauce roon back?' Alby shook his head:

'Oi dunno, boy. Seems loike they're sendin' boats wherever they want 'em on the spur o' the moment, now.'

62

'Bit silly, ain't it?' Harriet said: 'Oi mean, if yeh've got a crew that's got the drop of a partic'lar roon, knows its ins 'n outs, loike, it meks sense ter keep 'em on it, don' it?'

''Course it doos,' Alby agreed, 'Boot they don' seem ter think loike that, this noo lot. Oi 'ope they don' put oos on a coal roon...'

'Whoy's that, Dad?' Michael asked.

'Well, boy – it's 'ard enooff watching yew 'n the girls shiftin' them h'ingots, or 'umpin' barrels o' beer. Oi couldn' stand boy 'n see yeh shovellin' coal, that'd be too mooch.' Ginny rounded on him:

'If we do get a coal roon, yeh'll do 'xactly that, Dad! Oi ain't 'avin' yew strain yerself shovellin'!' Alby held up his hands:

'H'okay, h'okay! Oi'll do as Oi'm told!' Michael had been looking thoughtful:

'Boot, Dad – if we was ar own bosses...' Alby turned to him: 'Yew still think we could roon ar own boats?'

'Whoy not?' Alby heaved a sigh:

'Oh, Moikey! Think what's h'involved, boy! 'T'ain't joost 'avin' a pair o' boats, yeh've got ter deal wi' the gettin' o' loads, dockin' 'n maintainance, all o' that – 'n yeh'd 'ave no-one ter see yeh boy if things got 'ard. Loike in the freeze-oop two year back – Fellers's kep' oos goin' wi the loyin' money. Yeh'd 'ave none o' that.'

'No, Oi know, Dad. Boot we'd be able ter go wi' the work, 'n tek the loads we can 'andle 'stead o' joost doin' what we're told.'

'Yeah, mebbe – boot Oi can' see it workin', Moikey.'

'It moight work, Dad,' Harriet chipped in: 'Oi mean, Moikey's 'ad a lot o' learnin', 'asn' 'e? Ther's noo folks coomin' on the cut, mekin' a go of it. Loike that feller as bought the ol' Columba.'

'Oi s'pose so, loove – boot it ain't loike we're 'avin' trooble, is it? 'S long as we're h'okay as we are, let's leave well alone, roight?' Michael nodded reluctantly:

'Yeh, Oi s'pose yeh're roight, Dad. Any'ow — wher'd we get the money ter buy oos a pair, eh?' They all laughed – but Albert's eyes held a knowing smile.

Heavy raindrops suddenly speckled the water around them, and they all squeezed down into the butty cabin for a fresh brew of tea, too tired after their day to bother heading for the pub.

In the Windmill, Vi Hanney was concerned with the future as well – but it was her son's future she had in mind:

'So what's doin' wi' yew 'n Ginny, then?' Stevie looked uncomfortable under her scrutiny; he just shrugged his shoulders. His mother wouldn't let it go:

'Coom on boy! 'Ave yeh fell out with 'er, or what?'

'Not really, Ma, boot – well, Oi ain't gonna marry 'er. Oi know that's what yeh all thought, boot it ain't roight.'

''Ow d'yeh mean, son?' Her voice was softer now.

'Well – Oi do loove 'er, Oi s'pose, boot it's more loike she's moy sister, d'yeh see? Mebbe Oi've known 'er fer too long, if yeh oonderstand, since we was both kids. 'N Oi don' think Oi can loove 'er... that way, if yeh see?' Vi studied his troubled face; then she put her arm around his shoulders and gave him a consoling hug:

''Ave yeh told 'er that?' He shook his head:

'No – she don' wan' ter talk ter me.' Vi laughed:

'Oi ain't surprised, after she saw yeh wi' that girl at the Black Boy! 'Oo is she, any'ow?' Stevie suddenly smiled:

''Er name's Ellie, 'n she's really noice. 'Er dad's a carpenter, in Knowle, 'n she's stoodyin' ter be a teacher. She said – 'e's lookin' fer an h'apprentice, 'er dad, 'n 'e moight look at me – if she arst 'im, loike...'

'What 'bout the boats, lad?' His father had been listening; now, he put his question gently. Stevie looked guiltily at him:

'Well – yeh've been talkin' 'bout givin' it oop, 'aven't yeh? 'N Oi can get better money on the bank, 'n 'ave a bit o' free toime as well, in the evenin's. If Oi 'ad a reg'lar job.' Bill sat looking at his son, deep in thought; then he nodded:

'Yeah, yeh moight be roight, boy. Boot let's noone of oos be 'asty, h'okay? We'll go on as we are fer a whoile, boot Oi'll think 'bout what yeh said. Yeh won' roosh off 'n leave oos, will yeh?'

'Oi wouldn' do that, Dad.'

'Mebbe if Oi could get a job 'round ther' soomwher', we could mek a go of it on the bank – what d'yeh think, Ma?' Vi surprised her husband by leaning over to kiss his cheek:

'Oi'll go wherever yew go, Bill 'Anney, yeh should know that boy now!'

Josh had been following the conversation, his eyes growing wider and wider; now, his voice broke in with a tentative question:

'Does that mean – Oi could go ter school?' Vi smiled at him:

'Would yeh loike that, Josh?' The nine-year-old hesitated:

'Yeah – Oi think so...'

Chapter Twelve

''N no drinkin' yer load, Alby!'

All the barrels were aboard the two boats; Alby Baker chuckled at the flip comment from the loading foreman of New Warwick Wharf, an old FMC man kept on by the new management. Michael looked up grinning from his task of shifting the last few to trim the boats level for their trip:

'Oh! Can' we lose one or two on the way?'

'No way, mate!'

Their load was destined for a bonded warehouse at Park Royal, on the Paddington Arm. They all knew that any 'shrinkage' would be quickly spotted and severely dealt with, so the exchange was understood as being merely flippant. Not that it had always been so – in the past, less responsible boatmen had been known to tap off some ale from a barrel or two and make up the contents with canal water, to the benefit of their health but the detriment of the product.

With another waterproof load, as with the ingots they had just delivered, they didn't stop to cloth up the boats but set about quickly mopping down the cabins and sprucing things up for the journey. Alby was checking over the engine, oiling up the shafts and pivots, while Michael mopped off the foredecks; Carrie and Ginny were polishing brass while Harriet threw together some hot soup to warm them on their way. Into their hive of activity came a sheepish interloper:

'Ginny?' Stevie Hanney's voice was almost supplicating in its tone. Ginny, cleaning the brass rings of the butty's cabin chimney, looked around. She sighed:

'Hello, Stevie.'

'Can Oi talk teh yeh?'

'H'okay, as yeh're 'ere.'

'Ginny, look... Oi do loove yeh, boot...'

'Foine way yeh've got o' showin' it!'

'Oh, Gin! Yeh're loike a sister teh me, 'n Oi didn' mean ter 'urt yeh – If Oi've led yeh h'oop the garden path, Oi'm really sorry. Boot – Oi couldn' marry yeh. Oi loove yeh too mooch fer that, if it meks any sense...' The girl stared at him, her polishing cloth forgotten in her hand. Then she pushed the beret back from her brow, leaving a smudge of Brasso behind, and smiled:

'H'okay, Stevie – mebbe yeh're roight. Yeh're a foine chap, 'n Oi'd 'ave been proud... Boot Oi'll not be fifteen 'til June, 'n yeh're too old fer me. We can still be friends, can' we?' He smiled back at her, relief clear in his eyes:

''Course – broother 'n sister, eh? Loike we were before?'

'All roight, Stevie, Oi'll fergive yeh...' He stepped up close, took her by the shoulders and kissed her on the cheek:

'Thank yeh, Gin.' She gave him a weak smile and turned back to her polishing.

'Wher' are yer boats, Stevie?' Alby spoke from his engine-hole. He, like the rest of his crew, had been surreptitiously listening to the conversation.

'We're on the old wharf, next door. They've got oos a load o' sauce fer City Road, joost loadin' oos.'

'Huh! Pinchin' ar job, eh?' Michael had walked back from the fore-ends. Stevie chuckled:

'Swap yeh, if yeh loike? Oi could use a beer roight now!'

'Mebbe we can meet oop later, if yeh're not too long gettin' away?'

'Aye, that'd be good – Oi'll see what Dad says.'

'Wher'll we be ternoight, Dad?' Michael turned to Alby, who scratched his head with his pipe-stem:

'We'll not get down 'Atton terday. 'Ow about the Black Boy?' There was a mischievous twinkle in his eye. Stevie looked guilty:

'Oi dunno, Ooncle Alby...'

They all looked up at a shout from across the basin:

'Steerer Baker! Yew still ther', Alby?'

'Still 'ere, mate!' Alby called back; the foreman hurried over to them:

'We just 'ad a phone message for yeh, Alby, from Sampson Road. They said ter tell yeh Missus 'Anney's 'ad the baby. Li'l girl; they're callin' her Emily.' For a moment they all just stared at him; then everyone was talking at once:

'That's brilliant!' Michael grabbed Stevie's hand and shook it vigorously.

'Ah, tha's grand!' Alby grinned as he stuffed the pipe back in his pocket.

'Ginny, Ginny!' Carrie jumped into the butty's well and embraced the older girl.

'That's woonderful!' Ginny hugged her back. Harriet emerged from the butty cabin, her face alight with joy; Michael smiled over at her:

'Ar turn next, 'Arrie?' She returned his smile:

'Wouldn' it be grand, Moikey?'

The foreman stood there, a big grin on his face:

'Well, as long as yeh're all pleased about it...' He turned and left them to their celebrations.

'Oi guess that settle's ternoight's stop, Moikey.' The initial pandemonium had settled down; the twinkle was back in Alby's eye.

'Oi guess it doos, Dad! Top o' Camp 'Ill?'

''Course, boy. We've got ter stop 'n see 'em, wet the babby's 'ead.'

'Oi'll go tell Mam 'n Dad – we'll see yeh ther'.' Stevie gave them a last look around, the grin on his face almost comical;

Ginny caught his eye, and quickly looked away as he turned and hurried off.

Alby had already lit the blowlamp on the old Bolinder; now he climbed back into the engine-hole, set the throttle and stepped on the flywheel pin. The big engine gave its usual loud 'Boof!' and cloud of smoke from its exhaust, and settled to turning over at a fast, steady idle. After a few moments, he turned the throttle back and it took on the distinctive off-beat tick-over of its kind.

In minutes, they were away, and approaching the bottom lock of the Camp Hill flight. Six narrow locks, meaning that the butty had to be worked through separately – but in barely an hour they were tying on the towpath opposite the old Grand Union Company depot of Sampson Road. And then everyone was hurrying over the gates of the top lock and making their way around to the basin itself, where a smugly delighted Billy was waiting to greet them.

The girls all squeezed into the cabin of the Middlesex, to see the radiant but tired Sylvie and the tiny bundle in her arms; on the dockside, the men stood talking, Billy telling all about the delivery of his daughter while Alby packed and lit his old pipe.

Michael and Kim listened through his tale, but then while he and Alby chatted, Michael took Kim by the arm and led him a little way off:

'Stevie came boy this mornin', as we were loadin'.'

'Oh, ah?' Kim looked wary.

''E settled things wi' Ginny, said sorry to 'er.'

'Oh – are they...' Michael shook his head:

'They're joost friends, now. Boot Oi reckon she's pretty oopset about it. She was really sweet on 'im.'

'Yeah...' Kim sounded uncertain of how to take this: 'Is it – Oi mean, do yeh moind if Oi talk to 'er?' Michael shook his head, smiled at the lad:

'Oi don' moind – it's 'er choice, 'n yours. She likes yew, Kim,

Oi know, boot:' he paused: 'Don' yew 'urt moy sister. Yeh'll 'ave me ter answer to, if yeh do.' Kim looked up at the tall young man, understanding his concern and accepting the quiet warning in his tone:

'Don' woorry, Moikey. Oi won' do anythin' ter oopset 'er any more.'

'H'okay, Kim. Go easy on 'er fer now, all roight?'

'Oi will, Moikey.' Michael gave him a nod; then he smiled down at the younger man, walking back with him to where Alby and Billy were still talking:

'We'll 'ave a few ternoight, eh? Yeh'll be coomin' down the Marlborough, will yeh, yew 'n Billy?'

'Oi 'spect so, Moikey. As long as Sylvie's h'okay.'

'We'll be ther', Moikey! Ma'll stay wi' Sylv, keep an oiye on 'er – they'll be along any toime.' Billy confirmed as they approached.

'Aye – we'll 'ave a real party fer little Emily, eh?' Alby chuckled in anticipation of a few welcome pints later on as Michael stepped into the butty's stern. He peered down into the cabin, and his smile grew wider than ever:

''Ow are yeh Sylvie? Yeh're lookin' grand!' The new mother looked up:

'Oi'm fine, thanks, Mikey. Come and see my little girl!' He stepped down inside as she eased the blanket away and gazed at the tiny face sleeping soundly there:

'She's loovely, Sylv! Yeh moost be so proud.'

'Oh, we are, Mikey. Billy hasn't stopped bouncing around all day!'

'Aye – if 'e grins any more 'is 'ead'll fall in 'alf!'

'No sign of a little Baker yet then, Mikey?' He turned to smile at his wife, sitting on the stool by the open table-cupboard:

'We're workin' on it, ain't we, 'Arrie?' She smiled and nodded:

'We'll get ther', Sylvie.' Michael looked around:

'Wher's Ginny?' Carrie, snuggled in beside Sylvie on the side-bed, spoke up:

'She went back ter the boats, ter start on dinner. She's been very quoiet, terday, Moikey?'

'Oi know, Carrie – she's a bit oopset. We'll 'ave ter mek a special fooss of 'er, shan' we?' The little girl nodded:

'She's oopset 'bout Stevie.'

'Tha's roight. She'll get oover it, though.' Carrie chuckled:

''Specially if Kim's ther'!' They all laughed:

'Aye, mebbe so!' Michael agreed.

Chapter Thirteen

The landlord of the Marlborough plonked six pints of mild down on the bar and took the ten-shilling note from Billy's outstretched hand.

''Ere's ter little Emily!' Bill Hanney raised his glass, and the others lifted theirs in salute. Albert set his down again, felt in his pocket for his pipe:

''Ow's it feel ter 'ave a noo granddaughter then, Bill?'

'Brilliant, Mate, bloody brilliant! Oi mean, yoong Jack 'n Rosie, 'n little Gabriel are great – boot this'n's a 'Anney, ain't she?' They all laughed, and Billy said:

'Oi still can' believe it – Oi'm a dad!'

'Ah, yeh'll soon get used ter it, boy. Oop at all hours, changin' nappies – 'n a row o' clean'uns blowin' in the breeze wherever yeh stop.' Everyone laughed again at Bill's comment.

'Yeh stoppin' ter get 'er Christened 'fore yeh go, Billy?'

'Yeah, we thought so, Alby. Sylv's keen ter get 'er doon. Oi'll troy the local vicars in the mornin' – foreman says 'e knows oone or two 'oo're usually 'elpful.'

'No soign o' yew two mekin' Alby a granddad yet, Moikey?' Michael shook his head:

'No, Bill. We keep on troyin, boot it ain't 'appened yet.'

'Are yeh disappointed, Moikey?' Stevie asked; Michael shrugged his shoulders as Bill reassured him.

'Not ter woorry, lad! It teks a whoile, soomtoimes, fer the furst ones ter coom. Look at me 'n Vi – four years it were 'fore

Gracie turned oop, then anoother two 'fore 'e coom along!' He gestured at Billy as everyone laughed again.

'Ah, boot Oi was worth waitin' fer, eh Dad?' Another ripple of laughter ran around at Bill's non-committal grunt.

'Yeh never 'ad any more after Jack, Dad?' Stevie asked; Bill shook his head:

'No, boy. Yer Ma 'ad a bad toime with 'im, 'n Sister said as we shouldn', fer 'er sake.'

'Oh...'

'Yew plannin' ter pick oop any more kiddies, Alby?' Billy's eye held a wicked twinkle. More laughter as Albert growled:

'Not bloody loikely, boy! Oi've got enooff trouble wi' the oone's Oi've got!'

'Oh, coom on Dad! Wher'd yeh be without oos, eh?' Michael asked.

'Tooked oop voice 'n warm in a little cottage soomwher', prob'ly!' But Alby's hand reached across and squeezed Michael's where it lay on the table.

'Yeh're very quoiet ternoight, Kim?' Billy asked his crewman; the youngster shrugged as Bill laughed:

''E's missin' 'avin' Ginny around!' Kim looked up, a self-conscious smile on his face, but his embarrassment was saved by a hail from the door of the pub:

''Ave yeh got room fer a poor old Gran' Union man?' They all looked around; Billy beckoned to the figure on the threshold:

''Course! Coom 'n join oos, 'Enry!'

Henry Caplin strode over to the bar, his youngest son following in his wake; he put out his hand:

'Well doon, Billy! We've joost toied in Sam'son Road fer emptyin', 'n saw the girls. They told oos yeh were down 'ere.'

'Thank yeh, 'Enry.' Billy took the hand and shook it eagerly.

'Left Suey ther', 'ave yeh?' Alby asked; Henry nodded:

'Aye – she's mekin' a big fooss o' the babby. Along wi' the rest o' them!'

''What are yeh 'avin'?' Billy asked, but Henry shook his head: 'No, Oi'll get these, boy...'

'Oh no yeh don', 'Enry Caplin! It's Granddad's round.'

Bill intervened: 'Moild, is it?'

'Bitter fer me, if yeh don' moind, Bill. 'N a shandy fer Sam.' A chuckle ran around the group at the disgruntled look on the boy's face; Bill turned to the bar:

'Landlord! If yeh would, mate...'

A scraping of chairs, and a group of locals got up to leave the pub. Glasses refreshed, the boaters took over the vacated table.

'What yer got on, 'Enry?' Bill asked the newcomers.

'Timber. Should'a gone ter Gravelly 'Ill, boot the silly booggers 'ave shut the wharf. Tekin' it on by lorry from 'ere, they are.'

'Yeah. 'S'appenin' all oover, ain't it?' Bill sympathised.

''Specially after the freeze-oop two year ago,' Michael said. 'Coomp'nies switched ter usin' lorries 'n soom of 'em ain't coom back teh the cut.'

''S'roight, boy. Yeh can pass places we used ter unload 'n see the ol' basins loyin' empty, can' yeh?' Alby agreed.

''S gonna get wuss, 'n all. Soom fact'ries are turnin' oover ter oil 'stead o' coal, so we'll be losin' them loads.'

'That roight, 'Enry?'

'Oh, aye. Oi c'n see oos all lookin' fer jobs on the bank, oone day – t's only the coal keeps oos goin', really. From the coaleries 'round Suttons ter Nash, or Apsley, or Southall – 'n we're loocky if we get any koind o' back-load now, offen we 'as ter roon back empt.'

'Ain't they gettin' new loads though, 'Enry?' Billy asked: 'Oi 'eard as they're carryin' wheat down the Wellin'borough River now.'

'That's true, Will Bos'ells on that roon. Boot there ain't no back-load fer them, neither, they get sent back empt ter Brentford. Ain't worth 'em coomin' ter Birnigum, nor goin' ter Coventry neither, at least so they tell 'em!'

'The guv'nors, yeh mean?'

'Yeah!' Henry's voice was heavy with scorn. 'Too many bloody office wallahs gettin' in charge now. Lot's o' the old bosses 'ave gone, teken their chance when the goov'mint took oover. This noo lot don' know their arse from their elbow, 'alf the toime.'

'Is it really that bad, 'Enry?' Bill asked: 'We're still keepin' workin' all roight.'

'Oi dunno, Bill,' Alby put in: 'We've 'ad ter coom back empty once or twoice, lately. Oi reckon it's loike Moikey said, a lot o' stuff's goin' on lorries now that we used ter get.'

'Oh, Oi s'pose we keep goin', mostly.' Henry answered Bill's question: 'Oi think 'alf the trooble is they've got too many boats 'n not enooff jobs fer 'em. So it's easier ter send oos back empt rather'n troy ter foind oos a load. 'N another thing…' he waved an admonitory finger: 'They still 'aven' doon noothin' about all the drudgin' what's needed! Fixed oop a few rotten gates, 'ere 'n ther', boot yeh still can' get a full load along the bottom road, nor down the h'Oxford cut. 'N the Strafford cut's so shaller yeh can' even get an empty motor along, 'tween 'Ockley 'Eath 'n Kings Norton!'

'So what d'yeh think's gonna 'appen, 'Enry?' Bill asked; Henry shook his head:

'Not mooch! Oh, the cut'll keep goin' fer a good whoile yet, boot Oi can see the lorries tekin' oover in the end. Oi 'ope the trade'll see me out, moind – it'll be easier fer yew kids as can read 'n wroite, when it cooms ter gettin' noo jobs. 'Ear that, Sam? Moikey 'ere did yew a big favour these las' few years learnin' yew all that stooff!'

'Yes Dad.' The boy's tone of resignation suggested that this was a frequent comment from his father.

'Yew keep on with it, boy! Keep practisin'!'

'Yes Dad.'

'That goes fer all yew youngsters, roight?' Henry looked around at Kim and Stevie; they nodded sheepishly, chorused:

'Yes, Mr Caplin.'

'Ther's quoite a few men leavin' the cut fer jobs on the bank lately,' Albert observed.

'That's roight, Alby!' Billy confirmed. 'Mostly yoong fellers, goin' after better pay...'

'Yew ain't joined 'em then?' His father asked with a grin.

'Nah! Oi reckon, the more o' them as go, the more work ther'll be fer oos that's left. In the end, the bosses'll 'ave ter put our mooney oop ter keep oos on the boats, roight?'

'Yeh think ther'll still be work ter be 'ad?' Alby asked quietly.

''Course ther will! Oh, soom loads'll go ter the lorries, 'cause they're quicker'n boats, boot we'll still 'ave plenty, yeh'll see!'

'We've bin thinkin' o' packin' it in.' Bill's revelation was met with a stunned silence. He looked around their astonished faces and grinned: 'It's bin on me moind since we furst 'eard tales o' Fellers's closin' down at Moikey's weddin'. Oh, that don' seem loike the big problem we thought it moight be – but now Stevie's mebbe got soomthin' loined oop...' All eyes turned to the young man, who looked distinctly uncomfortable:

'It's only a chance, loike, nothin' defnite. Yeh know Oi've got friendly wi' the barmaid at the Black Boy...'

'We 'ad noticed!' Billy interrupted, causing a chuckle all round, which became a roar of laughter when Kim added:

'So did Ginny!'

'Yeah, well...' Stevie had the grace to blush as he went on: 'Ellie – that's 'er name – she's learnin' ter be a teacher. 'Er dad's a carpenter, 'n she reckons 'e's lookin' fer a noo h'apprentice. 'N she's gonna put in a word fer me, loike...'

'Yeh're that serious 'bout the girl, are yeh?' Henry asked; Stevie blushed again, but he nodded:

'Yeah, reck'n so. She's real noice, 'n very pretty...'

'A boatee 'n a teacher – that'll be a rare mixture!' Laughter echoed again at Alby's comment, but he looked over the table at Stevie: 'Good Loock teh yeh, lad.'

'What about yew, Bill?' Henry asked. Bill shrugged:

'Dunno, 'Enry. If Stevie really wants ter go, Oi wouldn' stop 'im. 'E's all boot noineteen now, 'n it's 'is future. We'd be sad ter leave the boats, boot Oi'd troy fer a job on the bank wi' the coomp'ny, mebbe lock-keeper or soomat. If soomthin' coom oop.'

'Not roight away, though?' His eldest son asked.

'Oh, no. Oi want Stevie ter be sure of what 'e's at, 'fore we do anythin'. 'N Oi'd want ter be soomwher' 'andy so's 'e can stay with oos.'

'Yeh'll 'ave toime ter get that load o' sauce ter Loonon, then?' They all laughed again at Alby's spurious question.

Later, as they were strolling back to the boats Michael fell into step with Stevie: 'Yeh're really serious about this, are yeh? Leavin' the boats?' His closest friend sighed:

'Yeah, Oi think so, Moikey. Ellie's – really special, yeh know? Oi think – we're meant ter be tergether. Loike yew 'n 'Arriet.'

'Yeh've not known 'er long.'

'Oi know. We ain't gonna roosh anythin', moind – Dad's gonna troy 'n stop boy Knowle when 'e can, so Oi can get ter see 'er. 'N Oi'd 'ave ter talk to 'er dad, about the job.' They walked in silence for a while, then Michael said:

'It won' be the same, without yew around.'

'Yeah. Yeh've bin a real good mate ter me, Moikey.'

'Yew too. Remember 'ow yeh got me ter steer the butty, that furst toime?'

'N yew troid ter 'it the bridge on Grafton straight!'

Their laughter echoed across the canal as they walked on.

Chapter Fourteen

A drab, colourless morning in October, and the gleaming maroon Rover 75 splashed through the puddles in Lincoln Road, Olton. It drew up at the kerb, and a non-descript man in a raincoat and a trilby hat stepped out into the steady drizzle; he reached back into the car for his briefcase, and then closed the door, carefully locking it before he turned away. Fumbling in his pockets for another set of keys, he crossed the pavement and then let himself into the premises of the Birmingham Building Society.

Charles Harrison had been the manager of the Olton branch for some six years. Nearing sixty, he had been with the Society for most of his working life – now, in the front office, he hung his hat on the stand in the corner and then took off his coat. Carefully adjusting it on a coat-hanger, he hung it below his hat and left it to drip disconsolately onto the lino flooring. He paused and looked around – and only then experienced a feeling of oddness, of something being not quite right. A frown creased his otherwise-unlined brow, and he walked across to the door which led into the back office, unconsciously brushing his hands down his black pin-stripe suit as he did so.

He opened the door, and gazed into the room which housed his own desk and the company's safe. The reason for his unease now struck him forcibly – the back door into the yard behind the row of buildings stood partly open, letting too much light into the back office, and it had been this added illumination which had unsettled him. And now he sensed also that something was missing. He looked around, uncertain of just what it was that he wasn't seeing. His frown deepened, and he stepped over to the desk, looked beyond it...

How long he stood there, his mouth open in horrified consternation, Harrison was never able, later, to decide. But the gap in his visual memory of the room was all too clear – the stubs of four sheared-off bolts, let into the concrete, delineated a clean square of floor, but of the company's safe there was no sign.

* * *

At around the same time that Charles Harrison was letting himself into his office, a Fellows, Morton and Clayton pair was drawing away from the top of Knowle locks into the ten-mile pound to Camp Hill. Although loaded, the boats were riding high, because the bulk of their load consisted of fresh air – but perhaps not so fresh, as most of it was contained within empty wooden barrels, the property of Mitchells and Butlers Birmingham Brewery.

Michael glanced back, and grinned through the drizzle as Carrie waved to him. For once riding at her ease on the butty, she was perched on the front of the cabintop, his old jacket drawn tight around her slim shoulders against the damp; beyond her, Alby, leaning in the hatches puffing on his pipe, echoed his grin. So high was it riding in the water that they had the butty on cross-straps, tight to the motor boat's stern, which left little for its crew to do – on cross-straps a pair works much like an articulated truck so that any steering input from the rear is more hindrance than help.

Settling himself in the motor's hatches, Michael smiled up at Harriet, herself perched on the roof by the slide where she had climbed as they left the last lock. Her brown eyes sparkled as she smiled back:

'Miserable weather, eh?'

'Aye.' But the look in their eyes was anything but down-hearted.

Michael reached out, and she touched his hand, quickly, briefly, the sudden shyness showing in her smile that he loved so much.

'Ginny'll be out wi' breakfuss soon.' Harriet just nodded.

In the cabin of the Antrim, the fifteen-year-old stood over the range, stirring the pot which contained a soup resurrected from the left-over juices from last night's mutton stew. They'd spent the last night at the Black Boy again, happening across Bill Hanney's boats there, and that meeting had left them all with conflicting feelings.

'They're lookin' fer a lengthsman, oop the maintainance yard,' Bill had informed them over the rim of his pint glass. Alby had held his gaze for a moment before asking casually:

'Yeh goin' fer it, then?'

'Dunno, mate. Ar Stevie's keen ter go fer this h'apprenticeship with Ellie's dad, so mebbe Oi'll 'ave teh. Boot, now it cooms ter it, Oi ain't sure Oi want ter leave the boats.'

'Oi know 'ow yeh feel, Bill.' Alby looked over to where Michael and Stevie were chatting, joined between customers by the pretty brunette behind the bar they leant against: 'E's bin offered it, 'as 'e?'

'We met oop wi' them in 'ere a few weeks back,' Vi told him: 'Carter, 'is name is, James Carter. Seems loike a decent feller, 'n 'is missus is noice girl; they've got a boy 'n all, Jimmie, twelve year old.'

'We all 'ad a long talk, 'n then 'e says as 'e'd be 'appy ter tek Stevie on, when 'e's ready. So, if Oi was ter get this job oop the yard, it'd settle everythin' noicely. Ther's a 'ouse ter be 'ad, goes wi' the job, so 'e could stay with oos. T'ain't far inter Knowle, so 'e could boike in ter work.'

'Meks a lot o' sense, Mr 'Anney – anyoone can see as Stevie's really stuck on that girl!' Harriet observed.

''E is that!' Vi laughed.

Six months on, Ginny was entirely reconciled to her split with Stevie. His sudden abdication had hurt her more than she'd wanted to let people know at the time, but in the following weeks she had accepted that the idea that theirs was a long-term relationship had been based more on habit than fact.

Now, she was happy to have him as a friend, a good friend, but only as a friend. But to think that he might leave the boats, that she wouldn't run into him at unexpected moments, in unexpected places, still left her with a vague empty feeling deep inside. But, she consoled herself, they'd still see him, and his mum and dad, when they passed through Knowle. And the ten-mile pound was a part of almost every trip they made, as the last remaining easy route south out of Birmingham, so they'd be that way week by week.

She gave the pot a stir, tasted the result. Another dash of salt to bring out the flavour, and she filled the five mugs waiting on the table-cupboard. Over the summer, she had settled into a kind of easy relationship with Kim Warden – but she knew in her heart that this, too, was only friendship and not romance. *After all, Oi'm only fifteen!* Kim was a grand fellow, kind and considerate as well as darkly good-looking, and it made her happy to spend time with him, enjoy the occasional kiss and cuddle, but she could never imagine marrying him. Like all boatees, their opportunities to meet were dictated by the job, restricted to a quick hello-goodbye as the boats passed, the occasional evening together at a stop somewhere.

'What're yew smoilin' about, girl?' Alby gave her a grin as she handed him a mug of the soup; she chuckled:

'Nothin' special, Dad.' She handed two more mugs to Carrie, who got to her feet and scampered off along the top-planks to hand them on to Michael and Harriet; Carrie's she left on the cabin-top for the child when she returned.

Alby put an arm around her shoulders, gave her a quick squeeze as she took a sip from her own soup:

'Good ter see yeh so 'appy, Gin.' She just smiled at him again. Thinking about boys had brought the twinkle to her eyes, the slightly self-conscious memory of the looks that would follow her sometimes, in the pub or on the wharf, the nudges, the uncertain smiles that would greet her. She knew that boys found her attractive, wanted to be with her (or be seen with her, perhaps!), and that knowledge secretly pleased her as much as it surprised her: *Oi'm nothin' special!* But at the same time she knew that she stood out from the crowd – most boat-people were on the short side, stocky, dark of hair and eye; slim, blond and blue-eyed, she was already as tall as her adopted dad.

She slipped her arms around the old boatman, cuddled into his embrace: 'Oi do loove yew, Dad.'

'Oi know yeh do, choild.'

Alby's own thoughts had been revolving around the future and its uncertainties. People, he knew, had been drifting away from the boats for a long time, since before the war even. Now, more and more were going – young men, looking for better money and easier hours in factories and warehouses; young women, marrying away from the cut for much the same reasons; and whole families, looking for a better future for their children or just losing heart as the waterways deteriorated around them and loads became harder and harder to get.

Now Bill, of all people. With Ben Vickers, retired since the closing of FMC's Braunston depot, Bill Hanney was Alby's closest friend, had been since their childhood, and his final decision to leave the boats felt like the end of an era. Bill had said that he was going to think things over during their trip, to City Road Basin with another cargo of HP sauce, but Alby harboured little doubt of what his decision would be. Melancholy gripped the old boat-man – they'd still meet, perhaps more regularly than ever with Bill working on the bank, but it would not be the same, somehow. And if Bill did leave, it left Alby wondering how much longer the rest of them could go on, how many more years would there be any trade for the boats, any loads for men like him to carry?

At his age, the future perhaps didn't trouble Alby too much for himself. But what of Michael and Harriet, Ginny, and little Carrie? What would the years to come hold for them?

Chapter Fifteen

Thank goodness we'll soon be at Camp 'Ill! Even Michael's spirits were getting dampened as the unending drizzle soaked into his donkey-jacket, weighing him down physically as well as mentally. And his surroundings didn't help – more than half way along the ten mile pound to the beginning of their descent towards Bordesley Junction and the New Warwick Wharf, the gloom of the day deepened as they ran through the long cutting which borders Ulverley Green. Harriet had retired to the cabin out of the rain; behind him, Alby still kept a watching brief in the butty's hatches while the two girls also sheltered within.

He glanced up at the high brick-arched bridge spanning the cutting as the boats swept towards it, raised a hand in response as an indistinct figure waved over the parapet. Suddenly the boat lurched under him; he grabbed the rim of the hatch to steady himself as his ribs slammed against the back edge of the slide, at the same time snatching out the clutch rod, while the stempost of the butty drove into the tipcats on the motor's stern, forcing it even harder onto whatever obstruction had brought it to such a dramatic halt.

For a moment, Michael just stood, dumbfounded, as he tried to catch the breath that had been driven out of him. His next thought was for his wife:

'Yew all roight, 'Arrie?' Harriet appeared in the hatches as he stepped back onto the counter, slipping her coat around her shoulders:

'Oi'm h'okay, Moikey. Whatever's 'appened?'

'We've roon oop on soomthin' in the channel. Soomthin' solid.'

'We're stoock?' He was bending over the side of the boat; he glanced back at her, a rueful smile on his face:

'Yeh could say that. Stern-end's six inches out o' the water.' He looked up at a gasp from the butty's fore-end, where Carrie could see the problem for herself:

'What are yeh on, Moikey?'

'Dunno, loove. Soomthin' 'ard and solid. 'Ang on – Oi'll see if she'll coom back off it.'

Harriet ducked back out of the way as he reached for the controls and reversed the engine. Pushing the clutch back in, he wound up the throttle in stages until it was at full speed, water boiling and foaming under the counter; he shook his head in frustration as they remained firmly stuck. Feeding in the oil rod, increasing the engine's power, only resulted in the smoke-rings emitted by the exhaust becoming thicker and blacker as the boat stubbornly refused to move.

After a few seconds, he gave it up and let the engine run down to its usual irregular tickover.

'We ain't gettin' off loike that!' By now Alby and Ginny had joined the gathering on the butty's fore-deck:

'Shaft 'er over, see if she'll coom off soideways,' Alby suggested.

'Oi'll go.' Harriet stepped up out of the cabin and made her way towards the fore-end of the motor, pausing to pick up the long shaft which lay on the beams over the open hold, above the barrels. Climbing around the deck-board, she braced herself on the fore-deck and pushed the bow sideways across the canal until it was all but touching the edge of the towpath; as the boat swung, it pivoted from a point somewhere under the cabin, where the obstruction had them wedged. Holding it over with the shaft, she waved to Michael. He nodded; reversing the engine again so that it ran forwards, he pushed the clutch in once more and wound up the power. The boat rocked; he could feel it trembling under him, trying to move in response to the tiller which he held hard over towards the towpath. But still it remained stuck fast. He tried the tiller the other way, trying to rock the boat off in the other direction, but that too was to no avail:

'Let's drop the butty out o' the way, Dad.' Alby nodded; they unhitched the cross-straps and drew the Antrim up alongside, and then pushed it over to the bank with Carrie still on board. She stepped off and held it on the back-end line while the others contemplated their situation.

Over the next half hour, they tried all they knew to shift the boat – shafting the fore-end from side to side to try and work it loose, standing on the gunwales and rocking with the same end in view, while Michael ran the engine hard in reverse. Pushing the fore-end over to the towpath again, Alby and Ginny stepped off; Michael threw the stern line to them, and they heaved and strained, first sideways and then backwards, as he used the engine in the same directions. But nothing had any effect – the boat stayed where it was, with inches of daylight and the top of the propeller showing under the counter.

They had been stuck there for well over an hour. And in that time, just when they could have used some help, not a single boat had passed – but now, as they paused in their struggles, cold, damp, dispirited and wondering what to try next, the sound of another engine echoed distantly through the bridge. Michael looked around with a smile of relief:

'Per'aps we can get a snatch!'

Minutes passed as they watched and waited; at last, the fore-end of a boat appeared in the bridge-hole, deep-laden, bearing the blue and yellow colours of British Waterways. The steerer, as he came into view, gaped at them in amazement for a moment before throttling back his engine and turning to take in his towline. He drew slowly alongside, passing them on the outside, and came to a halt beside the immovable Sycamore; under the bridge, his wife stepped off the butty and brought it to a stop, holding it on her stern line. The man looked over with a grin:

'Yeh 'avin trouble, Moikey?'

'Nah – joost stopped ter h'enjoy the soonshoine, Frank.'

'Ah.' Frank Shine put his boat into reverse and backed up far enough to throw his towline over to Ginny on the bank. Coming forward again, he took the end of a short snubber as Michael handed it to him and dropped it over the stern dolly of his own boat, and then ran slowly on until the rope drew tight. He turned and raised a hand; Michael waved back and pushed his clutch in, winding the engine, already running in reverse, up to full power. Over the deep note of the Bolinder, they could hear the staccato beat of the Dover's two-cylinder National; water foamed from beneath the two counters, and the rope thrummed like a bowstring. But still the Sycamore refused to budge; Michael began throwing himself from side to side, using his weight to rock the boat. Harriet, standing on the back-end planks in the hold, took the hint and did the same; and at last, rocking violently as it did so, the boat began to edge gradually backward.

A cheer rose from the people on the towpath – Alby and the two girls, and Betty Shine and her daughter, standing by their butty. Frank Shine had a broad grin on his face, echoed by the little boy who stood with him on his motor's gunwale, but a worried frown crossed Michael's face at the bumping and grating that he felt from beneath his feet – like all of the ex-FMC boats, the Sycamore had a flat wooden bottom bolted to her iron sides.

A few more feet, and they were floating free once again. Frank cast off the short line, and Michael coiled it in, dropping it on the cabin-top out of the way. He put the engine back to forward rotation and cautiously edged the boat in to the bank in front of the Antrim. Frank backed his own motor up and pulled in behind them; he stepped off as his son took the back-end line to hold the boat and walked up to them:

'Whatever were yeh stoock on, Alby?'

'God knows, Frank. Soomat solid, fer sure. Roight in the channel, 'n all.'

'Can't 'ave been there long, or soomeone would 'ave found it before,' Michael suggested.

'Aye – ther's alwes junk in this stretch. Oi'll bet soomeone chucked it in las' noight, from oop the bank.'

'Yeah. We were joost oonloocky ter roon over it – if we'd been deep-loaded, loike yew, we'd 'ave bounced off it, boot bein' loight we joost roon oop on it.'

'We'll 'ave ter let the coomp'ny know, Dad.'

'Aye – we'll stop in at Sam'son Road 'n tell 'em.'

'Oi'll tell the yard at Knowle, 'n all,' Frank said: ''N we'd best warn anyone we meet.'

'We'll do that.' Alby changed the subject:

''Ow's little Freddie been lately?' The boy had been poorly on and off for some time, and everyone had been concerned for him.

'Not so bad – Sister Mary give oos a bottle o' tonic fer 'im 'n 'e's bin mooch better since.'

'That's good!' Ginny turned and gave the little boy a cheery wave; he grinned and waved back.

'We'd best be on ar way.'

'H'okay, Frank. Thanks fer yer 'elp, mate.'

'H'any toime, Alby! Be seein' yeh!'

Frank returned to his boat and backed carefully past them; picking up the tow again, the British Waterways pair set off, going out wide to avoid the unknown obstruction in the canal. A final wave from its crew, and they were gone.

'Is ther' any o' that soup left, Gin?'

'Oi can mek it stretch ter anoother moog all round with a bit o' loock, Dad.'

'We ought ter get goin', Dad.' Michael said.

'Ah, boogger it, we've lost that mooch toime anoother 'alf an hour ain't goin' ter matter! We're all cold 'n wet – turn that injun off whoile we get soomat 'ot down oos!'

Chapter Sixteen

Ginny strode off and disappeared into the butty cabin. Michael climbed down into the engine-room and emerged with two mooring pins; he hammered one into the towpath beside the Sycamore, and tied the back-end rope to it to hold the boat while they all changed and warmed up over Ginny's soup. Then he did the same for the Antrim. Ginny called out to Carrie to go and get into dry clothes; the little girl eagerly obeyed, and Harriet went down into the motor cabin with her to do the same.

Michael and Alby slipped off their sodden coats in the engine-room and hung them up to dry in the heat from the Bolinder. Alby headed for the butty to join the girls now huddled around the stove; Michael stopped the engine, and then entered his own cabin to find a dry pair of trousers. He sat on the sidebed where Carrie normally slept to take off his boots, but in the silence his ears pricked up at an unexpected sound. He felt his heart sink: *Oh, no!*

One boot unlaced, he knelt down and quickly lifted one of the sections of the floor boards. He could hear it clearly now – the steady, rapid trickle of water. He whipped up the next section of floor – and there it was. A small fountain of water, pouring in a constant stream up through the bottom of the boat. He stared in angry frustration for a moment before hurrying from the cabin to tell the others.

'Dad – motor's tekin' water oonder the cabin.' Alby looked up from his mug:

'Bad?'

'Bad enooff, Oi reckon. Looks loike it's knocked some caulkin' out between two planks, ther's about six inches wi' water pourin' up through.'

'Can we stop it?' An old boater's trick was to throw ash from the range under the boat, which would often seal a small leak as it was drawn into the crack.

'Nah. It's too woide, caulkin's blown roight out boy the look of it.'

'Boogger! Lemme 'ave a look.' He followed Michael back to the Sycamore; they climbed down into the cabin, where Alby pursed his lips at the sight of the leak:

'We'll 'ave ter get goin'. If we keep poompin' we can stay ahead of it 'til we get ter Sam'son Road.'

'Roight. Oi'll start the injun again.'

'Don' forget ter put the poomp on.'

'No, Dad!'

Michael slipped on the belt which would drive the mechanical pump before kicking over the engine; the old Bolinder sprang back into life, and he peered over the side to see a steady stream of water emerge from the pump outlet: *That's joost about enooff ter cope wi' what's coomin' in!* Alby, meanwhile, had untied the butty, drawn it close behind the motor and reattached the cross-straps. Now, retrieving the mooring-pins, he untied the Sycamore and pushed it out from the bank, and then hurried to step onto the butty as it began to move.

''Ow bad is it, Dad?' Ginny asked.

'We're h'okay fer now, poomp'll cope with it. Boot we'll 'ave ter watch it – if any more caulkin' blows out we'll 'ave ter use the 'and-poomp as well.'

'Oi'll go 'n join Moikey, Dad, keep an oiye on it,' Harriet volunteered. She stepped up out of the cabin and made her way forwards. Michael looked around with a smile as she joined him on the motor boat; she stretched up to kiss his cheek and then squeezed past him into the cabin, where she looked down with a worried frown at where the water was pouring up through the boat's bottom.

'Give me a shout if it gets any wuss!' She looked up and nodded at Michael's words, and then settled herself on the sidebed her feet tucked up beside her clear of the exposed bilge.

As he steered the pair under the high bridge, Michael was swiftly calculating: It was about an hour to Sampson Road depot and the top of Camp Hill locks – they would need to stop there anyway to tell the company about the obstruction in the canal which they'd found in such dramatic fashion – then another hour with both boats down the narrow locks. Warwick Bar and the old FMC wharf of Fazeley Street depot was only a few hundred yards on then, past Bordesley Junction where 'The Garrison' turned off. They should make it all right, as long as the leak got no worse. He'd take a good look at Sampson Road – if it looked bad they could unload there, but he would only do that if it was really necessary. The boatman's pride in his job, instilled in him over ten years, said that only the direst circumstances would stop them getting their load to its proper destination.

Once unloaded, the boat could go to Saltley Dock. Down the five locks of the Garrison – the old Birmingham and Warwick Junction Canal – and on towards Salford; not too far, and there the damage could be repaired. They'd probably have to lift the boat out – the leak looked too bad to fix with it in the water. He heaved a sigh – if they did that, they'd want to give it a full docking, recaulk all of the bottoms, reblack the hull and repaint the cabin. That would mean a week or more on the dock even if they could start on it straight away, so he and his crew would end up with a change boat, a spare kept ready for any crew whose own boat was out of service for any length of time.

A deep sadness gripped the young man. For almost ten years now, since that fateful night when he'd run away from his loveless life in Wolverton and found himself adopted into the world of the canals, his home had been this old boat. The thought of giving it up to the dock-workers and moving into a different cabin with his wife and little Carrie left him with a hollow feeling inside, like the loss of an old friend.

And what boat would they get? The whole of the Fellows, Morton & Clayton fleet had been handed over to British Waterways back in July, to become part of the national operation, so they might not even get another Josher. Like all ex-FMC men, he held to the belief that their elegant boats, mostly built on Saltley Dock and known as Joshers' after Joshua Fellows, the founding director of FMC, were much superior to any other canal craft. The idea of being given one of the ex-Grand Union boats, with their bluff rounded bows and tapered sterns, filled him with horror! And that would mean getting used to a different type of engine, as well – FMC had always stayed with the single-cylinder two-stroke Bolinder, while the Grand Union boats, built in the 1930s at Woolwich on the Thames, or Northwich in Cheshire, all had two-cylinder National or Russell Newbury engines. *Oh well, Oi s'pose we'll manage, whatever 'appens...* The gloom which had assailed him earlier settled back on his shoulders.

At the top of the Camp Hill flight, he hurried over to the depot in search of the foreman while Alby took a close look at the leak. They'd left the engine running, the pump still returning the incoming water to its rightful place, but even so Alby shook his head, a worried frown creasing his brow. The water level in the cabin was measurably deeper than it had been an hour before: *Bloody poomp ain't keepin' oop!* The difference was not great, but they were undeniably losing ground, albeit slowly. He pushed back his hat and scratched his head – then, reaching a decision, he called for Carrie, chatting with Harriet and Ginny beside the Antrim:

'Roon over ter the depot, loove, tell Moikey ter get them ter telephone Fazeley Street. Tell 'em we're coomin', 'n we're leakin' bad, we'll need ter be emptied straight away.'

'Yes, Dad!' The little girl looked scared, but she dashed off to do as she was bid. In minutes, Michael was back:

''Ow bad is it, Dad?'

'Poomp ain't keepin' oop, lad. We'll 'ave ter use the 'and-poomp as well, part o' the toime any'ow. Yeh got the message ter Fazeley Street?'

'Yeah. Foreman's callin' them roight now. 'N 'e knows about the h'obstruction we 'it, 'e's sendin' soom men ter get it out.' He hesitated, then suggested: 'Should we get the barrels off 'ere?' Alby gave him a grin:

'Not if Oi can 'elp it! We'll get the booggers ter Fazeley Street if we 'ave ter carry 'em!' Michael grinned back:

'Roight-oh, Dad! Oi'll coom with yew, that way Oi can give the poomp a good go in the locks. 'Arriet 'n Ginny can manage the butty. Let's get goin'!'

Needing no more warning, Carrie grabbed her windlass and set off to the top lock. Michael stepped onto the back-end planks and swung out the stirrup pump which was mounted in the corner of the hold; a few quick strokes and it was primed, and then with each thrust of his arms a gout of slightly oily water poured from the outlet over the side of the boat. Alby had walked back to the butty to tell the girls what was happening and unhitch the cross-straps; now he untied the motor and stepped onto the counter. Pushing the clutch in, he eased the throttle open slightly and steered for the open lock.

Carrie gave him a slightly worried smile as he ran the boat in, and then leant on the gate to push it closed. Michael was still heaving up and down on the pump-handle; Alby pushed in the reversing rod, but the engine, instead of kicking against the compression and beginning to run backwards, simply gave a desultory cough and stopped altogether.

'Bloody 'Ell!' Alby grabbed the back-end line and jumped off of the boat, throwing his weight against the rope as he did so, but he was too late – the Sycamore's momentum carried it the last few yards until it hit the bottom gates with a resounding bang. Michael had braced himself, warned by his dad's shout, but even so he almost fell from the planks into the hold.

'Damn 'n Blast! Of all the toimes fer the boogger to go out...' Carrie gave Michael a half-scared, half-amused look – neither of them had heard Alby give vent to his feelings quite so forcibly before. They watched as he stepped back onto the boat and peered down into the cabin:

''Ell 'n Damnation!'

'What is it, Dad?'

'Boogger's knocked a chunk more caulkin' out. Bloody water's pourin' in now!'

'Must'a got cold, standin' above the lock.'

'Aye. Boot that don' 'elp now, boy.' They both knew that, to reverse successfully, a Bolinder had to be running hot – standing at tick-over in the cold damp weather, it had cooled down too much. Michael stepped up and peered over his shoulder, felt Carrie come up behind him too.

In the bottom of the cabin, water was now coming in through a crack which stretched all the way across from one side of the central keelson, which ran fore and aft the length of the boat, to the point where the timber bottom met the iron side. Carrie's voice quavered as she asked:

'What're we goin' ter do, Dad?'

Chapter Seventeen

'Oi ain't bloody givin' oop now! We're goin' ter get these barrels ter Fazeley Street coom 'Ell or 'igh water!'

Despite their dire situation, Michael couldn't help the grin which spread over his face. Albert turned from his contemplation of the damage:

'Carrie – go 'n tell the girls ter leave the butty wher' it is. We'll whistle the motor straight down on its own, coom back fer that'n later. Moikey – yew keep pumpin', boy, as 'ard as yeh can!'

They both hurried off to do what he directed. Alby dived down into the engine-hole – five minutes with the blowlamp and he had the Bolinder running again. In the mean time, Harriet and Carrie had run past him to the bottom gates and furiously wound up the paddles. By the time the narrow lock was empty, Ginny had hurtled past on the bike to set the next one.

They flew down the flight: Carrie ran ahead with Ginny to set the locks; rather than risk another mishap, Alby didn't try to reverse the engine but resorted to the old horse-boatman's habit of strapping the boat into a lock, dropping a heavy rope around the stump on the end of the top gate as the boat glided past, slamming the gate shut and stopping the boat's momentum at the same time. He and Harriet whipped up the bottom paddles in unison, and she pushed the gates open as he ran back to jump down onto the counter and drive the boat out. With the next lock already set, in seconds they were repeating the performance.

And all the time Michael thrust the handle of the stirrup pump up and down as hard and as fast as he could. By the third lock, he was flagging, gasping for breath, his arms feeling like lead; Harriet saw his distress, and jumped on beside him:

'Oi'll do that fer a bit, Moikey, yew 'elp Dad.' He hesitated, but then nodded: 'Joost fer a whoile, then Oi'll tek over again.' He looked over the side: 'We ain't keepin' oop, love, it's goin' down.'

'Soon as we're out o' the locks Oi'll start gettin' ar clothes and stooff out o' the cupboards.' He just nodded again, impressed by her matter-of-fact attitude, and stepped off as Alby ran the boat out of the lock.

At lock number five, he took over again. They exchanged only looks this time as Harriet, her cap awry and her breast heaving, let him take her place.

Lock six at last; Bordesley Junction before them, the Garrison going off to their right, and Warwick Bar, site of the one-time stop-lock into the Birmingham and Fazeley Canal, in sight in front of them. Cold, wet and dispirited in the continuing drizzle, all of them could see now that the Sycamore was settling – the water was halfway up to the centre guard around the counter, eight or nine inches higher than it should have been. His arms and shoulders on fire, his back feeling as if it could break at any moment, Michael kept up his steady rhythm on the hand-pump; Alby kept the engine running fast, the mechanical pump doing its bit.

As she and Carrie pushed the last gates open, Ginny called down: 'We'll go back fer the butty – yew go on!'

'Roight – Oi 'ope they're ready fer oos!' He paused in the lock-tail for Harriet to step on, and then threw the clutch in and wound up the engine. The two girls stood and watched for a moment before turning away to walk back up the flight to their waiting butty. Ginny saw the tears in Carrie's eyes and slipped her arm around the child's shoulders; they walked in sad silence back the way they had come.

In the Sycamore's cabin, Harriet stared miserably at the water lapping over the floorboards. The spinning propeller shaft, now completely submerged, made the oily surface ripple in waves like a miniature ocean; with a sigh, she dropped the sections of the floor which Michael had removed back into place and set to, frantically emptying all of the low cupboards. Carrie's spare clothes and shoes from under the sidebed, pots and pans from below the range and the table-cupboard, their own spare clothing and boots from beneath the cross-bed. She was starting on the crockery and provisions inside the table-cupboard when she felt the boat turn hard to the left.

At the tiller, Alby saw the depot foreman run out and wave at their approach. The man signalled him to run straight in; carefully but quickly, he turned into the basin and manoeuvred under the canopy. Men snatched the ropes to tie the boat up; one jumped onto the back-end planks beside Michael:

''Ere, I'll do that. Yeh look bloody knackered, mate.'

'Thanks!' Michael stepped off onto the wharfside and staggered against the side of the cabin. Men were now swarming over the hold, heaving the empty barrels out onto the bank; he watched them, his chest heaving as he tried to get his breath. The foreman came up to him:

'What 'appened, Mikey?' His breathing getting easier, Michael raised his head:

'We 'it soomthin' in the channel, oop boy Olton. Took oos nigh on two hours ter get off, 'n then the bottoms were leakin'.

'Yeah, we 'eard about that. Gang from Sam'son Road's up there now tryin' to fish it out.'

''S'roight. We were doin' h'okay 'til a load more caulkin' blew out at the top o' Camp 'Ill.' The foreman looked at the boat, lying deeper than ever now:

'Did well to get 'er 'ere, from the look of things!' Michael laughed:

'Yeah, well, moy Dad wouldn' give oop! We whistled down the floight, left the butty at the top, ter troy 'n mek it. Ginny 'n Carrie 'ave gone back fer it now.'

There was thoughtful admiration in the man's eyes as he said:

'Yeh've done a bloody good job there, all of yeh – I'll send a couple of men to give them a hand. You give your missus a hand to get your things out of the cabin while we empty 'er.' He glanced around at the men unloading the boat: 'Yon barrels are barely even wet!' Alby had come to join them; now he growled:

'Shame they ain't wet on the insoide – Oi could do with a beer roight now!'

Back at the top lock, Carrie stopped to raise the paddles and refill it as Ginny walked back to the Antrim. They had paused to close the bottom gates of the last three locks, knowing that no boats were coming in the opposite direction.

Ginny knew that her home was safe – she and her dad shared the cabin of the butty – but she knew how the others must be feeling. The Sycamore would have to go on the dock for repairs, and so they would be given a change boat. Even though all boat cabins were pretty much the same in design and layout, every one was different in small and subtle ways – drawers in slightly different sizes, cupboards slightly deeper or shallower, small things in different places. And every stove was different, each with its own idiosyncrasies, which would inevitably upset Harriet when it was her turn to cook.

She put the eye-splice of the long line over the looby at the top of the butty's mast and then untied the boat. Checking to see that Carrie had the lock ready, she threw her weight against the rope. At first, she seemed to be making no impression, but then, almost imperceptibly, the rope began to give against her shoulder as the butty started to move. Gradually, it picked up speed until she was able to take a step; then another, then another, and then she was walking forward, very slowly, the rope twined over her arms, the boat following obediently.

Win Barnet climbed out of her butty cabin into the now-easing drizzle with a cup of tea for her husband, who was standing chatting with a couple of the dockhands beside their boats in the Sampson Road depot. Just unloaded, they were waiting for orders; Harold would move the pair into the layby once he'd drunk his tea:

'Thanks, Win. Yeh want a coopa?' he asked the men.

'Nah, thanks – we'd better get back ter work 'fore we gets a rollickin'!'

'Eh, 'Arold – look oover ther!' Win had seen the Antrim begin to move. They had noticed the lone butty, left there on the towpath above the locks; and the tale of Alby Baker's woes had gone around the depot a little while earlier after Michael's hurried visit. Harold Barnet looked up from his oh-so-welcome drink:

'Eh, that's yoong Ginny bow-'aulin' it! Wher's Moikey?' Michael would usually take on the task of pulling the butty through the narrow locks, and everyone had heard him joke about playing the mule at Camp Hill.

'Dunno, loove' Win answered his rhetorical question, only for Harold to answer it as well:

'Oi'll bet they're stoock soomwher' wi' the motor... We can' 'ave a slip of a girl loike 'er doin' that! 'Ere, Alfred!' he called to his teenage nephew, who looked up from where he sat on the gunwale splicing their spare towline: 'Coom 'n lend a 'and, boy!'

'H'okay, Unc!' He'd followed his uncle's gesture and realised the situation. He got up and followed Harold, not entirely displeased at the prospect of helping out, and hopefully getting to talk to, the pretty blond girl he'd seen often but never met.

Ginny had drawn the butty into the lock, letting its momentum carry it the last few yards. She walked back to brace herself against the rope and stop it, only to realise that the boat was stopping anyway, apparently of its own accord; looking up, she met Harold Barnet's grin:

'We'll give yeh a 'and, girl!' He was leaning against the heavy strap attached to the stern shackle, braking the boat to a halt.

'What about yer own boats?'

'We're waitin' fer h'orders in Sam'son Road. Wher's Moikey 'n yer dad?'

'They're at Fazeley Street wi' the motor – we coom back fer the butty, me 'n Carrie.'

'Ah. Yeh know moy nephew, Alfred.' She smiled at the tall youth standing next to his uncle, who stammered:

''Ello, G-Ginny.'

''Ello, Alfred. Thanks fer coomin' ter 'elp oos.' The boy blushed pink:

'Tha's h'okay.'

The four of them worked the boat quickly down the first three locks. At the fourth, they met the two men despatched by the foreman from New Warwick Wharf:

'Mr Gordon's sent us to help these girls with their boat,' one of them told Harold.

'H'okay, mate. We'll go back ter ar own boats 'n leave yeh to it, then.' But Alfred offered:

'Oi'll stay 'n see 'em down ter the bottom, Ooncle 'Arold.' Barnet gave the lad a knowing smile:

'All roight boy. We'll be in the layboy at the top when yeh coom back.'

Soon the butty was descending in the last lock. One of the Fazeley Street men was standing ready to bow-haul it out and on to the depot; Ginny stood by the bottom gate with Alfred Barnet, who at last plucked up the courage to speak to her:

'Well – yeh're 'ere now, Ginny. Oi'd better be gettin' back.' Aware of the teenager's shyness, and grateful for his help, Ginny smiled at him.

'Thank yeh ever so mooch, Alfred.' He shrugged his shoulders, colouring slightly at her words; impulsively, she gave him a quick kiss on the cheek. With a bemused smile, he stammered:

'H'it's no t-trouble, really! A-any toime, Ginny.'

Chapter Eighteen

A forlorn sight met them when they reached the basin at New Warwick Wharf. Under the unloading canopy, Michael stood beside the stack of their meagre possessions with his arm around Harriet's shoulders as she gazed dispiritedly at their home; next to them, Albert stood silent, his hands on his hips. Several of the wharf hands were poling the Sycamore out into the basin rather than risk it going gunwales-under against the bank, in space they would need continually to load and unload other boats. One of their number was still frantically heaving on the hand-pump; they had stopped the engine, unable to keep it running now the engine-room was inches deep in water.

The two men manoeuvred the Antrim into the space vacated by their motor as Ginny and Carrie went to join the others:

'Oh, Dad!' Alby looked around at the hitch in Carrie's voice and gathered her into his arms:

'Don' fret, choild. Yeh'll 'ave a new boat ter play with now.'

'Boot it won' be ar boat!' With nothing to say to this, Alby just held her tight. The foreman came up to them, his face a mask of sympathy:

'Ah've sent ter Saltley fer a mechanical pump, they'll be 'ere any time. We'll put 'er against the side over there...' he gestured across the basin '...where it's shallow, so she'll just settle on the bottom without goin' under. They c'n pump 'er out 'n get 'er teh the dock when they're ready.'

Albert just nodded; the man went on, hesitantly:

'They've got no change boats down there. But Sampson Road have got a couple – they're goin' ter get one ready for yeh.'

'H'all roight – thanks, mate.' They all looked at Alby, hearing the quiet sadness in his voice; he saw their concern and gave them a weak smile:

'Oi've 'ad the Sycamore nigh on fifteen year now. Moy Rita doied in that cabin...' Michael reached out and took his hand, and Ginny put her arm around him, hugged him tightly; his smile grew easier as he looked around their faces:

'Boot that's all in the past, eh? Oi've got yew kids wi' me now – loife goes on, don' it?' Michael gave his hand a squeeze:

'That's roight, Dad.' He turned to the foreman: 'When'll the boat be ready fer oos, Mr Gordon?'

'In the mornin', Mikey. There's another batch of ale from Mitchells due then as well, so yeh might as well take that – I'll suggest it to the manager. We can get yer butty loaded ready, then load the motor as soon as they bring it down.'

''Ave yeh got soomwher' we can put our stuff overnight?' Harriet gestured to the pile beside her.

'Oh, sure! There's a few empty crates inside, by the wall – help yerselves to a couple o' them. It'll be safe enough in the ware'ouse til the mornin'.' He studied them for a moment: ''Ow will yeh manage tonight, all of yeh?' Alby laughed:

'It'll be a bit toight! Boot we'll get boy – it's only oone noight.'

'Look – we've got a spare room, me 'n the missus. You two could come to us, if yeh like?' He spoke to Michael and Harriet, who shook her head:

'Oh no, we wouldn' want ter put yeh out.'

'It'd be no trouble, really. Save you all being crammed in tergether.'

'Well, maybe, if yeh're sure yer missus won' moind?'

'Nah, she'll enjoy the company!'

* * *

Early the next morning, they met again on the wharfside, Alby, Ginny and Carrie emerging from the butty cabin, mugs in hand, to meet Michael and Harriet. Anna Gordon had proved to be an eager hostess, glad, as her husband had said, to have visitors – she had insisted on entertaining their whole crew to dinner, despite the restrictions of rationing. She had chattered incessantly as she cooked, her guests congregated in the small kitchen of the terraced house in the backstreets near the depot; and then, after the meal, she had been fascinatedly attentive as they talked about their life on the boats and the dramas of their last trip in the Sycamore.

It had been late when Alby insisted on taking the two girls back to the Antrim – Gordon had walked back with them to let them into the wharf. Michael and Harriet had spent a comfortable night in the spare bedroom, despite their concerns over whatever new boat they would be given. A quick breakfast in Anna's kitchen, and they walked back with Gordon through a bright but overcast dawn as he went to work for seven o'clock.

As they stood talking, he emerged again from the wharf office:
'Yer new boat's ready, Mikey.' Somewhere between relief and apprehension, Michael turned to him:
'What've they got fer oos, Pete?'
'It's called the Oakley.' He hesitated: 'You've always been josher men, aven't yeh?' Michael nodded; Gordon went on: 'Well, yeh'll find this a bit diff'rent. It's a Northwich boat, ex-G.U. Got a two-cylinder National in it.' He held up a hand as he saw the disappointment in Michael's face: 'They're not bad boats, handle well – and yeh'll find the 'elm's lighter than a josher. They'll carry two-three tons more, as well. And they've got a proper gearbox – no need to faff about reversin' the engine!' Not entirely convinced, Michael smiled none-the-less at the man's eagerness to placate them:
'We'll get used ter it! Are they roonnin' it down or shall we go 'n get it?'
'Prob'ly be quicker if yeh walk up 'n get it. They'll be busy

first thing. M 'n B's lorries'll be 'ere any time, so we'll get yer butty loaded, okay?' Alby replied:

'Roight-oh, mate. Ginny 'n Oi'll stay 'ere whoile yew tek 'Arriet 'n Carrie ter get the motor, Moikey.'

'H'okay Dad. We won' be long.'

But they were rather longer than they intended to be. After the brisk walk back up Camp Hill flight, the three of them went straight to the depot manager's office and knocked on the door.

'Come in!' Michael pushed open the door and stepped inside, to be greeted by a relieved smile on the moustachioed face of George Coker:

'Ah! Just the man – come on in, Mikey.'

'Yeh've got a change boat fer oos, Mr Coker?'

'I have indeed, but these gentlemen want to talk to you first.' Michael looked around – he hadn't seen the two men standing behind the door, one of whom wore the uniform of a police constable. He turned back to Coker, suspicion darkening his expression:

'What do they want with oos?'

The shorter of the men, his mackintosh unbuttoned, a trilby hat in his hands, spoke up:

'You're Mr Baker, with a boat called Sycamore?' Michael regarded him coolly:

'Moy Dad's captain.'

'But you were in charge of the boat yesterday?'

'Oi steer the motor, yes. Dad roons the butty, wi' moy sister.'

'So you were on the boat when you ran aground yesterday?'

'Oi was.' The man gave a patient sigh:

'Mr Baker – I'm detective-sergeant Norton, and this is PC Froome. We're not – accusing you of anything, we simply need some help, some information from you.' He looked around at the sound of a chuckle from Coker:

'I did warn you, sergeant! Boat people have little regard for authorities on the bank – they tend to get a rough time from a lot of your colleagues.' Norton sighed again, looking as uncomfortable as he obviously felt:

'I know, Mr Coker. Mr Baker – it turns out that the obstruction you ran aground on in the canal was a safe. It had been stolen from the offices of the Birmingham Building Society in Olton, some time the previous night. Because you effectively found it for us, I just need to know what you can tell me about that.' Michael gave the man a smile:

'Oi'm sorry, Mr Norton. What did yeh want ter know?' Norton visibly relaxed:

'What time was it when you ran aground?'

'Oh – 'bout nine, I'd guess.'

'You saw nothing at the time, nothing suspicious?'

'What sort o' thing?'

'No-one on the bank, at the top of the cutting, for example?' Michael shook his head:

'No, not as Oi remember.'

'You didn't see anything thrown into the canal?'

'No – Oi could've gone 'round it if Oi 'ad!' Norton actually smiled at this:

'Yes, I suppose you could! It caused you quite a problem, I understand?'

'Yeah – two ruddy hours we were stoock on it! 'N it damaged the boat's bottom – we only joost got ter Fazeley Street 'fore it sank. That's whoy we're 'ere, ter pick oop a change boat.'

Harriet and Carrie had stood in the doorway listening to all this; now the little girl piped up:

'Did they steal mooch money?' Norton smiled at her:

'About forty thousand pounds.' Her eyes widened in astonishment:

'Tha's an awful lot!'

'They actually took the whole safe?' Harriet asked.

'Yes – they cut it from its mountings and took it away. Then they broke it open, took the money, and tossed it into the canal from a back-alley behind some houses at the top of the bank above where you found it.'

'Is ther' anythin' else, Mr Norton?' Michael asked.

'No, I don't think so. Can you stay in the area in case I need to talk to you again?' Michael bridled at this suggestion:

'We can' do that! We've got a load waitin' ter go ter Park Royal – 'n we don' get paid fer sittin' around goin' nowhere!'

'I can always reach Mr Baker if you need to see him again, sergeant,' Coker put in; and the constable spoke for the first time:

'With respect, sarge, I doubt if Mr Baker can tell us any more than he has already.'

'No, you're probably right, Froome.' Norton turned back to Michael: 'You'd be happy to talk to me again next time you're here, if I need you? Or perhaps talk to an officer in London, on my behalf?'

'Yes, I guess so.'

'Thank you, Mr Baker.'

'Good loock – Oi 'ope yeh catch 'em!' Michael put out his hand and Norton shook it, smiling:

'We'll certainly try, Mr Baker!'

Chapter Nineteen

After the two policemen had departed, Michael asked the manager:

'Can we get the boat, 'n get started? They've got a load waitin' fer oos down at Fazeley Street.'

'Yes, I know, Mikey. The boat's all ready, over in the layby – Harold Barnet's there, with his pair, get him to show you over it. His motor's the same as the Oakley.'

'Roight-oh, Mr Coker. When can we get our own motor back?' Coker hesitated:

'I don't know, Mikey. It'll be up to the people at Saltley to decide what to do with it.' Michael frowned:

'Well yew tell 'em we want it fixed, 'n we want it back, soon as maybe!' Coker shrugged:

'I'll tell them, Mikey.'

They made their way around the extensive basin of the Sampson Road depot to the layby where pairs tied to await orders for loading. There, Michael soon spotted the Oakley; he didn't know whether to be pleased or upset. After the slim elegance of a josher boat, the bluff lines of the town class were less pleasing even if they held the promise of a greater loading capacity, as Gordon had said. And fresh off the dock, the paintwork gleamed in the early morning sun – but it was the drab, uninspiring blue and yellow of the national fleet which met their eyes.

'Not what yeh're used teh, eh?' They turned around to see

the older boatman smiling at them: 'Mr Coker said yeh'd be along ter get it any toime.'

'Hello, Mr Barnet!' Carrie greeted him with a happy smile; he grinned at her:

''Ello again, Carrie – yeh got ther' h'okay then?' Michael replied:

'They did – thank yeh fer 'elpin' the girls, 'Arold. We 'ad our 'ands full wi' the motor.' Barnet chuckled:

'So Oi 'eard! Wher' is it now?'

'Sittin' on the bottom in the shallers 'cross the basin. Saltley's men are s'posed ter be coomin' ter poomp it out 'n get it ter the dock fer fixin'.'

'Aye. Well, coom on, let's show yeh what this'n's all about.'

Barnet stepped onto the counter of the Oakley and opened the cabin doors; he stood back and waved Harriet inside:

'Yew 'n Moikey 'ave the motor cabin, don' yeh?' She smiled at him:

'Tha's roight – 'n Carrie. Dad 'n Ginny share the butty.' She lowered herself into the cabin and began to look around as he walked along the gunwale to the engine-room. Michael and Carrie followed, and all three climbed down to inspect the engine. Barnet gave the little girl a surprised look, which made Michael laugh:

'Carrie's our second motor steerer,' he explained; Barnet asked her with a grin: ''Ow old are yeh, Carrie?'

'Oi'm twelve!' He chuckled:

'Good fer yew, girl!' He turned to the engine: 'T'ain't what yeh're used to, eh Moikey?' Michael shook his head:

'We've alwes 'ad a Bolinder, 'Arold.'

'Ah well – these Nationals ain't so bad. This'n's only joost bin put in 'ere. Two cylinders, bit quoieter than yer ol' Bolinder, 'n mooch quicker ter start. No need ter 'eat 'er oop, joost woind oop the bracket a bit.' He reached over his head and turned the throttle shaft with his hand; 'lift the taps,' and he flipped over two small levers on the cylinder heads; ''n woind 'er oop!'

He grabbed the starting handle with both hands and began to
turn the engine over, picking up speed until it was spinning rapidly
with a quiet, rhythmic clicking and chuffing sound:

'Drop the taps!'

Michael did as he said; as the first tap closed, the one cylinder
began to fire with a solid – donk – donk – donk'; with the second
tap, both cylinders were running, and the engine picked up to a
fast tick-over: 'donk donk donk donk donk donk...' Harold let it
run for a few seconds before reaching up again to turn the throttle
shaft back; he let the engine slow until it settled to a steady idle.
He looked around with a grin:

''N that's all ther' is to it! Yeh can start 'em on yer own boot
it's easier wi' two o' yeh.' Michael nodded doubtfully:

'Yeah – Oi s'pose it'll save oos a few minutes in the mornin's...'

'Oh, coom on, boy! Piece o' piss after a Bolinder! 'N they're
mooch easier ter droive 'n all – coom wi' me!' He led them back
around to the stern of the boat:

'Yeh've only got two wheels, roight? This'n...' he pointed to
the bigger of the two heavy brass control wheels, to the left under
the cabin roof: 'controls the gearbox. Yeh turn it this way...' he
spun it to the right '...ter go forrards': The boat surged gently
forwards as the propeller began to turn under them, and Michael
looked over the stern to see the water pushing out from below
the counter. Barnet went on:

''N this way...' he spun the wheel to the left '...ter go
back'ards'. The boat settled as the forward drive ceased, and
then eased back against the dockside as the stern gear took hold,
water bubbling along each side of the hull. Settling the wheel
back to its central, neutral position, he pointed to the smaller wheel
to its right:

''This'n's the throttle. It woinds oop ter the roight.' He
demonstrated, and the engine picked up speed until it was revving
quite hard. Michael frowned again – after the slow, steady beat
of a single-cylinder Bolinder, the National seemed to be going at

a phenomenal rate. Harold spun the wheel back again, and the engine returned to idle:

'Ther'. What d'yer reckon?' Michael shrugged off his doubts, at least in front of Carrie and the other boatman:

'Oi guess we'll get used ter it, 'Arold.'

Half an hour later they were well down the flight. The two boatmen had stood discussing the state of the canals and their trade until Harriet emerged from the cabin and reminded Michael that a load awaited them at New Warwick Wharf. With that, he had gingerly eased the engine into gear as Carrie loosed off the single line tying the boat stern-on to the layby and manoeuvred slowly and carefully out onto the main line. They found the top lock ready-set for them; Michael ran the unfamiliar boat in and used the gears as Harold Barnet had shown him to bring it to a halt.

But that unfamiliarity caught him out – the fast-revving engine stopped the Oakley quicker than he had anticipated. Feeling embarrassed, he had to go into forward gear again to nudge up to the bottom gates, his blushes not helped by Carrie's giggles. But within minutes he had got the feel of the boat and was stopping it as accurately as he ever had the Sycamore. In fact, he found himself beginning to enjoy the way it handled, appreciating the much simpler controls of the more modern engine.

Out of the bottom lock, and he paused to pick up the girls before running the few hundred yards to the Fazeley Street basin. Here he wound the engine up for the first time, and felt the big boat lift under him with its rapid acceleration; a tentative smile crossed his face. The Sycamore had had the enormous pulling power of the old Bolinder, but that engine had needed time to pick up speed – in contrast, the Oakley felt almost like a speedboat.

And another surprise awaited him: Travelling faster than he had earlier coming out of Sampson Road, he swung into the right-angle turn to enter the basin – and almost fell out of the hatches.

After the heavy tiller of a josher, the Oakley 's helm moved easily against the flow of water; he had to grab the slide and quickly correct his turn before the boat's fore-end hit the copings on the inside of the corner: *Boogger me! Oi wonder what it'll be loike with a load on?*

Soon after, he was able to find out.

By the time he'd run the boat into the wharf alongside the Antrim, the butty was loaded and the men waiting to put the rest of the barrels into the motor. Feeling a lot less down-hearted at the loss of their old boat, he stepped off onto the dock with an almost jaunty air; but then he caught sight of Albert's expression. The old boatman said nothing, but the look on his face spoke for him – it said that he wanted nothing to do with the 'oogly boogger' ex-Grand Union boat.

By lunchtime, the job was done, and they were quickly mopping down the boats ready to depart.

With full barrels this time, to be delivered to the bonded warehouse in Park Royal, the boats sat well down in the water; even so, it was apparent to Michael that they could have taken a few tons more on the Oakley. The Mitchells and Butlers trips had never seen the Sycamore loaded to capacity, but he could see that there was a bit more freeboard with the town class boat: *Pete was roight – Oi reckon we'd get twenny-seven ton on this 'n!*

And setting off, drawing forward out of the wharf, picking up the tow with the butty on the twenty-foot snubber, he felt the responsiveness of the northwich boat and the urge of the two-cylinder engine again: Oi could get used ter this! But glancing back he caught sight of his dad at the butty's tiller, and knew that his captain was going to insist on getting the Sycamore back as soon as it was repaired: *Oh well...*

Later, in the bar of the Cape of Good Hope, he gave air to his thoughts:

'These Gran' Union boats ain't so bad, Dad – it 'andles pretty good, 'n Oi reckon we'd get an extra ton or two on if we troyed.' Alby looked disdainful:

'T'ain't a josher though, is it?'

'No, but...'

'Oogly boogger of a boat – no shape to it.'

'Maybe, but...'

'Colours are 'orrible.'

'Yes, but...'

''N the h'injun goes too bloody quick – sounds tinny.'

'Yes, Dad.' Michael gave up, saving his opinions for another day.

And by the following morning, he was revising his own views.

''Arrie – moy blanket's all wet!' Harriet turned over as Carrie spoke. She pushed back the curtain between the bed-hole and the rest of the cabin:

'Wet? Is the roof leakin'?'

Carrie pushed back the slide and put her head out into the fresh morning air; she ducked back down:

'T'ain't rainin'.' She riddled the fire in the range and put the kettle on to boil. Harriet watched her, puzzled, as Michael stirred beside her:

'Hey!' She turned to him at his exclamation; he had stretched in waking, and his bare foot had touched the cabin-side: 'It's wet in 'ere too!'

'What?' She sat up and looked around. Water beaded the walls of the cabin and obscured the glass of the portholes. Michael propped himself up on his elbows; he reached behind his head to touch the cabinside. It felt cold, and his fingers came away wet:

'Condensation. What's it loike outsoide, Carrie?'

'Broight 'n chilly,' she called back. He looked at his wife:

'Bloody steel cabin! It's joost our breath, condensin' on the walls.'

'What can we do 'bout it, Moikey? We can' 'ave ev'rythin' gettin' wet!' He thought:

'Should 'elp if we mek sure all the vents are open. We'll ask yer dad, or Joey, nex' toime we see 'em, they know these boats.'

'Yeah – h'okay.' She sounded unconvinced.

Chapter Twenty

The pre-war Austin Ten saloon crunched through the snow as it turned into the car park opposite the Galleon public house in Old Wolverton.

The man who stepped out of the driver's seat, wrapped up against the cold, was white-haired, tall and slightly stooped; he reached inside to pick up an old trilby hat, but looked around in surprise as he went to place it on his head:

'Grandad!' A tall slim teenage girl in dungarees ran across the road and threw her arms around him: 'Yew came!'

'Did you think I'd miss seeing you?' He kissed her cheek and then held her away to look at her: 'You're prettier than ever, Ginny. And you've grown again, too!'

'Coom on insoide – they're all waitin'.'

Fred Morris let his granddaughter lead him over the road to the pub. There, seated around a pair of tables pushed together in the main bar, were a whole lot of familiar faces; the men all stood up to greet him, and he shook each proffered hand:

'Henry – good to see you again!'

'Bin a long toime, Fred.'

'Joe – how are the children?'

'Foine, Fred, foine. Gracie's stayed wi' them on the boats, boot she moight pop oop fer a quick'n later.'

'Ernie – How old are you now?'

'Noineteen this month, Mr Morris.'

'Happy birthday! And Sam – how you've grown since the wedding!'

'Oi'm fifteen now, Mr Morris.'

'Yes, I suppose you must be. Same age as Ginny!' The boy coloured slightly and glanced at her as he nodded. And lastly:

'Alby – how are you, my friend?'

'Oi'm very well, Fred, not that yeh'd think so the way Ginny goes on at me! What 'bout yerself?' Fred almost staggered as the boatman clapped him on the shoulder:

'Very good, thanks. Getting stiffer as the years go by, but I suppose that's only to be expected.'

There was only one lady seated at the table; Fred bent to kiss her cheek:

'Sue – you must be so proud of Harriet!'

'Oh, we are roight enooff, Fred!'

Ginny had stayed beside him all this time, her arm around his waist; now Carrie came up to him and he enfolded her in his spare arm:

'Carrie – how are you, sweetheart?' The little girl just smiled up at him and held him tightly.

Michael and Harriet had stood to one side through all the greetings, arm in arm, but now they came forward. Fred released the two girls to embrace Harriet:

'It's lovely to see you again, my dear. Are you well?'

'Oi'm joost foine, thank yeh, Grandad. 'Ow d'yeh feel about...' she nodded down at her stomach. Fred laughed:

'Being a great-grandfather? I'm so excited, I can't wait! When's the baby due?'

''Bout mid-June, Sister reckons.' He held her, smiling into her dark eyes:

'Boy or Girl?'

'We don' moind. Do we, Moikey?' Michael stepped to her side and put his hand on her shoulder:

'Oither oone'll be foine fer oos.'

Fred let go of Harriet and turned to his grandson:

'Michael...'

'Grandad...' And then they were in each others arms, hugging tightly, and Fred felt Michael slapping him on the back: 'It's so good ter see yew!'

After a while they eased their embrace and Fred held the young man at arms length, just looking at him. He felt sudden tears burning behind his eyes:

'Michael...' Warm grey-green eyes smiled into his, and he found it difficult to speak:

'Ten years ago – today?'

'Yesterday.'

'Ten years ago... If you'd told me then that I'd be holding you now, looking at you...' He broke off as his throat tightened up and drew a deep breath: 'When those policemen came to our door and told us you were missing, that you'd run away... We all thought you were dead – yes, even me! Only your mother refused to accept it. But she was right, God bless her! And now look at you – you're taller than me, you young rascal!'

'Oi'll be twenny-oone this year, Grandad.'

'I know, lad, I know! You're making me feel old – not to mention making me a great-grandfather.'

'Coom 'n sit down. Dad's got a beer in fer yeh.' Fred let himself be guided to the seat at the head of the combined tables.

'Point o' the landlord's best bitter, Fred.'

'Thank you, Alby.' He took a long draught of the cool beer and looked around their smiling faces before turning to his grandson again:

'You ought to be here in the seat of honour, Mikey!' Michael shook his head:

'No – yeh're the last of ar old family, Grandad, 'n Oi'm... Oi wanted ter say sorry fer roonnin' off loike that.'

'You did what you had to, Mikey. And just look at you now! A job you love, a lovely wife, and soon to be a father! I'm so proud of you, my boy.' He half-emptied his glass and then laughed: 'And I'm not quite the last – don't forget your Uncle Tony, even if he is twelve thousand miles away!'

They all laughed with him; then Joe Caplin asked:

'Weather was pretty mooch loike this that noight, wasn' it, Moikey?'

'Ten year ago? Yes it was, Joey – Oi remember croonchin' through the snow all teh way ter the cut. Oi was goin' ter joomp off the bridge, joost 'ere boy the Galleon, boot Oi couldn' cloimb the bank it was so slipp'ry. So Oi joost took a roon at it.'

'Didn'reckon on Billy 'Anney seein' yeh doive in, did yeh?' They all laughed again at Alby's comment, but the mood sobered as Michael said:

'Oi'm bloody glad 'e did, though. Oi'd 'ave been dead if 'e 'n 'is dad 'adn't fished me out – 'n look what Oi'd be missin'!' His arm curled around his wife's shoulders, and he pulled her close to kiss her.

'Bill should be here with us,' his grandfather said; Alby agreed with a chuckle:

''E shoud, of all folks! Mr Noob'ry at Bulls Bridge said as 'e'd tellyphone 'em 'n tell 'im we'd be 'ere ternoight.'

'We saw Billy 'n Sylvie th'oother day, goin'ter Leicester wi' timber,' Harriet told them.

'Oh ah? 'Ow's littl'un?' Suey asked.

'Emily? She's lookin' grand!'

'It was roight 'ere, as yew... yeh know?' Sam asked Michael hesitantly.

'Tha's roight, Sam. Joost th'other soide o' the bridge ther. Oi spent moy first noight on a boat over there...' he gestured vaguely '...opposite the ol' wharf in Vi 'Anney's cabin.' Behind him, the door had opened as he spoke:

'S'roight! We din' know if 'e was aloive or dead when moy man got 'im out!'

'Vi! Bill! Coom on over 'ere!' Michael leapt to his feet and held his arms out; Vi Hanney gave him a long hug, while Bill shook his hand. Josh dashed past them to throw his arms around his sister, and promptly began a long and eager tale of his time at school; behind his parents, Stevie stood with a grin on his face:

''Moikey – 'ow are yeh, mate?'

''Foine, Stevie – 'ow 'bout yew? Wher's Ellie?'

'She's workin' tonoight, boot she sends 'er love.' He shook Michael's hand: 'It's grand ter see yeh!' Michael laughed:

'Not loike las' toime we met on the boats, eh?'

'Ah – well...' Stevie looked embarrassed; Henry Caplin asked, a twinkle in his eyes:

'What 'appened then, Stevie?' He'd heard the story from Alby, but delighted in the prospect of discomforting the young man. Stevie smiled sheepishly:

'Well – It was in Bugby locks, 'n – well, Oi wasn' thinkin' what Oi was at. Oi went ter close oop 'n fill the middl'un. Din't see 'im coomin' th'oother way, did Oi? Not 'til 'e pops oop through the bridge.'

'So what did yeh say, Moikey?' Henry prompted; Michael chuckled:

'Oi told 'im Oi din't think it was a good oidea, turnin' the lock 'round in front o' me.' Ginny laughed, and quoted:

''E said, "Yew turn that lock round, Stevie 'Anney, 'n yeh'll be learnin' ter swim in it!" We all 'eard yeh!' Laughter filled the bar, and Stevie joined in sheepishly. As it died down, he changed the subject:

'Yew still got that northwich motor, Moikey?' Michael nodded, his expression darkening:

'Yeah. We keep askin' fer a change, boot nothin' 'appens.'

'These new bosses don' listen, do they?' Henry sympathised: 'We 'ad the same trooble wi' the Towcester, boot the ol' guv'nor sorted it. All them northwich boats were the same – those steel cabins use'ter sweat soomat awful. 'E 'ad our'n teken off 'n a wooden cabin put on fer oos.'

'We'd rather 'ave the ol' Sycamore back,' Alby told him, but Michael disagreed:

'Oi don' moind the boat – it 'andles foine, loighter than a josher. It's joost that bloody cabin! Condensation's real bad, 'specially in this cold weather.'

'What did they do wi' the Sycamore?' Bill asked.

'Dunno,' Alby replied: 'They poomped it out 'n towed it ter Saltley, 'n we ain't seen it since.' The look on his face said that he didn't want to talk about it, but his smile returned as he in his turn changed the subject: ''Ow's yer new job, Bill?'

'Grand, Alby. Oh, h'okay, Oi miss the boats, boot Oi'm still on the cut, 'n Oi see 'em all goin' boy, 'as a good ol' chat. 'N it's noice ter 'ave a bit o' free toime in the evenin's. 'N Soondays off, o' course!'

''Ow's the pay, Bill?' Henry asked.

'Thinkin' o' joinin' me, eh, 'Enry?' They all laughed as he went on: 'Not bad – 'n it cooms every week, whatever 'appens!' He looked around them: 'So wher' are yeh all 'eaded fer, then?'

Fred Morris sat back in his chair and let the conversation flow around him as the boaters talked of loads and routes, friends and acquaintances, lives and deaths, weddings and births. And, just being there, he knew himself to be privileged – he, too, had become a part of his grandson's new life, accepted into the proud and very private world of the boating people. He gazed across the table at the tall sandy-haired young man, caught the laughter in his eyes as he smiled back: *Your mother would be so proud of you...*

Chapter Twenty-One

'Oh no – not anoother bloody 'old-oop!' Michael cast his eyes to Heaven; the loading charge-hand raised his hands in a gesture of resignation:

'I'm sorry mate – there ain't nothin' I can do about it.'

'Wha's the trooble, Moikey?' Alby asked as he strode up after tying the fore-ends; the colliery's man answered him:

'We ain't got the coal ter load yeh with, captain.'

'What? They tol' oos this was a roosh job!'

'Aye, well – they're s'posed ter 'ave 'ad another train o' wagons 'ere, but the shunter's broke down. They're 'avin' ter fire up the spare, 'n that'll take time.'

'Oh, bloody 'Ell!' Alby looked at the sympathy in the man's eyes and sighed: 'Don' woorry, t'ain't yer fault mate. It's joost been one o' those trips.'

'Tell yer what – I've got about thirty ton 'ere. We could start loadin' that, 'n by the time that's done with any luck the rest'll be 'ere.'

'Yeah, h'okay mate. That'll about fill the butty – we'll put it oover for yeh.'

'Right-oh – I'll chase 'em up about the other wagons.' He went off to the office to telephone while the two boatmen moved the Antrim onto the loading dock.

It had, as Albert said, been 'one of those trips'. They'd set off from Brentford all right, loaded with forty-nine tons of aluminium ingots bound once again for James's foundry in Birmingham. And the run there had gone well, through the early summer's quiet weather – but then things had begun to fall apart. They had arrived at the foundry to be told that they would once more have to wait to be unloaded – a consignment of scrap had been delivered by road and had to take precedence.

So they had kicked their heels for the rest of the day. The delay had at least allowed time for them all to take the bus to the nearest public baths; but then, on their return, feeling fresh and clean, they had found a message awaiting them from the traffic manager at Sampson Road depot. They were to run empty to Griff colliery and load for Dickinson's paper mills at Apsley.

Until now, they had been lucky in avoiding the carriage of coal. The traffic departments had remained considerate of Albert's weak heart, and latterly of Harriet's developing pregnancy, in keeping them on other work where heavy shovelling was unnecessary.

But they had all known that the time would come, as other trade dwindled and coal became the only major southbound business for the waterways; and now it had. Michael felt angry and frustrated – it couldn't have come at a worse moment, with Harriet only a week or so from the birth of their first child. Alby had not suffered a recurrence of his heart attacks since his stay in hospital over two years before, but they were all aware of the risks of allowing him to over-exert himself, so that left only Michael and Ginny to cope with the heavy job of levelling the load in the boats and shovelling to clear the holds at the other end of the trip. Carrie would help, of course, but she was still only twelve, and could only do so much.

Discussion in the pub that night had hinged around Michael's displeasure with their lords and masters:

'Of all the toimes ter land oos with a coal roon!'

'Ah, we'll manage. Oi can lend a 'and wi' the levellin' – 'n the shoovellin' out. Apsley's got a big grab as teks most o' the coal out – we've seen it workin' when we've bin boy.'

'Oh no yeh won', Dad!' Ginny's eyes flashed as she rounded on him; then she turned on Harriet before she could speak: ''N yew ain't doin' nothin' either, not in your condition! Moikey 'n me'll do it, even if it doos tek a bit longer; Carrie'll 'elp, won' yeh?'

'Course Oi will,' the girl agreed; Alby shook his head:

'Oi can' stand boy 'n let yew do it all...'

'Oh yes yeh can!' Ginny told him.

'If we was ar own bosses, we could tek the jobs we wanted. We wouldn' 'ave ter put oop wi' this!'

'Oh, Moikey! Would we get any loads at all, eh?' Alby took up their old argument; Michael gave him a slightly guilty look:

'Oi did 'ave a little chat wi' Mr Noob'ry, las' toime we were in Bulls Bridge. 'E says they could offer oos work if we 'ad our own boats. 'N Oi've 'eard that Barlows tek on noomber oones fer soom o' their jobs.'

'Boot that'd be coal all the toime, boy! D'yeh want ter be doin' that?'

'No, Dad – Oi'm joost sayin' we could get work. If we got our own pair.'

'We can' do that roight now, can we loove?' Harriet injected some cool reason into the discussion: 'Let's deal wi' this load, 'n we'll think about it later, eh?'

'Oh, Oi suppose so.' Michael let the idea drop, still unhappy with their lot. He smiled at her: ''Ow'd we buy a pair, any'ow?' He was looking at his wife; only she noticed the little smile on Albert's face, but she said nothing.

The next day, the boats had been emptied and they had set off along the 'bottom road'. Down Farmer's Bridge and Aston lock flights to Salford; then the length of the Birmingham and Fazeley Canal, further downhill via Minworth and Curdworth locks; a right-hand turn onto the Coventry Canal, back uphill through

Glascote two and then Atherstone eleven locks. It was halfway up Atherstone that the next delay caught them – emergency repairs to a failed paddle lost them half a day. And now they'd arrived, only to find that the colliery didn't have enough coal at their dock to load the boats...

At the colliery, men ran the wagons they had alongside and set about preparing to tip the coal into the butty, Michael went up to the chargehand:

'Listen, mate – moy missus is 'avin' a baby in a coopl'a weeks, 'n moy dad's got a bad 'eart...' The man studied him for a moment, realising both the boatman's problem and the implied request; then he nodded:

'Okay mate. I'll get a couple o' the men ter level the load for yeh, bein' as we're messin yeh about. Will that 'elp?' Michael smiled his relief:

'Yeah – thanks mate, that'll 'elp no end.'

'We 'aven't seen yeh before, 'ave we – yeh don't usually take coal, eh?'

'No – we've been on metals, sugar, tinned stooff. Boot they tol' oos this was a roosh job.'

'Yeah – the road 'aulage firm they use fer some o' their deliveries let 'em down.'

''N now we're pickin' oop the pieces fer 'em!' The man just shrugged as Michael grumbled: 'We seem ter be playin' second fiddle ter the bloody lorries all the toime nowadays!'

The man was as good as his word. The two dock-hands he detailed to level the load in the boats were obviously not happy at the prospect, but they did as he bid them, clambering down into the hold with their shovels and setting to as the coal was tipped in from the wagons on the wharf above. Michael worked with them, keeping an eye on the trim of the boat, until all the available coal was on board; at that moment, the chargehand came over again:

'The other wagons are on their way, mate. D'yeh want ter get yer motor over now?' Michael looked up:

'Yeah, h'okay. We'll shove this'n over on the towpath.'

The two men climbed out, and Michael and Ginny poled the butty across the basin. They tied it up, and Alby cast a critical eye over it:

'T'ain't properly level, Moikey.' Michael stood on the cabintop, looking forward over the hold:

'It's only a gnat's whatsit off, Dad – It'll do fer now.' Albert gave a disgruntled shrug as the younger man jumped down and went to move the motor:

'Yeh got that kettle on, 'Arrie?' he called; a reply sounded from within the cabin:

'Nearly boilin', Dad!'

Ginny and Carrie were still on the loading dock, waiting for Michael to tie the Oakley alongside. Alby stood looking at the butty, still unhappy that it was lying a little to one side; Harriet emerged and handed him a steaming mug:

'Oi don' loike ter see moy boat loyin' oover like this, girl,' he grumbled.

'Oh Dad – it's not enooff ter woorry about. Yeh'll never get it dead roight wi' coal on – 'n yeh know what Ginny'll say if yeh start shovellin' at it!'

'Oh, Oi s'pose so...'

He took a sip at the hot tea as she stepped down inside again to start preparing their dinner. He put the mug down, and stepped up onto the cabintop to feel the tilt of the boat, as Michael had done; it was, indeed, only a fraction off, but still he shook his head. Brought up in the old traditions of the boating world, even that slight list was too much for him; he looked around, spotted the big shovel in the fore-end: If Oi joost move a little bit, around that middle stand...

He climbed down and walked forward, bent and picked up the shovel. Back in the middle section of the hold, he began to move some of the heaped-up coal across the boat, then stopped and checked its trim again: *Tha's better! Joost a bit more...* He bent to his self-imposed task again, moved another one, two, three shovelfuls, reached for a fourth...

Over by the loading wharf, Michael and Ginny were stood in the boat, talking to the chargehand while they waited for the train of wagons to arrive. Carrie sat on the edge of the cabintop, listening and swinging her legs to and fro; she looked across at the butty and raised her hand to wave to her new dad, only to frown as she realised he was moving coal: *After Gin told 'im not to!* She was about to call out to him, as he bent down for another shovelful, but her expression turned to one of horror:

'Dad! DAD!' She leapt to her feet; Michael and Ginny both turned at her shout, in time to see him crumple into a heap on top of the coal...

Chapter Twenty-Two

At Sutton's Stop, the junction at Hawkesbury where the northern Oxford Canal joins the Coventry, boats lined the banks. Mostly in the blue and yellow livery of the national fleet, interspersed with immaculate Barlows pairs, some loaded, others empty and waiting for orders, men and women stood in every open hatch, bare-headed. Not a word was said, but none was needed; sadness and sympathy radiated from every figure and every face.

Around the tight 180 degree turn under the iron bridge, the shallow stop-lock stood open and ready; the tall figure of Henry Caplin doffed its hat as he waved the approaching boat in. The gate slammed shut; paddles were raised, and in minutes they were away again. Sitting on the back-end planks, Ginny's arm around her shoulders, Carrie felt the tears streaming down her face again, knew that her companion was crying too, deeply moved by the display of respect from the boaters hurrying them on their way.

Despite his annoyance at their orders, part of Michael had been looking forward to this trip. He had passed this way, on the old boater's 'bottom road' out of Birmingham, once or twice as a boy in the dark years of the war, and he still felt a quiet thrill at the idea of unfamiliar territory. But now he felt only an aching sorrow – instead of the twenty-five tons of coal they should have been carrying, the hold of the Oakley was empty except for the simple pine coffin strapped to the planks. In true boater's tradition, he had laid the top-planks along the beams at gunwale level; the deckboard and cratch were in place, the strings holding them down scrubbed white; and Albert was making his last journey back to Braunston in pride of place, behind the mast.

* * *

At the colliery, they had run around the basin to the butty at Carrie's shout. Michael had leapt onto the heaped coal and knelt beside Alby, carefully turning him onto his back; Ginny had dived into the cabin to scrabble in the ticket-drawer for his medicine bottle. Harriet, unaware of the drama as she chopped carrots in the cabin, dropped everything to follow her out as she said:

'It's Dad, 'Arrie – 'e's 'ad a bad turn!'

They found the old boatman cradled in Michael's arm, his face grey and drawn, barely conscious. Ginny scrambled up beside him, shook a pill from the bottle and held it out, but he shook his head, feebly waved her away:

'Not this toime, girl.' His voice was weak, croaky.

'Coome on Dad, yeh've got ter take it!' His head shook again, and he smiled weakly at her; she turned to Michael:

'Moikey! Tell 'im!' She saw the tears running down her brother's face, felt her own beginning to flow, as Alby spoke again:

'Moikey?'

'Yes Dad?'

'Yer boats...'

'Don' woorry about them now!' The grey head shook again:

'Talk ter Ben, Moikey. Go 'n see Ben Vickuss. Moy savin's...'

'What do yeh mean, Dad?'

'They're yours now, son. Buy yer boats, if that's what yeh want...'

'No, Dad! We'll talk about it when yeh're better!' Alby just smiled and shook his head again. He glanced around, saw Harriet standing beside the boat, her brow furrowed with concern; his eyes met Michael's again:

'Tell moy grandson about me, eh?' Michael took his hand in his own free one:

'Oi will, Dad. We'll name 'im for yeh, 'n all.' Alby's smile grew wider:

'That'll be noice, boy.'

His eyes travelled around their anxious faces, and Michael felt the hand in his own tighten its grip: 'Oi'm so proud...' The hand released its grip, and a long sigh escaped Alby's lips as his head sank back against Michael's arm.

The tableau held for a moment, none of them wanting to believe what had happened.

'Moichael?' Ginny sounded lost and afraid; he could only shake his head as he turned to her; kneeling there on the coal, its sharp edges cutting into their legs, she flung herself into his arms and began to sob quietly into his shoulder. On the bank, Carrie's look of disbelief crumpled; Harriet drew the girl into her arms and held her tightly, feeling her body trembling as she too dissolved in tears.

And then pandemonium had broken out. A doctor, summoned by the colliery foreman, had arrived; the chargehand, his face a mask of shocked sympathy, had quietly taken them under his wing as the ambulance arrived and had some of his own men move the Oakley over and tie it next to the Antrim. The doctor had confirmed what they already knew but didn't want to believe; he had departed to prepare the death certificate, and Albert had been taken away to a local undertakers.

A little later, a heavily built man in a pinstripe suit had knocked on the cabinside and introduced himself as the colliery manager. Having expressed his sympathy, he told them gently that the colliery would arrange for a coffin:

'Would you like me to arrange the funeral for you, here in Nuneaton?' Michael shook his head:

'No, thank you. We'll tek 'im home, ter Braunston. 'Is woife's buried ther.'

'Oh, yes, I see. Would you like me to get in touch with the church there, perhaps?'

'That would be very koind, thank yeh.'

'Right then! Leave it to me, I'll get everything arranged for you.' Ginny gave him a weak smile.

'Thank yeh, Mister...'

'Raison, Bernard Raison.'

'It's really good of yeh teh do so mooch fer oos, Mr Raison.'

'We really do 'ppreciate it, Mr Raison,' Michael agreed.

The following morning, the undertaker's van had brought Albert back to them.

Michael had spent his evening preparing the Oakley, keeping his mind on making the paintwork gleam and the brasses shine as they never had before. He had scrubbed all the ropes securing the cratch and refitted them, and laid the top planks along the crossbeams.

Harriet and Carrie had sat, silent and shattered, in the motor's cabin, lost in their memories. Carrie had descended into tears again from time to time, to be comforted by her sister-in-law, as she thought of the man who had taken her in when she'd been orphaned, whom she had come to love as her 'new dad'.

Ginny, unable to be still, had walked the towpath for hours, uncaring of where she went, barely seeing her surroundings. Cloud had gathered during the day, and now a gentle drizzle covered the hedges with tears; seeing them, she offered up a prayer, thankful that the world was sharing her pain and loneliness.

And at last they'd slept – badly, fitfully, disturbed by their grief and by thoughts of the future without their ever-smiling, ever-cheerful Dad, afraid to face the next few days, the pressure of others' sympathy.

'We'll keep an eye on the butty for yeh,' the chargehand had told them as Michael tied down the coffin behind the mast.

'Thank yeh, mate. I guess we'll be back fer it in a few days.' The man had just nodded, his face lined with compassion.

* * *

At the long turn approaching the three duplicated locks of Hillmorton, they found the same scene awaiting them: A number of loaded pairs tied to the bank, waiting for the locks, and in the hatches of each, the boatwomen doffed their bonnets at their approach, waving them past to take precedence through the flight. And as the locks came into sight, they saw the bottom gates standing open for them, the boatmen ready, windlasses in hand.

The single boat with its tragic cargo swept into the bottom lock; gates swung to, and paddles rattled up. Not a word was spoken; the men worked them through swiftly until, in mere minutes, they were ready to set away from the top lock on their level run all the way to Braunston. As Michael wound the engine into gear, the last man, waiting to close the gate, told him quietly:

'We'll be there, lad, ter see 'im off.' Michael nodded his thanks, too choked to speak.

Chapter Twenty-Three

The priest climbed the steps into his pulpit; he removed his glasses, and surveyed the packed church in silence for a moment before speaking:

'Over the years that I have been the Rector of Braunston, I have come to know many of you, and I have come to know the boating people as a proud and independent community, almost a race apart from other, land-based folk. And I know Albert Baker was one of the proudest and most independent-minded of all of that select group.

'And rightly so. I cannot claim him as a friend, but I knew him. And I knew him to be a good man, a truly Christian man in the very best sense of the word. Oh, he may not have darkened the door of this or any other church from one year's end to the next, but I'm sad to say that going to church does not necessarily make one a Christian. No, it is rather by one's way and manner of life that we should judge who is truly Christian, and who is not. And from the way he conducted his life, the way he treated his fellow human beings, his neighbours as our Lord would have put it, I can safely believe that Albert was, in all ways that matter, a true Christian. And I can also safely trust that in departing this life, he has been called to the presence of the Father.

'If you need proof of what I say, take a look at the family he leaves behind him. His children – Michael, Ginny, and Carrie; and Harriet of course. I call them his children, but not a one of them is truly related to him, at least not in a biological sense! You will all know that his beloved wife, Rita, passed away in the first months of the war; and that his only son Alex was killed in the tragic sinking of H.M.S. Hood, barely eighteen months later. And yet he leaves a loving and grieving family!'

The priest turned to look down upon the front pew and its occupants:

'Michael – I remember you as a young boy, the famous "boy off the bank" who was the subject of such curiosity and speculation among the boating folk for so long. You came to be the son he longed for, and I know that you have for many years thought of him, loved him, as your true father.

'Ginny – when you were left alone after your mother died, he brought you to join your brother where he felt that you belonged rather than see you banished to the dreary life of a council orphanage. You were, I know, the daughter he had always wanted.

'And you, Carrie. A second daughter, you brought him even greater joy when he took you in too after your parents died in that dreadful accident in Regent's Canal Dock. I know how you all loved him, and how he loved you – a love which took no notice of blood ties, or the lack of them. I feel your sorrow, all of you, at his passing, but I can assure you that he is now resting in the bosom of our Lord in Heaven.

'Harriet – I remember clearly the look of love and pride in Albert's eyes as he watched you and Michael taking the vows of marriage in this church. He was so happy for you both that that joy radiated from him like the warmth of the sun. It is perhaps a further sorrow to you that he didn't get to see his first grandchild – it will come as no surprise to anyone here that your baby is due literally any day now! But I hope that your joy in that birth, when it comes, will help to assuage the sadness you are all feeling now, and will help to give you the strength to pick up your lives and carry the next generation of Bakers into the future.'

He raised his eyes to the congregation once again:

'I urge you all, in the coming days and weeks, to offer your prayers not only for the soul of Albert Baker, but for these young people he leaves behind. Pray that they will indeed find the strength to get beyond this painful time; pray that joy and happiness will once more invade their lives, and pray also for the safe delivery of Michael and Harriet's firstborn child, and that that joyful occasion will help them to believe that life really does go on, even after such sorrow as they face now.'

* * *

'It seems so dreadfully unfair!' Fred Morris fumbled for his handkerchief and mopped the tears which threatened to spill from his eyes: 'I mean – he meant so much to you, he'd done so much for you, been such a wonderful father to you all. And now he's gone, while a useless old codger like me is still hanging around!'

'Don' say that, Grandad! Yew know we love yew, too!'

'Ginny's roight. Oi know we don't see as mooch of yeh as we'd loike, but joost knowin' yeh're there means so mooch to oos.'

The old man smiled at their reassurances:

'I suppose so – thank you for saying so! But he was so much younger than me, it just seems wrong that he's not here any more.'

They were standing in the churchyard as the crowds drifted away towards the Old Plough and the intended celebration of Alby's life that would inevitably follow now that the burial was over. Michael heaved a sigh, wearied by the endless shaking of hands and the well-meant but unhelpful words of sympathy, feeling the weight of anticlimax descending onto his shoulders with the knowledge that the ceremonial was all done. He looked around at them with a tired smile:

'Coom on, let's go 'n say goodbye to 'im the way 'e'd loike.'

Fortunately, the day had dawned dry and warm if overcast. The crowd, too large to all fit within the old village pub, spilled its celebration over not only into the garden but into the street as well; and down to the canalside during the afternoon closing time. It seemed that everyone they knew was there – some with their boats, loaded or empty as the job dictated, others, tied elsewhere, had travelled by bus or train to join them, as had Bill and Vi with little Josh. Stevie had brought his Ellie, and introduced her proudly; Billy and Sylvie had made their way up from Bulls Bridge where they were waiting for orders, leaving a disgruntled Kim in charge of the boats:

'Boot Billy – what 'bout Ginny? Oi oughtta be ther'.' Billy, not unsympathetic to the boy's plight, had clapped him on the shoulder:

'Oi need yeh ter be 'ere 'case they call fer oos, mate. Don' woorry, we'll give 'er yer sympathy. 'N yer loove, eh?'

But Ginny had never-the-less found herself with an escort for the day. Sam Caplin had made it his business to be by her side, supportive but unobtrusive, only stepping back while the funeral service was in progress. And as the day went on, she found herself grateful for his presence, appreciating his quiet sympathy, the way he was there, silent but attentive, whenever she felt the need of someone. In the graveyard, when she found the tears rising again, it was Sam who'd proffered a shoulder and a handkerchief, and been the recipient of her thankful smile.

* * *

The next morning, they were all sitting rather self-consciously in the cosy front room of the little cottage in Welton Road.

'Everything seemed to go very well yesterday.' Ben Vickers spoke quietly.

'Yes – thank yeh both for coomin'. Michael looked up with a smile as Vickers' wife bustled in with a tray.

'I'm only sorry we couldn't stay longer at the pub, my dear. But I don't drink, and Ben's tummy gives him gyp if he has too much beer these days!'

'That's all roight, Missus Vickuss, it was good to see yeh both at the church.'

'He had a good crowd to send him off, didn't he?' Ginny nodded:

'It was good to see so many people ther' fer 'im.'

'Are you going to have a cup with us, Olive?' Vickers asked his wife; she shook her head:

'No, Ben – I've got a pile of washing to do, and you folk will have things to talk about. Enjoy your tea, and tuck into the biscuits!' Her smile swept over them all as she turned and left the room.

'So, Michael – your dad told you that he had left his savings with me, I suppose?'

'Sort of. The only toime 'e mentioned 'em was when we got caught in the big freeze-oop. Boot then 'e said, joost before...' He paused, blinking back his grief: ''E said ter coom 'n talk ter yew.' Vickers nodded:

'Well, whatever he had is yours now, Michael. I hear you've got ideas of buying and running your own pair, is that right?'

'Oi'd thought about it, yes. Oi thought we could tek the work we wanted, instead of joost doin' what we were told, yeh see.' He felt his anger rising again: 'If they 'adn't sent oos on that bloody coal roon, 'e'd still be 'ere!' Harriet, beside him on the sofa, put a hand over his:

''Ush, Moikey, ther's nothin' we can do about it now.' He rounded on her:

'Oi know! Boot if we'd been ar own bosses, we could've turned it down! Ther' was no need fer 'im ter doie now – they killed 'im with their bloody roosh job!' She held his eyes, her own awash with compassion. Her voice was soft:

'What's doon is doon, Moikey. We can' change nothin'. He stared at her, feeling his fury subside under the weight of his sorrow.

She drew him close, held him tightly for a moment; in the

other armchair, Carrie, sitting on Ginny's lap, dabbed at her eyes with her handkerchief.

Michael eased out of his wife's embrace, and turned to Vickers who had been keeping diplomatically silent. He smiled ruefully:

'Boot Oi suppose buyin' a pair o' boats wouldn' coom cheap, eh, Mr Vickuss?'

'Not as much as you might expect, Mikey. The Transport Commission have got a lot more boats than they can use, and they don't seem averse to getting rid of a few of them. You might get a pair in decent condition for about four or five hundred pounds.'

'Four or foive 'undred! We could never raise that mooch!' Vickers held up a restraining hand:

'Hold on, Mikey. How much do you really know about your dad, about what he did before the war, for example?'

'Well – not that mooch, Oi suppose. 'E'd alwes been on the boats, 'adn't 'e?'

'That's right. He was born the year after me – his father was a Fellows Morton captain before the merger with Claytons. We were good friends, from our childhood. When he married Rita, the company gave him his own pair – horse boats, to begin with, but they soon realised he was a first-rate man and made him captain of a steamer, on the London to Birmingham fly-runs. After the war, they replaced the old steamer with a new motor boat – they'd been switching over to Bolinders since they built the Linda in 1912. Your dad became one of the most respected captains in the Fellows's fleet – and one of the highest paid!

'Then when the second war came, the government took everything over and the old traffic patterns were ignored in favour of the needs of the war. Rita died, just before that Christmas, as you know; Alex had joined the Navy, and it was only because you came along, Mikey, that he was able to keep on boating.'

Michael nodded:

'And because Bill 'Anney lent 'im their Gracie, ter 'elp teach me what was what!'

Vickers laughed:

'He was so nervous of taking you on!'

'Not sure what 'e'd let 'imself in fer, Oi s'pose.'

'Oh no – I think he was afraid that a boy who'd had five years of schooling would never take to the boating life, that he was getting his hopes up only for you to give up and go back home, and leave him stuck on the bank again. And like a lot of boaters, he was very wary of people with an education anyway – a part of him was almost scared of you!'

'Yeh're kiddin' me?' Michael sounded astonished.

'I'm not, believe me! Anyway, the point is, Mikey, that during the time between the wars, he was earning enough to put some money by. And he had me put it into a Post Office savings account for him. Once the war came, he didn't have enough to go on adding to it, but it has been earning interest all these years, of course.'

'So 'ow mooch is ther', Mr Vickuss?' Ginny was almost afraid to ask. Vickers laughed again:

'With all the interest, it amounts to nearly nine hundred pounds.'

Michael felt his jaw drop; he looked at Ginny, to fmd her expression was just as comical:

''Ow mooch?'

Chapter Twenty-Four

'Oh Moikey!' Michael felt his wife's hand tighten on his arm as he stared across in disbelief at his sister. He turned back to Ben Vickers as he heard the man's chuckle: 'Say that agen, Mr Vickuss?'

'You've got the best part of nine hundred pounds in the Post Office, Mikey.' He grinned at the young man's expression: 'If you really want to try running your own boats, you can do it. And have some money by in case you need it.'

'Yeah...' Michael still found it hard to grasp. It was Harriet who picked up the discussion:

'What d'yeh reckon, Mr Vickuss? Should we give it a go?' Vickers frowned:

'I don't know for sure, Harriet. It's a risk, but the Transport Commission's biggest problem at the moment is the lack of crews. So many men are deserting the boats, going for jobs on the bank, that they're struggling to cover the contracts they've got. You could get work, subcontract for them and possibly for the other still-independent carriers like Barlows, and the rate would be better than you're getting now. But if the loads become harder to get as time goes by, you could find yourself dropped in favour of their own men.'

'Is that loikely ter 'appen?' Michael took up the subject.

'Who knows, Mikey. I think it's probable, eventually – the government seem to want everything to go on the roads these days, so they aren't putting anything into promoting the canals, or the railways for that matter. The big freeze back in '47 saw a lot of jobs go that way – another hard winter would push more work away onto the lorries.'

'Seems crazy ter me! We can carry so mooch more than even the biggest lorry!'

'Yes, but they're so much quicker. And people seem to want things delivered yesterday, nowadays, they don't want to wait. There's another problem, too: A lot of factories are changing over from coal to oil, and that's going to lose a lot of contracts in the long term. It seems stupid to me, to rely on foreign oil when we've got coal under the ground here in England, but that's the way of it.'

'So yeh don' think it's a good oidea?'

'Oh, I didn't say that, Mikey! I was looking on the black side – it doesn't have to be that way. Canal carrying can have a future, and a good one, but it'll take a change of heart by the government; and don't forget we've got a new government now, a Tory one. It still makes a lot of sense to move bulk cargoes like coal and roadstone, maybe grain and cement, things like that, by boat – the cost is low, and the urgency isn't an issue. But it'll need men in charge who believe in what they're doing – too many of the new managers they've put in aren't canal people; they don't have the commitment, and they don't understand the cut and how it works. Or the boatmen.'

'That's roight!' Michael's anger flared again: 'Sendin' oos on that damned coal roon, joost when we didn' want it...!' He subsided with a rueful smile as Harriet gently shook his arm.

'As a number one, you'd have more freedom. You'd be able to choose the jobs you take, and I know that's important to you – and you'd earn more for what you did. But you must remember that you'd be responsible for your own maintenance on the boats, and keeping track of the tolls and so on. And no-one to bail you out, no laying money if you're stuck because of ice or stoppages.'

'Yeah...'

'I'll tell you what, Mikey – why don't you think about it for a while? Go and pick up your butty, finish the job you're on, and then come and see me again next time you're by. In the meantime, I'll put a few feelers out, shall I, see if there are any decent boats we could buy?'

'Yeah... Yes, h'okay, Mr Vickuss! That'll give me toime ter think about things, toime ter mek oop moy moind.' Vickers' choice of words struck him. 'Yeh said "we", Mr Vickuss?' Vickers grinned:

'I wondered if you might like me to act as a kind of traffic manager for you, Mikey? I'm here, with a telephone to hand – I could try and arrange loads for you, co-ordinate things so you weren't wasting too much time either moving empty or waiting for orders.'

'Yeh'd want payin' fer that, o' course?'

'Of course! A small percentage, on commission, of any jobs I found for you? It would supplement my pension a bit!' Michael grinned at him:

''N it'd solve the biggest woorry Oi 'ad – 'ow ter foind the loads! It's a deal, Mr Vickuss, as long as we decoide ter go fer it.' Vickers got to his feet, held out his hand; Michael stood up and shook it:

'Thank yeh, Mr Vickuss!'

'I think it's about time you started calling me Ben, Michael, if we're going to be partners!'

'Er – yeah – Ben!'

* * *

'Yeh ain't sayin' mooch, Moikey!'

Michael looked up from the prolonged contemplation of the half-full beer glass in his hands and smiled at his wife:

'Sorry, loove.' He sighed: 'It joost don' seem roight, ter be goin' on without Dad.'

'Oi know.' Her hand reached for him; he put the glass down on the table and took it in his:

''Ow are yeh feelin', 'Arrie?' She patted her expansive tummy:

'Oi'm foine – 'n so's 'e!' This brought a wider smile to Michael's face:

'Could still be she,' he reminded her, but Harriet shook her head, her eyes twinkling:

'Dad knew it'd be a grandson fer 'im.' He gazed at her, fascinated by the certainty in her voice, but he decided not to question it:

'We'll be in Stoke Bruin termorrer – we're stayin' ther' so's Sister can look after yeh.' The hand holding his gave him a squeeze:

'That'll be good, Moikey – Li'l Albert won't be long now.' He chuckled, and leant over to kiss her cheek.

Following their discussion with Ben Vickers, they had returned to Griff Colliery. The Oakley had been loaded, and they'd picked up the already-loaded Antrim, but over the intervening days their orders had been changed – they were now to deliver to Bulls Bridge, the coal to be trucked from there to the nearby Nestle factory. Stopping overnight outside the colliery arm, the next day had seen them to the top of Long Buckby locks and the New Inn.

Michael had been quiet and thoughtful ever since the funeral, and the revelations from Ben Vickers. The girls had all left him in peace, knowing that he was considering their future at the same time as trying to get over the loss of Alby, a loss which had left each of them feeling the same sorrow, the same emptiness. Words were never needed anyway, for working the boats – they all fitted together for every task, each knowing what the others would do, working like a well-oiled machine.

The two of them sat alone at a table in the corner of the bar. Carrie was outside, in the evening sunshine, talking or playing with a couple of other boat-children, and Ginny, once again wanting to be alone, had taken herself off for a walk around the fields towards the junction with the Leicester Line of the canal.

They sat hand in hand for a while, not talking, hearing without listening to the hubbub of conversation around them, the rattle of glasses and the whoosh of beer drawn from the hand-pumps.

'Oi do miss 'im so mooch.'

''Course yeh do, Moikey. 'E was yer Dad, after all.' He looked around at her with a smile:

'It ain't joost that, loove. 'E was the oone in charge, the oone 'oo decoided what we did. Oi feel – koind o' lost, if yeh know what Oi mean. Oi'm woorried in case Oi get it wrong, mek the wrong decision.'

''Bout the boats, yeh mean?' He laughed:

''Bout everythin'. She gave the hand she held a gentle shake:

'Yeh'll be foine, Moikey! Yeh're ar captain now, 'n yeh know as mooch about the cut as 'e did. We all troost yeh, we know yeh won' let oos down.'

* * *

The next day saw them duly tied up near the old mill in Stoke Bruerne, soon after midday.

Michael hurried Harriet along to the sister's surgery while the two girls tidied the boats, only to be reassured that all was well; they sat with Sister Mary for quite a while, reminiscing about Alby, hearing of one or two of his escapades which he had never let on to them about, while Carrie helped Ginny with a load of washing. And after a dinner of rabbit stew, the rabbits provided by another of the sister's visitors, they retired to the Boat Inn for the evening.

'Oi'm goin' back ter the boats, Moikey.' Michael looked up, concern creasing his brow:

'Are yeh all roight, 'Arrie?' She gave him a broad smile:

'Oi'm foine! Joost a bit toired, tha's all.'

She patted her tummy: 'Boot Oi think yeh moight be a daddy boy this toime termorrer!'

Michael took her hand and gave it a squeeze, noticing the same rosy glow about her face that he'd seen on Sylvie's the day before little Emily was born:

'Oi 'ope so, Oi can' stand mooch more o' this waitin'!' He watched her leave the bar, and then turned to Carrie: 'Go along with 'er, will yeh loove? Joost in case, eh?'

'H'okay.' She got up and followed Harriet out. Michael went back to contemplating the pint glass in front of him; Ginny sat looking at him for a minute until her impatience got the better of her:

'What're we goin' ter do then, Moikey?' He looked up again: 'Eh?'

'Are we goin' ter get ar own boats? Oi think...' She stopped as he held up a hand, a frown on his face:

'Gin, don' pester me, h'okay? It's moy job ter decoide what we do.'

'Boot...' The hand was up again:

'Look: Dad was ar captain, 'n we all did what 'e said, roight? Me 'n all. Boot now 'e's... now 'e's gone, Oi'm the oone 'oo 'as ter decoide things, Oi'm captain, h'okay? It's moy choice, roight or wrong.'

'Yes, Moikey.'

That was the way on the boats, she knew – the captain, the steerer, which usually meant the man of the family, was the one in charge, the one whose decisions would go unquestioned by his wife and children, his crew.

But after a moment the rebellious, independent part of her insisted on being heard:

'Oi reckon we should 'ave ar own pair!'

'Ginny!' He looked at her in despair; but then he laughed:

'Oh, Gin! Yeh 'ave ter get yer say in, don' yeh?' He laughed again as she nodded, grinning at him:

'Oi ain't med oop moy moind yet, h'okay? Oi know 'Arrie's not sure about it, she's woorried about the future fer littl'un, 'n any oother kids we 'ave. Give me anoother day or two, eh? Oi'll decoide boy the toime we're next in Braunston, Oi promise.'

* * *

'Wha'…?'

'Moikey! Moikey, wake oop!'

'Wha' toime is it?'

'Middle o' the night!' He heard the chuckle in Harriet's voice, but then she gave a gasp of pain, and he was instantly awake:

'What is it, 'Arrie?' She chuckled again:

'Soomthin's movin' down below!'

143

Chapter Twenty-Five

Once more, the Rector of Braunston Parish mounted the steps leading up to his pulpit. But this time joy lightened his step; he took off his spectacles, laid down his prepared notes, and looked up to survey his congregation. As he saw them gazing back at him, his face creased into a broad smile:

'You have no idea how delighted it makes me feel to welcome you all back to this ancient church! I see before me so many of the faces whose eyes were clouded with sorrow a scant fortnight ago – to see now the light of joy and happiness in those same eyes is a tonic to raise the spirits of God himself, let alone a crusty old man like me.' He looked down into the front pew:

'Michael – Harriet – it lifts my heart more than I can describe to see the love and joy on your faces, and above all to welcome your first-born child into the family of the Church, and into the community of the boats...'

* * *

It had been an eventful ten days, since Harriet had awoken her husband in the middle of the night. Instantly grasping the import of her jocular words, he had leapt from their bed and scrambled out of the cabin, dragging on his trousers as he went. He ran along to Sister Mary's cottage and hammered on the door, which was opened to him with such promptitude that he suspected the good Sister had been waiting for his knock. Her calm, proficient manner had served to calm him too, as she told him to go and wake Ginny, and get some water on to boil; she followed him back to the boats, her medical bag under her arm.

By the time they returned, several other boatwomen were gathered around the stern of the Antrim, wakened by some instinct he never did understand and ready to offer whatever assistance was needed. Sister Mary took charge, and such was their implicit trust in her that everything she required was done without question; only the baby had other ideas.

But at last, he gave up the unequal struggle and ventured into the light of day. For day it was – Albert Michael Baker drew his first protesting breath at 11.43am. And Alby had been correct – whether by some dying intuition, or by sheer chance (the odds were, after all, only two to one), he had known that Harriet would bear him a grandson.

They had stayed another two nights in Stoke Bruerne, to let Harriet recover from the pain and stress of childbirth, and, as Michael put it to Joe and Gracie in the pub that evening, to give him time to come down to Earth again. The Birmingham and the Andromeda had stopped there on their way North during the afternoon after 'Littl' Alby' had arrived and stayed to wet the baby's head in traditional fashion; and the following day, the Towcester and the Bodmin had turned up, heading South with Warwickshire coal for Dickinson's Langley Mill. Henry and Suey had of course heard the news from their son, and in their turn stayed over to celebrate with the new parents. Which pleased their youngest child immensely, and appeared not to displease Ginny too much, either – the two of them spent most of the evening sitting side-by-side in the stern well of the Antrim, with a glass of shandy each while a procession of boatwomen came by to greet Harriet and fuss over the new baby.

On the move again, three days had seen them at Bulls Bridge, unloading their coal; then a two-day wait until they had had orders to load metal ingots from a lighter in Brentford Basin for James' foundry in Birmingham. Then a steady run Northwards; Littl' Alby was ten days old by the time he was dressed in his finest – a crocheted christening gown presented to them by Suey Caplin – and carried joyously up to Braunston's elegant church.

As the Vicar had observed, many of the same people were there as had attended Alby's funeral: Henry and Suey Caplin, with Sam of course, had stopped over after reaching Braunston the night before, Vi Hanney had travelled by train, her husband and son both being at work; Joe and Gracie had left their boats, awaiting orders at Sutton's Stop with Ernie in attendance, and caught the train from Coventry. Jack and Maggie Warden had boated almost through the night to be there, but once again their eldest son was cursing his luck – the Skate and the Middlesex were loading that day at Brentford. And Fred Morris, all but speechless with delight at the sight of his great-grandson, had driven up from Buckingham in the car.

The baptism, where Sam Caplin had once more danced a quiet and apparently not-unwelcome attendance on Ginny, was inevitably followed by a prolonged celebration in the Old Plough in Braunston High Street; but during the afternoon closing time, Michael and Ginny had gone back to the cottage in Welton Road with Ben and Olive Vickers, while Harriet and Carrie had returned to the boats, taking both the baby and a very merry crowd of well-wishers with them.

'Tea, Michael, Ginny?' Olive showed them into the front parlour where Ben waved them into the cosy armchairs.

'Yes please, Missus Vickuss.' They relaxed gratefully, nodding their thanks.

'So – you've come to a decision; Mikey?' Vickers asked; Michael gave him a rather self-conscious smile:

'Oi 'ave, Ben.' Ginny laughed:

'Not without a bit o' pushin'!'

'Oh?' Michael's smile turned rueful:

'Well Oi know as 'Arrie's not too sure, she's woorried 'bout the future fer Li'l Alby 'n any oother kiddies we 'ave. Boot Oi can' work fer this dozy boonch any more!'

'What's happened?' Ginny laughed again, and took up the story...

A hot summer's afternoon in the layby at Bulls Bridge, and amid the murmur of conversations, the happy voices of children and the reverberating clamour of the nearby dock, the tall slim teenage girl in a t-shirt and dungarees laboured at her dolly tub. She looked up at the approach of a man in a suit and bowler hat:

'Hello – is your captain on board?' She surveyed him suspiciously for a moment:

'No 'e ain't.'

'Oh – it is steerer Baker, isn't it?'

'Yus.'

'Can you tell me where he is?'

''E's oop the h'office.'

'Oh – will he be back soon?'

'Reckon so. Yeh c'n wait, if yeh loike.'

'Oh – thank you.' She returned to her labours while the man stood self-consciously to one side, aware of the half-questioning, half-amused stares of the other boaters around the layby. Trying to sound relaxed, he made an attempt at conversation:

'You're his daughter, are you?' The girl looked up contemptuously:

'Oi'm Ginny Baker. Oi'm 'is sister.'

'Oh! I see. How many of you are there on your boats?' She laid the dolly to one side:

'Foive of oos, h'includin' Li'l Alby – that's Moikey – that's moy brother – 'n Arriet's baby.'

'That's four?'

'Ther's Carrie 'n all. She's moy little sister.'

'Oh. You're waiting for orders, are you?'

'As usual! Rooddy coomp'ny can't get back-orders h'organoised ter save it's loife.' She'd already placed the bowler hat as an official of the 'rooddy coomp'ny', and now kept her inner amusement in check as he replied, startled:

'Oh! I see...'

'Now, if yeh'll h'excuse me, Oi'ye got me washin' ter finish.'

'Oh – yes, of course. I'm sorry to have interrupted you.'

As she turned back to her tub, Michael returned, strolling back from the office: 'All roight, Gin? Wher's 'Arrie?'

'She's oop the loine, wi' Maggie Warden. Carrie's in the school 'ouse.'

'Good girl...' The man in the suit stepped forward, his hand outheld:

'Steerer Baker?'

'That's me.' Michael took the hand and shook it.

'Mr Baker – can I have a word with you?'

''O course.'

'In private?' It was Michael's turn to be suspicious:

'Yeh c'n say anythin' yeh got ter say in froont o' moy sister.'

'Oh – right. I'm Lionel Bartram, fleet co-ordinator for the Grand Union South region, and it's my job to keep track of our boats in this area. I note that your movements have been a little unconventional of late?'

''Ow d'yeh mean?' Michael found his instinctive dislike of the man matching his growing annoyance at his manner.

'Well – you abandoned your butty at Griff Colliery, a few weeks ago, and took an unauthorised trip to Braunston with the empty motor. And then, on your last trip to unload here, you stopped in Stoke Bruerne for several days, again without our agreement. Can you explain these incidents for me?'

Ginny saw the fury in her brother's eyes and fought to keep her own feelings in check. Michael rounded on the man, grasping him by the lapels of his jacket:

'Yes Oi bloody-well can! We went ter Braunston wi' moy father's body, ter 'ave 'im buried after 'e doied shoovellin' coal on your bloody boats, doin' a job 'e should never 'ave been asked ter do! 'N we stopped in Stoke Bruin fer moy son ter be born – the grandson moy dad'll never 'ave the chance ter see because yer bloody h'orders killed 'im! Now go on back ter yer bloody h'office 'n put that down in yer damned books!'

'Oh! Oh, yes, I see. I'm sorry, but no-one told me...'

'Mebbe if yeh'd teken the toime ter troy 'n foind out instead o' coomin' 'ere wi' yer 'igh 'n moighty bloody questions, if yeh took soom int'rest in the folks as work fer yeh instead o' joost keepin' yer books 'n countin' yer mooney things would roon a bit better around 'ere! Now boogger off before Oi lose me temper!'

'Oh – yes – I'm sorry to have bothered you...'

'BOOGGER OFF!'

A ripple of laughter and derisory applause followed the man as he scuttled away.

'I wish I'd been there! To see the look on Bartram's face – it must have been a picture!' Michael laughed:

'Yeah – Oi c'n see the foonny soide of it now, boot Oi was joost so angry at the toime.'

'I can imagine. Too many of these men they've brought in as managers are from other backgrounds, they've got no idea of what the cut's all about, so it's hardly surprising they get no respect from men like yourself.'

'That's roight, Ben. Any'ow – Oi'm goin' ter look at buyin' oos a pair o' boats, lookin' after arselves from now on.'

Chapter Twenty-Six

'That's definite, is it, Mikey?' Amusement gleamed in Vickers' eyes. Michael caught his look and laughed:

'Coom on, what 'ave yeh got fer oos, Ben?'

'I said I'd put my feelers out, didn't I? And I think I've got a result for you!'

'Oh ah?'

'Yes. I've not seen them, mind, so I could be wrong. I put the word out that I was after buying a decent pair of boats, in good trim and with as much equipment as possible intact. A few days ago I heard from Jimmie Hawes, the lengthsman who lives in the lock cottage at Widewater – he says there are a number of boats left abandoned in the flashes at Harefield, just below the lock.'

'Aye, that's right. We've seen 'em as we've coom boy.'

'Well, Hawes says that some of them are not worth the bother, but amongst them are a good original pairing of big Woolwich's. Like your Oakley, but built by Harland and Woolf – you'll know the type.'

'Aye, of course. They'll 'ave wooden cabins though, eh?' Vickers chuckled:

'Yes! No trouble with the condensation like you have with your motor. And the Northampton has got a National, just like yours. Butty's the Northchurch; as I said, they're an original pairing from 1937.'

'They sound oideal, Ben.' Ginny chipped in:

'Yes – Sister Mary was quite woorried 'bout the damp in ar motor, she says it moight give Li'l Alby the h'assma.'

'She's right – and you don't want that!' Olive Vickers commented as she bustled in with the teatray. She set about pouring as Michael asked:

'Can we go 'n tek a look at 'em?'

'Yes – next time you're passing that way, let me know when you expect to be there. Jim Hawes has said he'll take you out to them, on the quiet – I think he's quite upset to see good boats just lying there idle.'

'Boot can we buy 'em?'

'I think so. I've spoken to the Transport Commission people, and they don't seem averse to letting us have them. The price they're asking is a bit steep, but I think I can talk them down – I'll lay it on about the need to dock them for a thorough overhaul, and if you can tell me about any problems you spot, it'll give me more ammunition.'

'Roight-oh, Ben. We'll tek a look as soon as we can, eh Gin?'

* * *

'Ah! Thought it might be yew as wants 'em!' Jim Hawes always jovial face split into a wide grin as he opened the door to see Michael on the step outside. He stepped out to join them, going on in garrulous fashion: 'Knew yer ol' man was a big mate o' Ben Vickers – 'n we've all 'eard about yer bust-up wi' the bowler 'at down Bulls Bridge! Come wi' me, I'll tek yeh out to 'em in me dingy.'

Michael and Ginny followed him, slightly bemused, if only because he hadn't allowed them time to actually tell him why they had called on him. The flow of words continued unabated: 'Known Ben meself fer thirty year or more! Decent bloke, ain't 'e? Said as someone would be comin' by terday ter 'ave a look-see at 'em. Good boats, they are; do you a good turn 'n no mistake!

Only bin there a month or two, they 'ave – Danny Foster's 'ad 'em since the end o' the war, took 'em over from 'is old man when 'e got killed by that doodlebug as 'it the Star 'n Garter in Stepney 'Igh Street. Gawd knows what 'e was doin' in there, mind. Story is 'e'd gorn ter meet 'is fancy woman, 'n got a bigger bang than 'e'd reckoned with!'

'They've been used reg'lar then, 'ave they?' Michael managed to get a question in, only to prompt another torrent of words:

'Oh, aye! Bernie Foster ran moonitions Wolver'ampton ter Brentford most o' the war with 'em, back-loading wi' tinned stuff ter Sam'son Road – then Danny's bin on the lime juice ter Boxmoor, last year or two. Gone on the bank, 'e 'as, silly bugger! Workin' fer a 'aulage firm in Southall, part o' BRS it is now, o' course. Learned 'ow ter drive in the war, in the h'army. Can't blame 'im, I s'pose – says as the money's good, 'n 'e gets ter go 'ome every night, 'n 'ave Sundays off.'

The 'dingy', which had proved to be a small rowing-boat, bumped against the side of the empty town-class butty, and Hawes reached up to grab the gunwale and haul them around to the stern. He quickly tied the painter to the t-stud, and clambered up into the well behind the cabin:

'Come on – 'ave a gander at these two! Always kep' 'em nice, did Danny 'n 'is missus. Bloody shame ter see 'em stuck 'ere like this – good pair o' boats should be workin', not goin' ter rack 'n ruin. I've kep' an eye on 'em since they've bin 'ere, thought as 'ow someone might want 'em – not like the rest o' the old 'ulks 'round 'em!' He waved an arm: 'Ol' wooden boats, most on 'em, rotten 'n fallin' apart. But these two... well, you come 'n see!'

* * *

'He can talk, can't he?' Ben Vickers laughed at Ginny's description of their encounter with Jim Hawes. They'd stopped at the Halfway

House, below Widewater Lock, on their way back South in order to take a look over the boats in Harefield Flashes. Another week had seen them back in Braunston again, once more bound for James' foundry; although that load itself had left Michael with a feeling of gloom and despondency. With Harriet and Carrie looking after Li'l Alby on the boats, Michael and Ginny were once more in the Vickers' front room:

'So what are these boats of yours like, Mikey? Are they as good as he led me to believe?' Michael laughed:

'They ain't moine yet, Ben, oonless yew know soomthin' yew ain't told me! Boot Oi reckon they're pretty good. They ain't been lyin' ther' too long, 'n they'd been well looked after before. Cabins'll need cleanin' out, mast-box on the motor's goin' rotten 'n the top mast's missin', 'n a coopla the top-planks are rotten too. 'N ther's no top-cloths on oither o' them. Boot they both look sound enooff ter me.'

'What about the engine?'

'We got 'er goin'. Took a few troys, but she ran well enooff once she started. Joost needs a proper service.'

'Right – I'll put those points to the people at the Transport Commission, ask them if they'll replace the missing stuff or drop the price a bit more – that would be best for us, because I expect I can get the bits we need from Frank Nurser. He's prepared to dock them for you, give them a thorough going-over, black them round and repaint them.'

'Sounds h'okay, Ben.' Vickers gave him a puzzled look:

'Is anything wrong, Mikey? Are you having second thoughts?'

'No, no. Boot... 'ave yeh found oos any work fer 'em once we got 'em?'

'I've not taken any orders, if that's what you mean – it would be premature until we've got the boats here and back into proper trim.'

'Boot 'ave yeh got anythin' loined oop?'

'Nothing definite – but I've got some good prospects. Barlows, here in Braunston, could give you regular work, but it would be all coal – as you know, that's all they do – and it would be mostly down the Oxford cut. Hard going with all those single locks. I've spoken to the central traffic office at the Docks and Inland Waterways, and they say they can probably fmd you loads on a fairly regular basis. And I've got a line on a firm who import a lot of timber – they're using lorries mainly, but I'm hoping we might persuade them to give us some loads out of Brentford.'

'Ah – don't sound so bad, then.'

'What's up, Mikey?' Michael shrugged:

'Oh, it's joost... We've got another load o' h'ingots fer James's, on the So'o loop. Boot they tell me it's the last trip – fact'ry's closin' next month. 'N... well, Oi know it's daft, but... furst trip Oi ever did on the cut, wi' Bill 'n Vi, was oop ter James's. That's wher' they was goin' when they fished me out boy Galleon Bridge.'

'Yeh never tor me that!' Ginny turned to her brother; he shrugged again:

'Didn' seem important, Oi s'pose.' She took his hands in hers:

'Oi woondered whoy yeh were so oopset when they told oos it was the last roon! Oh, Moikey...' He gave a self-deprecating grunt:

'Oi'll get oover it, Gin! 'Specially if we're 'avin' ar own boats!'

'I'll go ahead then, shall I? I'll get the best deal I can out of the Transport Commission, and find someone to bring them here to be docked.' Michael smiled over Ginny's shoulder:

'Please, Ben. We can get 'em here arselves, though.'

'Might be better if you carry on with whatever orders they give you, Mikey. You'll have money coming in, and we don't know for sure how long it will take to get your boats ready. I know one or two retired boaters who'll cheerfully bring them up from Harefield for us.'

'Yeah – h'okay, Oi s'pose yeh're right, Ben. Now – are yeh coomin' down the Plough with oos ter celebrate ar h'independence?'

Chapter Twenty-Seven

'Moikey! Ginny! What're yeh 'avin'?'

An unexpected reception was waiting for them in the bar of the Old Plough:

'Billy! 'Ow are yeh, mate? Good ter see yeh!'

''Ello Billy – Sylvie with yeh?' Ginny asked.

'Nah – she's back at yer boats, comparing kiddies wi' 'Arriet 'n Carrie. 'Ello, Mr Vickuss!' He'd spotted Ben Vickers, following them in through the door.

'Hello, Billy – How are you all? How's little Emily?'

'Ah, she's grand, thank yeh. Coom on, what're yeh drinkin'? Mr Vickuss?'

'I'll have a pint of best, thanks Billy.'

'Me too, mate. Shandy, Gin?' Michael suggested.

'Yeah, please, Billy.'

Billy turned to the bar, attracting the eyes of the landlord; Kim Warden got up from the stool where he'd been sitting and came to meet Ginny, a smile of welcome on his face. His order placed, Billy gave Michael a grin and whispered to him:

'Kim's been real oopset wi' me! Oi needed 'im ter stay wi' the boats when we coom oop fer Ooncle Alby's do, 'n then we was loadin' the day o' Alby's christenin'.'

'Oh, 'e'll soon mek oop fer lost toime!' Michael glanced around to where the two had sat together in the window of the bar.

'Ther' yeh go, Mr Vickuss. Ther's yourn, Moikey. What's

this Oi 'ear about yew packin' it in?' Michael laughed – for once, the towpath telegraph had got things slightly awry:

'We ain't packin' in, Billy – we joost ain't workin' fer British Waterways no more!'

''Oo yeh goin' teh, then? Barlows?' Michael glanced at Ben Vickers, who said with a laugh:

'Tell him, Mikey! Put him out of his misery!'

'We're buyin' ar own pair, Billy.'

'Yeh're what?'

'Ben 'ere's found oos a good pair o' Woolwich boats, loyin' oidle in 'Arefield Flashes. We're 'avin' 'em brung oop 'ere fer Nurser's ter dock 'em, 'n when they're ready we're goin' on ar own. 'E's got soome work loined oop fer oos, already.'

'Well, boogger me! Yeh're goin' ter be a noomber oone, then?'

'S'roight. Dad left 'is savin's wi' Ben, 'n we've got enooff ter buy the boats 'n 'ave 'em sorted, 'n leave a bit oover in case o' trouble.'

'Gaw, yew loocky beggar!'

The usual boater's talk of loads and destinations and the state of the road went by the board that evening as the three men launched into an eager discussion of the practicalities of working as an independent owner-boatman. In their window-seat, Ginny and Kim were engrossed in their own conversation until the party broke up and they left the pub in the fading light of the summer's day. Vickers bid them all good night and set off along the High Street to Welton Road, and the others headed back down the lane to Butcher's Bridge and the canal.

Michael was still in buoyant mood as they parted at the bridge, Billy and Kim heading toward the locks to where their boats were tied. Part of the way along to the old Stop House, where they'd left the Oakley and the Antrim, he noticed that Ginny was unusually subdued:

'Are yeh h'okay, Gin?' She looked around and smiled at him:

'Yeah – Oi'm foine, Moikey.'

'Yeh sure? Yeh're very quoiet.'

'Oi'm h'okay, really!' There was a hint of annoyance in her voice, so he let it drop. Back at the boats, Harriet was already settled with the baby; Ginny shooed Carrie off to her bed, the younger girl prattling eagerly:

'It was loovely seein' Sylvie agen; 'n little Emmy, she's brilliant! Oi can' wait ter get growed oop 'n 'ave kiddies o' me own!'

'Yer turn'll coom, soon enooff – now go on, get off ter bed!'

* * *

The next few weeks passed in a fever of excited anticipation. By the time they'd unloaded in Birmingham, circled around via the old 'bottom road' to the Warwickshire coal fields and loaded for Apsley Mills, then run on empty to Bulls Bridge, a message was waiting for them:

> *Michael: Boats are secured, at a good price. I've got Eric Collis and Brian Franks to bring them to Braunston, and Frank Nurser will dock them as soon as he can. Come and see me when you can – our love to you all, Ben.'*

This further boost to their spirits also, conversely, sparked a feeling of poignancy in Michael – he found himself deeply and sorrowfully aware that this opportunity to realise what had become a real ambition for him was only there because his beloved dad was no longer with them. Sometimes, in the evenings, he would fall silent, losing the thread of whatever conversation was flowing around him, an emptiness overtaking him at the absence of Alby's gruff tones, the smell of his pipe tobacco, the sound of his laughter. He knew that the others all missed him too – he felt the occasional hollowness behind Harriet's quiet sufficiency and her obvious devotion to their son, and Carrie would sometimes come to him and put her arms around him, hiding her face in his shirt. Ginny would, when the mood took her, disappear for an hour or more, walking alone in the fields or on the towpath. And the mood of withdrawal that he'd noticed after the evening with Billy stayed with her, on and off.

Whether his strong words for Bartram had had a direct effect or someone had taken the hint, they found themselves on an easier job for those weeks. Almost a reversal of the beer run they'd sometimes had under FMC, they would load full barrels of Guinness at the bonded warehouse in Park Royal, on the Paddington Arm, and carry them to the now-British Waterways wharves at Birmingham's Fazeley Street, returning with a load of empties.

On their first such trip Northwards, they paused in Braunston long enough to meet Ben Vickers and take another look at their boats, lying in the arm awaiting docking:

'Look, Alby! These are our boats – ain't they grand?' Michael smiled over Harriet's shoulder as she proudly showed the pair to their month-old baby. He was pleased that she had lost her doubts about his decision, largely as a result of Ben's confidence that he could provide them with a steady flow of orders. The other girls had never needed any persuading, and now clambered over the boats chattering eagerly; Harriet ducked down into the motor cabin with little Albert, leaving him on the dockside with Vickers:

'Pleased with them, Mikey?' Ben's grin said that he knew the answer already.

'Oh, yes!' Michael felt the emotion welling up in him: 'Oi joost wish Dad was 'ere ter see 'em.' Ben clapped him on the shoulder:

'I know, son. He was so proud of you, of how you turned out, you know that. And now his name'll be on the side your boats.'

'Yeah – yeah, Oi 'adn' thought o' that!'

'What are you going to call yourself, Mikey? We'll need to tell the signwriter – Michael Baker, Canal Carrier?' Michael grinned:

'Sounds grand, doesn' it?' He paused: 'Moichael Baker 'N Soon!' Vickers laughed:

'Of course, Mikey! We'll put my phone number on there as well, okay? Can't waste an opportunity for advertising!'

'Yes, o' course.'

'What about colours? On the cabinsides?'

'Oh – yeah...'

'You want something smart, and distinctive. Stand out from the rest – you've got the BW blue and yellow, and quite a lot of the old GU or FMC colours still around. Barlows dark green and oak graining, Harvey Taylors' black and white – doesn't leave a lot of choice! What do you think?'

'Oi don' know...' He stood deep in thought for a moment: 'Oi'd loike red panels, loike the old FMC boats, boot if we 'ad different borders 'stead o' the green... Yellow'd be too broight, blue'd look loike GU... 'Ow 'bout white?'

'With a black coach-line? That'd certainly stand out!'

'Aye – be pretty smart, eh?'

'What about decoration?'

'Oh, not too mooch, Ben. Few di'monds on the fore-end, mebbe, 'n the odd swag o' roses. Real fancy stooff, loike ol' Joe Skinner's boat – it's noice, boot it looks koind o' ol' fashioned ter me.'

'All right, Mikey. I think I've got the feeling of what you want – will you leave it to me to talk to Frank?'

'Yeah, sure, Ben.' Vickers hesitated:

'What about names, Mikey? For the boats – do you want to keep Northampton and Northchurch?'

'Oh – Oi thought it was bad loock ter change 'em?'

'Unless they're out of the water, so they say. But we're docking these – so if you wanted to?'

'Yeah...' Michael raised his voice: ''Arrie! Ginny! Carrie! Coom 'ere, all of yeh!' A scrambling of boots, and his family gathered around him, all grinning excitedly: 'What're we gonna call 'em?'

'Are yeh gonna change their names, Moikey?' Ginny asked.

'Whoile they're on the dock, we can if we want.' Harriet's eyes shone:

'Ther's only one thing we can call 'em: The Albert 'n the Rita.' Michael felt tears burn behind his eyes as she echoed his own thoughts; he took her in his arms, cuddling the baby between them, as Ginny's voice at his side confirmed softly:

'That's roight. The Albert...'

''N the Rita.'

Carrie finished her sentence for her.

Chapter Twenty-Eight

A Friday morning in early August, 1950. A pair of empty boats climbing the straggling flight of six narrow locks at Camp Hill in Birmingham, in an intermittent drizzle. The butty rising in the top lock, the motor standing back by the top gate ready to take up the tow; the gate swings open, pushed by a girl about to enjoy her thirteenth birthday, in dungarees and an old flat cap as an older girl, similarly dressed, drops the paddles. At the tiller, a woman of twenty in more traditional dress with a coat pulled over her pinafore, an old-fashioned bonnet on her head; on the motor boat, their captain, a tall young man of twenty-one, his thatch of sandy hair bared to the weather, his donkey-jacket glistening in the rain, reaches to take one cross-strap and drop it over the dolly on his stern.

The boats are, to some eyes, a strange mixture – the motor, a big, bluff shape typical of the new Grand Union boats of the 1930s, in the blue and yellow livery of the national British Transport Waterways fleet, the butty, older, slimmer in appearance with its elegant double-curvature bow, in the now-defunct colours of Fellows, Morton & Clayton Ltd. Both look pristine, the paintwork gleaming, its brightness given an added sheen by the moisture, all the visible brasswork on portholes, chimneys and chains and sundry fittings shining despite the dullness of the weather.

The pair sweep around with careless, unhesitating perfection into the basin of the Sampson Road depot. The crew swing the stern of the butty into line; a burst of reverse thrust from the motor, and it glides easily backwards in to the layby area; casting off the one strap, the captain eases his powered charge back alongside as one of the girls hurries to the fore-end of the butty and throws a line across to tie the bows together. Moments later, both are secured by the stern, and the captain steps down to shut off the steady beat of the engine. In the sudden quiet, ignoring the bustle of activity opposite on the loading bays, the crew gather on the bank by the butty's rudder, an air of sadness about them.

'Well, that's that.' Michael broke the silence.

'Yeah... Ginny turned to look at him, and he saw the sheen of tears in her eyes; she looked away, shaking her head, and he put his arm around her:

'Bin a long toime, Gin.'

'Yeah...' The catch in her voice was clear now; Carrie hugged her from the other side:

'Coom on, Gin – we'll be in ar own pair tonoight!'

'Oi know! Boot – it's not joost leavin' the boats, it's loike leavin' a part o' Dad be'ind...'

'Yeah...' Carrie felt her own sadness well up, and buried her face in the older girl's shirt; Michael gently withdrew his arm and went to give his wife a cuddle. Harriet turned her face up to his:

'Oi know 'ow yew all feel. Yeh'd 'ad the H'Antrim all the toime yeh were tergether, 'adn' yeh?'

'S'roight, loove. The motor don' matter, it was never 'is. Boot...'

'Oi know.' She looked down at the baby cradled in her arms: 'Boot we've got a new start fer 'is grandsoon, fer all of oos, ain't we?' Michael nodded, his sigh drifting into a smile:

'We 'ave that!' He looked up: 'Coom on, all of yeh – Ben'll be 'ere soon with 'is motor-car, we've got ter git ar stooff ready!'

The sorrowful tableau broke, the thought of their new boats subduing the sadness of the moment. The two girls stepped over into the stern well and vanished into the butty cabin; Harriet passed the baby to Michael and stepped down into the motor. The drizzle had eased now, the cloud overhead beginning to break; a sudden shaft of sunlight struck his shoulders and he turned his face to it, self-consciously aware of the symbolism, and stood facing the brightness of their future with his infant son in his arms: *Oi'm goin' ter mek 'im as proud ter be moy soon as Oi am ter 'ave bin yours, Dad!*

* * *

The aged Alvis shooting-brake creaked heavily on its springs as it turned from the main road into the back of Nurser's Dock in Braunston. It seemed to give a sigh of relief as the doors opened and five people got out, stiff after the drive from Birmingham. Carrie grabbed Ginny's hand and the two of them went to run around to the dockside, eager for the first glimpse of their newly-docked boats, but a bellow stopped them in their tracks:

''Old on, yew two! Tek soomat wi' yeh fer goodness sake!' Michael's shout was good-humoured, and they turned back, grinning at him.

'Yes, Captain!' He aimed a playful cuff at Carrie's ear, and she ducked, laughing. Ben Vickers opened the back doors, and they each sought out their own bags of clothing before hurrying away. Ben took a roll of bedding under each arm; Michael grabbed the first things which came to hand, and they all walked around the buildings, Harriet with Albert junior in her arms. They found the girls standing on the edge by the boat-building shed, gazing across at the two boats tied on the other side – their eyes were wide, their mouths open; Ginny recovered enough to turn to her brother as he approached:

'Oh, Moikey! They look brilliant!' He chuckled:

'Stand out o' the crowd, don' they?' He had refused to tell any of them, Harriet included, the colours he'd chosen for them,

163

and the sight of the bright Signal Red cabinsides, with their wide white borders separated by a neat black coachline, came as a spectacular surprise for them.

'Moichael – they moost be the smartest pair on the cut!' Harriet sounded just as stunned: '"Moichael Baker 'n Soon, Canal C... Carriers".' She read off the signwritten legend on the cabinsides.

They walked around, past the two dry-docks, and approached the immaculate pair more closely. Depositing their burdens by the butty's cabin, they passed on to inspect them in turn from stem to stern:

The name *Rita* painted on the upswept top bend of the butty stern, a small neat panel of bright-coloured diamonds in front below the stern end of the cabin, the side of which was graced by a square landscape panel; the simple but elegant signwriting in cream shaded in two colours of blue, repeated on the motor's cabin as well, and the name *Albert* set high and proud on the sides of the engine-room; both fore-ends, a simple white finish on the top-bends sweeping around with a single swag of roses set centrally against the white. Over the way, the craftsmen building a new wooden butty under the shed looked up at the sound of their excited voices, and then bent, smiling, to their skilled labours again.

Michael was as impressed as anyone with the final result:

''Arrie's roight, Ben – they're the smartest pair Oi've ever seen! Yeh've doon a brilliant job!' Vickers laughed:

'I'm pleased you like them, Mikey! But the credit goes to Frank and his men, they've done it all. I just told them what you'd said you wanted, and they did the rest.'

'Oi'll 'ave ter go 'n thank 'em meself – They look woonderful!'

'I had them regrain inside both cabins, as well, and you've got all new decoration in there, landscapes on the table-cupboards, flowers on the doors, and everything.'

'Thank yeh, Ben – it moost 'ave cost, though?' He laughed again:

'Not as much as you might think! I've called in a lot of old favours for you, Michael – just make a job of working them, and make it all worthwhile!'

'We will, Ben, never fear. Fer Dad, 'n yew, 'n everyone 'oo's 'elped oos oover the years.' Vickers clapped him on the back:

'We're all proud of you, Mikey, all of you. I'll bet my old mate is up there now, on his little cloud, with a big grin on his face!' Michael gave a chuckle:

'Oi 'ope they let 'im 'ave a beer now 'n then, 'n smoke 'is poipe – 'e'll be roight pissed off if they don't!'

* * *

Later that afternoon, they were settling in, putting everything away in its rightful place. Michael was down in the engine-hole with Ben checking over the newly-serviced National, when a hale sounded from outside:

'Wher's the captain o' these boats? Oi want a word!' Michael stuck his head out of the side doors at the familiar voice:

'Bill! What're yew doin' 'ere?' He climbed out onto the dockside, grabbed the proffered hand: 'It's great ter see yeh!'

'Good ter be 'ere, lad! Vi's h'inspectin' the butty, 'n Stevie 'n Ellie'll be along in a minute. Ben tol' oos yeh'd be coomin' fer yer boats terday, so we coom down on the train. Josh's out o' school roight now, 'olidays.'

''E's 'ere 'n all?'

'Talkin' noineteen ter the doozen wi' Carrie, o' course!' Michael looked around and got a furious wave from the boy standing with his sister beside the butty cabin:

''Ello, Ooncle Moikey!' He waved back and called out:

''Ow are yeh, Josh? H'enjoyin' school?'

'Yeah – Oi'm near top o' moy class!'

'Good lad! Y' ain't missin' the boats, then?' A shrug of the shoulders:

'Yeah, Oi do – boot... yeh know!' Michael laughed, turned back to Bill:

'He's really coom on lately, ain't 'e?

'Aye – 'e's a great kid. 'E's even 'elpin' Stevie with 'is stoodies, in the h'evenin's.'

'Yeh're pleased yew 'n Vi took 'im on, then?'

'Oh, yeah. Oi 'ad me doubts, yew well know, boot 'e's turned out grand. 'Ow 'bout Carrie?'

'Oh, she's a good lass. She can read 'n wroite as well as me now, prob'ly better!'

'Hey, Moikey! Them boats look champion!' They turned, to see Stevie and his girl walking towards them along the dockside:

'Stevie, mate! Good ter see yeh – wher've yeh bin?'

'Gettin' soomthin' fer yeh!' Stevie chuckled as Ellie gave Michael a hug and a kiss on the cheek.

'Oh?'

'Yeah. Yeh're s'posed ter smash a bottle o' champagne over a boat when yeh launch it, boot bein' as they're already in the water, we thought it'd do more good ter drink it!' He held out a large bottle; Michael laughed:

'Sounds like a mooch better oidea ter me! Let oos finish toidyin' oop, 'n we'll drink ter yer 'ealth!'

'Nah! We should drink ter yer new boats, teh yer future!'

166

Chapter Twenty-Nine

Another flight of narrow locks, and another immaculately-turned-out pair of boats working quickly and efficiently uphill. And there the resemblance ended: The locks were the picturesque flight at Watford, lifting the Leicester Line of the Grand Union Canal up to its summit level, and the boats were a matched pair of ex-Grand Union Town Class, renamed and repainted in a private livery. The weather was kinder, dry and warm if rather overcast; even the demeanour of the crew was different – there was a jovial eagerness about the way they worked, in the occasional word passed between them.

At the top, the gate swung open under the effort of the same young girl in her dungarees; but now she had a helper – a little boy, a year or two her junior. The waiting motor boat set back to pick up the cross-straps, and the same young man bent to them, dropped them over the dollies on his stern; he looked up, called cheerfully to the lock-keeper just dropping the paddles:

'Thanks, mate! We'll see yeh later!' The man raised his windlass in salute:

'Aye – good loock, boy! Yer boats are a picture – yew look after 'em!'

'We will! Thank yeh!'

The boats swept away, around the series of long, easy bends that form the first part of the Leicester summit, their unusual red and white colours beginning to gleam under the lightening skies, every piece of brass glittering as the sun tried to break through. And, despite their recent trials, five hearts were light and swelling with pride – only the baby boy, cradled in his mother's arms as she sat on the back-end planks of the empty motor, was too young to know the significance of the day.

* * *

They'd stayed the weekend in Braunston, Michael deciding that for once they all deserved a short break to give themselves time to get used to their new boats, to the fractional differences in the cabins and the performance of the new ranges, to the marginal differences in the way they sat in the water.

On the Friday evening, bouncing like a bunch of children with a new toy, they'd taken them out for a 'trial run' – out of the dock, up to Braunston turn and away along the Oxford Canal towards Wigrams and Napton, where the lonely windmill stands high on its hilltop above village and canal. In a wide bend where the Southam Road crosses the canal, Michael let the butty up alongside the motor and turned the pair, enjoying the responsiveness of the Woolwich boats and the quick power of the on-song National engine.

On the return, he'd stepped away and let Bill, and then Stevie, take a turn at the tiller, both of them grinning like Cheshire cats at the feel of a pair of boats under their hands again. And then Carrie had taken over, to bring them back over the last mile or two into Braunston. Back on the dockside, in the fading light of the day, they'd broached Stevie's bottle of champagne and toasted their future success. It was then that Josh had looked wistfully at the boats and said:

'Oi wish Oi was coomin' with yeh...'

'Whoy don' yeh?' Harriet asked; Carrie looked around eagerly:

'Can 'e, Moikey?' Michael hesitated, but Vi chipped in:

''E's orf school fer a few more weeks, now. If yew'll tek 'im, we don' moind, do we, Bill?'

'H'okay, then. Fer a whoile, any'ow – we'll put 'im on the train soomwher' when yeh want 'im back – or when 'e's 'ad enooff!'

Brother and sister joined in an impromptu jig on the dockside in their delight.

The following afternoon, as Ginny was tackling a heap of washing in her dolly-tub and the two younger children were off watching the men at work under the boat-building shed, three more familiar figures appeared under the iron bridge over the dock entrance. Her back to them, Ginny didn't see them approach, and the gentle touch on her shoulder made her jump; she turned, ready to yell at whoever had startled her – but her face switched instantly to a happy smile:

'Sam! What're yew doin' 'ere?' His smile was just as eager: 'We coom boy ter see yeh – we've 'eard all about yer new boats.' Ginny looked up at the sound of a chuckle from beyond him.

''Ello, Mr Caplin, Mrs Caplin – it's noice ter see yeh! 'Arriet's in the motor, wi' Li'l Alby, 'n Moikey's polishin' 'is injun. Agen!'

''Ello, Ginny loove!' Suey Caplin stepped forward and gave the girl a warm hug as Michael's head appeared in the engine-room doors:

'Coom 'n 'ave a look at me injun, 'Enry!' Henry Caplin ruffled Ginny's hair as he passed her to join his son-in-law.

'We brought yeh soomthin' ter wish yeh well.' Suey held out a brightly painted water can to Harriet as she emerged from the cabin of the Albert. She took it, and looked closely at the decoration:

'Mam! Is that a Boockby can?' The water cans from Anchor Cottage, in the flight of locks at Long Buckby, were a badge of wealth and one-upmanship among the boaters. Suey smiled proudly:

'Aye, it is – noothin' boot the best fer moy girl 'n 'er man!'

'Oh Mam! Moikey'll be so proud – thank yeh!'

Later, they were all gathered in a corner of the bar in the Admiral

Nelson. Outside, a soft summer rain was falling; within, the atmosphere was equally warm as Suey made a huge fuss of her grandson, attended by his mother and his aunt and uncle; the two younger children sat together, talking and giggling, happy to be in each other's company; and Michael and Henry discussed the prospects for the success of an independent boatman in the 1950s.

Michael, naturally, was full of enthusiasm; Henry, true to form, took a more pessimistic view of the future, although he was clearly trying hard not to deflate his son-in-law's spirits too much:

'If anyone c'n mek a go o' things, Moikey, yew can. Yeh're a fust-class boater, 'n yeh've got yer scholarin' be'ind yeh. Boot Oi en't sure 'ow long its all goin' ter go on, boy. Soom fact'ries are closin', oothers're turnin' oover ter usin' h'oil 'stead o' coal, 'n loads're bein' lost ter the lorries. Them booggers are mooch quicker'n oos, yeh can' denoy it, 'n folks want their stooff fast now, they en't goin' ter wait. Anoother big freeze-oop, wi' the boats stopped fer a few weeks, 'n that'll be it, yew mark moy words!'

'Yeah, ther's soomat in what yeh say, 'Enry, Oi know that – boot ther's more work out ther' than ther's boats ter 'andle it! Ben's bin lookin' inter things fer oos, 'n 'e reckons as the Waterways, 'n oother folks loike Barlows, ain't got the boats – or mebbe the men – to cope wi' the loads they got!'

'Yeah, that's as mebbe, boy. Boot that's now – 'ow long's it goin' ter go on fer? 'Alf the wharves wher' we use'ter h'unload en't ther' any more!'

'Oh, Oi s'pose things're changin', 'Enry. Boot it'll settle down, surely? Ther'll alwes be soom things as'll go on the boats – 'n it might joost be that we'll be best placed ter carry 'em, bein' ar own bosses. We c'n go wher' we're needed, 'n mebbe do the job cheaper'n big coomp'ny's wi' lot's o' men ter pay, eh?'

They both looked around as the door in the corner of the room opened: 'Ah! I thought I might find you all in here!'

'Ben – what're yeh drinkin'?' Michael went to meet him, and Henry joined them at the bar:

'Oi'm getting' these, Moikey.' He turned to the rest of the group to ask who was ready for a fresh drink, but he paused and gave Michael a nudge, nodded in their direction. Michael followed his gaze, and felt his own eyebrows lift in surprise at the sight of young Sam's arm around Ginny's shoulders, a situation that seemed not to have perturbed her in the least. The three men exchanged amused glances:

'Oh, ah?' Henry chuckled quietly:

'Ah indeed!'

'I thought she was sweet on Kim Warden?' Ben Vickers asked, sotto voce; Michael replied, equally softly:

'Not any more boy the look of it!' Henry raised his voice:

''Oo needs their glass refillin', then?' Heads turned, and Sam's arm was quickly withdrawn.

Seated once more, fresh pints to hand, Michael asked Henry:

'Yew know Ben Vickuss, don' yeh? Used ter be Fellers's manager 'ere in Braunston.'

'Course! We met at Alby's do, 'n then at littl'un's christ'nin'.' The two shook hands:

'How are you doing, Henry?'

'Ah, pretty fair, Ben. Moikey was sayin' that yeh've bin lookin out fer 'im, wi' these noo boats?'

'Ben got everythin' sorted fer oos, 'Enry. Found oos the boats, 'ad 'em got 'ere 'n docked, 'n now 'e's getting' ar orders.' Ben laughed:

'It's been great – I'm really enjoying myself, getting involved with the cut again! And I've got your first job for you, Mikey.' Michael leant forward in his chair:

'Yeah? What've we got, Ben?'

'I've agreed that we'll try a couple of runs for the Transport Commission – they're short of the pairs they need for this job...'

'Not rooddy coal, is it?' Henry laughed:

'That's all we get, boy! Coal ter Dickinson's, oone o' the mills boy Apsley or Croxley, 'n back empt! Booggers can' h'organoise

171

a backload ter save their loives.' Ben grinned at them, spoke to Michael:

'You're going to Leicester, to Belgrave Wharf, and loading steel. Sheet steel, in rolls – it'll be craned in, and out again into lighters at Brentford. Five tons to a roll, four rolls in the motor, five in the butty. You could take more, but the summit there's getting shallow and I wouldn't recommend it.'

'When do they want oos ther?'

'I've said you can be there to load Wednesday.'

'That's foine, Ben! We'll get away Moonday mornin', 'ave another day ter get settled in, 'n still 'ave plenty o' tonne.'

'D'yeh know the road, Moikey?' Henry asked.

''Aven' bin that way since Oi was a lad, in the war – we used ter go ter Nottin'am soomtoimes, wi' sugar 'n stoof loike that.'

'Ah, roight. Oi en't bin that way fer a long whoile oither. Oi 'ear as it's slow goin', loike Ben says. 'N don' forget yeh've got them narrer locks at Foxton 'n Watford.'

'Yeah, Oi remember; Boot the rest o' the way's woide.'

'And at least the narrow locks are all concentrated in those two flights – it won't be too bad having to bow-haul the butty through.'

'That's roight, Ben. It'll be noice ter get off the Joonction fer a change!'

''Ave yeh got 'em a backload, Ben?' Henry's tone sounded as though he doubted the prospect, but he was surprised to hear Vickers chuckle:

'I reckon so, Henry! You remember I told you I'd spoken to that firm of timber importers, Mikey?'

'Yeah?'

'They've got shiploads coming in on a regular basis, and one's due around the time you'll be unloading the steel. I've told them you're available, and they're going to offer us a load, see how it goes. You might have to wait in Brentford for a day or two, until the ship docks and they can get the lighters around to you but if we can show them the boats are a viable option, we'll get more loads from them!'

'Boogger me! Oi wish yeh was workin' fer ar lot, Ben!'

* * *

Monday night, they tied at the bottom of Foxton Locks. Dinner taken on the long run over the summit from Watford, Harriet opted to stay on the boats with little Albert; Josh and Carrie enjoying each other's company in the gathering dusk, Michael set off for a pint in the Black Horse and found Ginny tagging along.

Since the weekend, she had seemed more cheerful, more like her old self than he remembered since Alby's funeral. He bought her a shandy, and a pint of mild for himself; they sat side by side on stools at the public bar, talking quietly, just happy to be alone together, brother and sister, in a way that was not often possible in the confined life of the boats. A brief silence fell between them; then Ginny looked up:

'Moikey?'

'Yes, loove?'

'Yeh loike Sam, don't yeh?'

'Sam? Which Sam?' His teasing brought a flash of her usual spirit:

'Sam Caplin, yew idjit! Yer woife's brother!'

'Oh, that Sam!'

'Yeah...' Her tone was hesitant now: 'Yeh do loike 'im?'

''E's a decent lad.'

'Boot – yeh *loike* 'im?' He looked at her, saw the gleam in her eye, her smile; and something in that smile made him pause. There was a strange gentleness about it, a look which reminded him of someone else; a moment's thought, and he realised – it was the same look he'd always loved in Harriet's smile, a kind of shyness. And the one thing he'd never accuse his sister of was being shy. *Oh ho! Oi think Oi know wher' this's goin'!*

'Yes I do. 'E's grown inter a real noice yoong feller.'

'Yeh won' moind – if Oi see a bit more of 'im, then?' He laughed at the unaccustomed nervousness in her tone:

'Oi don' moind, Gin! Boot don' yer think 'e'd best ask fer 'imself?' Her smile became a big grin:

'Oi'll mek sure 'e doos! If Oi can tell 'im yeh'll be h'okay about it...'

'All roight, girl! Boot what about Kim?' She shrugged:

'That was only friends, Moikey. Oi tol' 'im that, las' toime we saw 'im – 'e was a bit oopset, boot Oi think 'e's all roight.' She laughed, and he could hear the joy in her voice:

'Oi'll send Sam ter see yeh nex' toime we meet oop wi' them!'

They laughed together, his arm around her waist.

Chapter Thirty

The echoing clatter of a diesel engine exhaust suddenly diminished into a steady even beat as a deep-loaded narrowboat emerged from the darkness of Braunston tunnel. The dark-haired teenager at the helm glanced back to watch the equally-heavy butty follow him, seconds later, at the end of its long line, his mother comfortably settled at its tiller; the tall figure of his father climbed out of the cabin to join her in the stern well, raising a hand to his son who waved back.

Despite the gleam of polished brass, the uninspiring blue and yellow colours of the British Waterways boats took on an added drabness in the deep shade of the long cutting, but the boy's heart was full of hope. Another half-hour would see them past the junction with the canal's Leicester section and at the top of Long Buckby locks – and that would put them on the same water as someone he so much wanted to see again...

Sam Caplin had been carefully working it out as he steered the pair through the blackness of the tunnel. His girl – was it wishful thinking to call her that yet? – should have set away from Leicester with their load of steel the day before. So by now they ought also to be approaching the junction – would they be in front of his boats, or behind? His father had not been pleased, but Sam was secretly glad of that delay, waiting for orders at Sutton's. How far would they get today? It was already late, afternoon shading into evening, so Stoke Bruerne would be too far: *An hour from 'ere ter the bottom o' Bugby, mebbe anoother coopl'a hours 'fore we stop – Weedon? Boogbrooke if Dad's feelin' loike pushin' on...*

The boats gradually came out into the open as the sides of the cutting at last levelled out beside them. Past the feeder from Daventry reservoir, and under the succession of red-brick bridges until the heavier bridge before the junction appeared in the distance; Sam felt the nerves trembling in his stomach: Would there be a message for him at the top lock? *Bless yew, Moikey!*

It had been partly at his father's insistence that Sam had stuck with the impromptu lessons that Michael had for some years been giving him, along with many of their other friends amongst the boating youth. But now he was grateful for that limited learning – at least he knew how to read and write, and that meant he could exchange messages with Ginny: A piece of chalk, and a black-painted balance beam as a ready-made blackboard...

At the junction, Henry Caplin stepped off of his butty, windlass tucked over his shoulder. Sam had already slowed the engine to little more than tickover, and Henry hurried forward to the top lock. As he approached, he could see the gates closed against him: Dammit! A bad road would slow them down, losing the extra time taken to close up and fill each lock before they could work through, and he'd still hoped to be well along the sixteen-mile pound before they tied for the night.

Seeing the same scenario in front of him, Sam let the boats drift, slowing until they came to a virtual standstill in the wide reach above the lock. His father hurried around, closing up the bottom gates and paddles before whipping up all the top paddles to fill the lock; the draw as the water poured in began to move the boats slowly forward again, but Sam had judged it right, with the skill of long practice – Henry was swinging the gates open in time for him to clutch in again and run them in. His mother steered the butty up his left side as he braked the motor; he took the breasting string and dropped it over the stern dolly; the two boats snatched together, the impetus of the butty just sufficient to take them up against the bottom gates. Suey quickly tied the breasting line, through the shackle on the motor's gunwale and back to her T-stud, as her son ran forward and threw the fore-end line to tie the bows tightly together.

Henry had heaved the top gates closed; now he wound up the bottom paddles. Amid the roar of water echoing under the Watling Street bridge which spanned the tail of the lock, he grabbed the bike from where it lay on the motor's cloths and headed off to set the next. Suey stood by the one bottom gate, ready to push it open; she watched her son with a smile on her face as he dashed back to the top gates, inspected one balance beam and then, disappointment on his face, crossed over to her side. And suddenly a beaming smile split his face:

SC 5 Bells Thurs GB

Suey chuckled at the instant change in her son's demeanour, called across to him as he almost ran back across the lock and up to his bottom gate:

'Wher' are we goin' then, Sam?'

'Boogbrooke, if Dad'll do it!' His eagerness lit his eyes, making her laugh again:

'Yeh c'n alwes use the boike!' He joined in her laughter:

'Mebbe Oi will!'

The second lock of the Buckby flight is almost half a mile from the top one. Henry breathed a sigh of relief as he pedalled into sight and saw the uphill pair just drawing out, their own lock-wheeler coming to meet him on an equally tired old bicycle. The man skidded to a halt as they met, held up four fmgers:

'Four ready fer yeh, 'Enry!'

'Thank yeh, Chippy. 'Ow yeh doin'?'

'Not bad, mate. Better go or the missus'll give me 'Ell at the top'un!' Henry laughed:

'Roight y'are! Seen anythin' o' Moikey Baker's pair?'
'It's them what's in froont o' yeh! Look 'andsome, don' they?'
'Aye! See yeh later, Chip.'

The two bicycles headed off in opposite directions. *Oi wonder if Sam 'll be arskin' ter use the boike later?* Henry grinned to himself as he pedalled on to the lock.

* * *

It had been about half an hour before that the Albert and the Rita, resplendent in their fresh red and white livery, had passed through the top lock. And one member of their crew had been as much on tenterhooks as Sam.

They'd loaded, on schedule, first thing on Wednesday morning, and then run as far as the top of Foxton locks that day. The road, thus far, was not too bad; uphill from the Soar valley and through Saddington Tunnel to the junction below Foxton where the arm to Market Harborough branches off.

But the next day, Michael had been glad that he'd resisted the temptation to ignore Ben Vickers' advice and load an extra two rolls of steel. That would have given them a total of fifty-five tons, which the boats were easily able to handle, and a better payout at the end of the trip; but Vickers had said to take the lighter forty-five ton load. And even at that, the going had been slow over the twenty-two mile summit level – they had followed the twisting canal through its scenic territory, Michael all the time aware of the boat's bottom dragging through the accumulated mud and silt, seeing behind him in the water the churning clag stirred up by his propeller.

Setting away early around seven o'clock, it had nevertheless been near three in the afternoon when they'd reached the far end of the summit at Watford. Down the flight of narrow locks, Michael bow-hauling the butty, and then around the pound to the junction and the top of Long Buckby.

Over her plate of the mutton stew which she had first put on to cook while they were still on the summit, Ginny had tried to work it out as they ran past the Stag's Head and Watford village. She knew that the Caplins had gone to Sutton's to await orders, and that that usually, now, entailed a delay of a day or two. So they would be somewhere not too far away – but in front of them, or behind? Like Sam, she had no way of knowing. But she decided on her strategy – she'd ask Michael where he intended to stop that night, and chalk a message on the top lock. Then, if Sam saw it, he'd know where to meet them. If he saw it – if his boats weren't already past, minutes, hours, maybe even a day ahead. But then, in that case, maybe there would be a message for her?

But no chalkmarks showed on the beams when she hurried to look – so her cryptic note had been appended. And now, as they cleared the last of the seven locks and headed off along the straight towards the eerie gloom of Brockhall Spinneys, all she could do was pray that he was following her, and would be close enough behind to catch up with them after they'd stopped.

Later, the boats tied by the derelict coal-wharf on the edge of Bugbrooke village, she and Michael strolled around the road to the Five Bells; Carrie had taken to staying with Harriet of an evening, delighting in her role of auntie to little Albert, and Josh of course stayed with her. Over a pint of bitter for him and a glass of shandy for her, they chatted desultorily, Michael speculating about what return load Ben would have for them once they'd seen the rolled steel craned out into its lighters in Brentford basin, but getting only a distracted response from his sister.

And then, looking over his shoulder, her eyes lit up. He turned to see Sam Caplin closing the door and looking over at them with a rather sheepish smile; Ginny got to her feet, and Sam took both her hands in his as they met:

''Ello, Gin.'

''Ello, Sam – yeh saw moy note, then?'

'Yeah – thanks. Oi din't know if yeh were in froont of oos or be'ind 'til Oi spotted it.'

'Yer boats 'ere?'

'Uh-uh. Weedon. Oi coycled down ter catch oop wi' yeh.' Her eyes were glowing:

'Oh, Sam!' Looking embarrassed, the boy just shrugged.

Michael had been following the conversation, amused and at the same time eerily reminded of his own feelings when he had first started seeing Harriet, seeing the same nervous reticence in Sam: This looks awful serious! He decided it was time to make his presence felt:

'It's good ter see yeh, Sam. What brings yeh 'ere?' Sam turned to look at him as if only just realising he was there:

'Er – well...' Ginny gave him a nudge with her elbow:

'Go on, Sam!'

'Er – well, it's loike this...'

'Sam!' He looked at her and visibly braced himself, raising his eyes once more to Michael:

'Moikey – Can Oi – Oi mean, is it all roight if Oi, sort o'... coom 'n see Ginny? Now 'n then, loike?' Michael restrained his desire to laugh:

'Loike yeh 'ave already, ternoight, yeh mean?' Sam blushed scarlet:

'Er – well – yeah, Oi s'pose...' Michael put on a stern expression:

'Bit late ter be arskin' then, ain't it?' Sam dropped his eyes to the floor and just nodded; Michael held his silence until the boy looked up at him, the appeal clear in his expression:

'Oi'm sorry, Moikey! Oi din't mean ter oopset yeh...' Unable to contain himself any longer, Michael roared with laughter and put his hands on Sam's shoulders:

'Oh, Sam! If yew could'a seen yer face joost now!' Sam's expression slowly cleared into a beaming smile.

'Doos that mean yeh don' moind?'

'Oi saw this coomin, Sam – we saw yeh, in the Nelson, wi' yer arm around moy sister!'

'Oh...!' The youngster coloured again, making Michael laugh even harder:

'Listen – if yew want ter see Ginny, that's foine boy me. Yeh're a good lad, Oi know that, 'n not joost 'cause yeh're 'Arriet's broother. Boot joost remember – if yew 'urt or oopset moy sister, yeh'll answer ter me, roight?'

'Yeah, o' course, Moikey.'

'Roight then – yew coom 'n see 'er whenever yeh want. Yer only young, both o' yeh, so don' go gettin' too serious, not yet, h'okay?'

'Yes, Moikey!' Two voices chorused.

Chapter Thirty-One

'What the Hell are you doing here?' Stan Holland stared up from his desk in the small traffic office at Brentford: 'You're not supposed to be here until tomorrow!'

The tall young boatman before him grinned, his hat held between his hands like the cap of a naughty schoolboy:

'Oi'm 'ere, Mr 'Olland, 'n yer nine rolls o' steel're 'ere as well! What would yeh loike me ter do wi' them?'

'Oh – God, I don't know! I'll try and find you an empty lighter, and get them craned out for you. Leave it with me, will you? Go back to your boats, I'll give you a shout when I've got things organised.'

'Roight-oh, Mr 'Olland!'

Michael had gone to the office to report his arrival, half expecting that kind of reception. He'd wanted to make an impression with their first load, and circumstances had for once played his game.

They'd deliberately made a very early start from Bugbrooke, and on the deeper water of the Grand Union main line the relatively light load had seen the boats clipping along at a very good speed. That night they'd made it all the way across the bottom level of the canal, dropping down through Stoke Brueme and then Cosgrove locks, and up again to the top of the Chilterns, finally tying, quite late, at Cowroast ready for the descent into the Thames valley the next day.

The only one not entirely happy with their progress was Ginny, well aware that they were drawing further ahead of Henry Caplin's pair. But, to her delight and everyone else's amazement, Sam had turned up, hot, sweaty and tired, on the bicycle, barely half an hour after they'd tied up. His father had stopped in Marsworth, by the Red Lion, somewhat earlier, and he'd cycled all the way through the village, up the seven locks and along the three miles of the Tring summit to catch them.

Offering the youngster a bottle of pale ale from the few he kept on the boat, Michael refrained from comment – but the boy's dedication raised him further in his estimation: *Not Kim, nor even Stevie, would'a doon that!*

Another good run the following day had seen them tied not far from the entrance lock into Brentford basin. Barely eight o'clock the next day, and he was strolling back to the boats to await Holland's call to unload.

That call came around eleven, a message carried by one of the dockers. They swiftly moved the breasted pair alongside the lighter he indicated; a dockside crane sprang into life, and in short order the steel was gone, the boats now riding high and light as they moved them to a clear space on Brent Meadow Wharf to await whatever orders Ben had arranged for them.

Michael made his way back to the office; Holland looked up as he entered: 'Oh, it's you! Got your boats unloaded?'

'Yes, thank yeh Mr 'Olland. Thanks fer gettin' oos sorted so quick.'

'No trouble, Mr Baker, it's what I'm here for. You're lucky, mind – don't forget it's Sunday today, I'd have had a job to get a spare lighter normally, but I pinched that one from a job that's not due until late tomorrow. Now – I had a message for you...'

He scrabbled through papers piled on his desk:

'Ah, here we are...' He picked up a hand-written note and opened his mouth to read it out, but Michael stopped him with a grin:

'From Ben Vickuss, is it? Oi c'n read it fer meself, thanks, Mr 'Olland!'

'Oh – ah, right. Sorry – you get so used to dealing with people who can't, you know?'

'Tha's all roight, Mr 'Olland.' Michael took the note and read through it:

> *Michael – Barker and Freeman, the timber people, have got a ship docking in London early on Sunday. They're sending a load to Brentford by lighter, should be there midday on Monday – forty-seven tons of planked pine, to go to the timber merchants on the old wharf at Wolverton. If you can get it there for Friday, I think they'll be quite impressed! And there's another load of steel for you from Leicester the Wednesday following.*
>
> *Hope you're all well, and the steel trip went all right, Ben.*

He lowered the sheet of paper:

'Moonday termorrer, yeh said, Mr 'Olland?'

'That's right.'

'H' okay – we've got a load o' timber due from the docks, fer...' he checked the name again: 'Barker 'n Freeman. D'yeh know about it?'

'Oh, yes, Mr Baker. Someone'll let you know when it arrives – tomorrow's my day off.'

'Roight, then. Thank yeh, Mr 'Olland.' A smile overlaid Holland's normally hassled expression:

'No trouble, Mr Baker.' He stood up and held out his hand: 'Good luck to you – it's good to see someone with the courage to do what you're doing. I hope it goes well for you.'

'We'll do ar best, Mr 'Olland!'

None of them objected to the enforced twenty-four hour rest; that Sunday afternoon, an outing by bus to the nearest public baths left them all feeling fresh and bright, and a stroll around Brentford filled an hour or two. By now, a number of other pairs were also tied around them, similarly waiting on the morning to load their various cargoes. Fish and chips from the local shop made a special treat, especially for Carrie and Josh, and then a friendly drink with the other boaters in the Five Bells rounded the evening off.

In the thin light of early morning, Nationals and Russell Newburys, the occasional Armstrong or Lister, sprang into life around them as the other boats dispersed to be loaded. They took a relaxed breakfast for once, and then spent their time tidying, cleaning and polishing, taking pride in making the Albert and the Rita look as splendid as any pair on the system. Nearing lunchtime, a fleet of barges and lighters began to arrive through the tide lock from the river; Michael kept an eye out for their timber but saw no trace of it.

Eventually:

'That's yourn, mate!' A voice called out, and a hand pointed to a barge entering the basin from the river lock, piled up with timber and covered with a roped-down tarpaulin. It was by now late in the afternoon; the lighterman, a short, stocky man in blue overalls and a flat hat, manoeuvred his unwieldy craft over and tied it close by where they waited.

''Ow do, cock!' He strolled up to Michael.

''Ello. That's ar timber, is it?'

'Yus, mate.'

'H'okay – c'n we get it loaded?' The man laughed:

'Termorrer, mate!'

'Eh? Can' we get started now?'

'Ah, well – I goes 'ome in 'alf an hour, see?'

'Boot we don' mind workin' later!'

'Ah – that's as mebbe, mate. But 'oo'll put the sheets back, eh?'

'We c'n do that if yeh loike.' The man drew a sharp breath through his teeth:

'Yeh can't do that!'

'Whoy not?' The man took him by his upper arm:

'Lighterman's job, that is! If I let you touch them sheets, we'll 'ave the 'ole bloody union out on strike! No, I 'ave ter get 'em orf, 'n I 'ave ter put 'em back, see?'

'Boot we c'n shift the timber?'

'Oh, yeah, that's a'right. But you touch them sheets...' He shook his head, lips pursed. Michael wanted to argue the toss, but realised he was up against a brick wall of demarcation rules; he sighed:

'H'okay! What toime c'n we get started in the mornin'?'

'I'll be 'ere by seven, 'n get them orf right away, mate.' Michael shrugged:

'H'all roight – we'll see yeh then.'

The lighterman gave him a beaming smile, then turned and hurried away.

Chapter Thirty-Two

As good as his word, at seven the next morning the lighterman was untying the sheets covering the timber as Michael and Ginny manoeuvred the boats alongside and tied them to the barge. With all hands getting stuck in, and the lighterman himself – 'Terry Biggs, mate; call me Tel, everyone does!' – heaving the planks up out of his hold, they had the whole load transferred by early afternoon. With no instruction to cover the timber, they laid the top planks along the beams with just the cratches in place; an hour spent mopping down the paintwork again and repolishing the brasses, and Michael pronounced the boats fit to depart.

Slowed by a bad road left by other pairs running before them, they tied for the night at Bulls Bridge. To everyone's delight, they happened there upon a reunion of the Caplin clan – Henry's pair had been joined by his son's, and now both were awaiting fresh orders. Eschewing the pub on such a pleasant summer evening, the men sat or stood around on the layby, talking and drinking tea, while the women all gathered around Harriet to continue their fussing over little Albert. The children, Carrie and Jo and Jack and Rose, played with the other kids whose families were tied there, while eighteen-month-old Gabriel Caplin toddled happily around, getting under their feet.

Even before they had tied up on their arrival, Sam had spotted the distinctive red and white livery of the Albert and the Rita. He'd greeted Michael with a nervous grin; at his nod, he'd taken

Ginny by the arm and the two of them had strolled off together, out of earshot but observing the niceties by staying in sight.

A better run the next day, and a good early start, saw them as far as Boxmoor; and it was a rather startled manager who found a pair of boats, with its crew already begun on the task of unloading, tied at his wharf in Old Wolverton at eight o'clock on the Friday morning. A couple of the yardmen pitched in to help, and by lunchtime the timber lay in neat stacks on the wharfside, a snorting fork lift truck, still wearing its ex-army olive drab paint, snatching it away a bit at a time.

The manager came over to them as they were tidying up the boats. Michael looked up from the depths of the Albert's hold, wiping his hands on a piece of rag, as the man addressed him:

'Mr Baker?'

'Yes?'

'Williams, Harold Williams, I'm the manager here. I have to say I was against the company using your boats for this delivery – I never thought you could get the goods here in time.' Michael grinned:

'Oi'm glad we proved yeh wrong, Mr Williams!'

'You did, Mr Baker. I have to thank you for that – some of that timber is needed for delivery to our customer tomorrow. If you can maintain this kind of service, I'd be happy to have you carry for us again in the future.'

'We'll certainly do ar best fer yeh, Mr Williams!'

'Would you accept this as a gesture of my thanks – and contrition?' The man held out his hand with a crisp ten-shilling note. Michael hesitated, but then grinned and reached for it:

'Thank yeh, Mr Williams! We'll 'ave a drink on yew ternoight.'

'You do that, Mr Baker – and I hope we'll see you again.' Williams smiled and walked away.

'Got oos a tip, then, Moikey?' Harriet approached, a mug of tea held out for him.

'Aye – 'n what sounded loike a promise o' more work!'

'Tha's grand!' She squatted on the wharfside to smile into his eyes. He took a sip of his tea:

'Wher's Alby?' Her smile grew wider:

''E's asleep in 'is cot fer the moment.' Michael chuckled; the 'cot' was in fact the drawer under one side of their cross-bed, pulled out and lined with a spare blanket.

''E's a 'appy sort kid, ain't 'e?'

''E's no trooble at all. Cooms of 'avin' 'appy folks around 'im.'

'Are yeh 'appy, loove?' He was still aware of her previous doubts about their venture into self-employment, but the warmth in her eyes reassured him.

'As 'appy as can be.' She read the thoughts in his mind: 'We're getting' work, thanks ter Ben, 'n getting' better paid fer it inter the bargain. 'N now we've got 'til Wednesday ter get ter Leicester, 'n the soon's shoinin' – it's loike 'avin' a 'oliday!'

'Loife's woonderful, ain't it?' Ginny chipped in as she heaved a shovelful of sweepings over the side of the hold. Michael grinned at his wife:

''Tis when yeh're in loove, eh?'

'Oi ain't in loove!' Ginny faced him, her hands on her hips.

'Oh, really?' She held his gaze for a scant second before her eyes dropped and she blushed pink:

'Well – not really. Not yet...'

'Yew sure?'

'Leave 'er alone, Moikey!' Harriet intervened in his good-natured teasing; he laughed as Ginny took the opportunity to change the subject:

''Ow far d'yeh want ter get terday, Moikey?'

'Top o' Stoke? We can 'ave a h'evenin' in the Boat.'

Ginny's eyes lit up: *If 'Enry got loaded Wednesday, they'll be gettin' oop this way terday...*

* * *

'Terday is Froiday, en't it?' Sam called across the lock to his mother.

'Yes, Oi reckon so – whoy?' He gestured at the cryptic message he'd found chalked on the balance beam, a grin on his face, and she nodded:

'Ah! Wher' to, Sam?'

'Top o' Stoke!' Suey laughed:

'We'll mek that all roight! Suit yer dad 'n all, an ale or two in the Boat!'

The blue and yellow pair, loaded with tinned tomatoes bound for Sampson Road depot, were rising in Cosgrove Lock as the low evening sun dappled off the reed-grown water of the abandoned Old Stratford Arm, reflecting on the pebble-dashed wall of the lock-cottage. They'd received orders on the Wednesday morning to drop down to Brentford, and, with such an easy-handling load, had been on their way back before the day was done. Two days with a good road before them, and they were getting well ahead – but even so, they'd finish the flight in the dark if they pressed on to Stoke Bruerne. They'd eaten on the Fenny pound, running through Wolverton on their way to Cosgrove, and now the attractions of a beer in the Boat Inn was drawing them on. To say nothing of Sam's determination to catch up with his girl.

It was nearer to ten o'clock than nine when they cleared the top lock and tied outside the old stables attached to the pub. Sam's heart gave a leap as he spotted, gleaming through the dusk, the red and white of the Albert tied opposite by the old mill basin, the butty tucked inside it against the bank. And a pair of Joshers, further away near the narrows of what had once been Rectory Bridge, were familiar too...

A joyful evening it proved, indeed. The three Caplins strolled into the canalside bar to find the music well under way, with someone playing a melodeon and several couples step-dancing on the tiled floor. Henry gave his wife a ten-shilling note to get the drinks while he returned to the boat for his banjo after quickly greeting Michael and kissing his daughter on the cheek; Sam, inevitably, made a bee-line for Ginny who wriggled aside on the bench where she sat to allow him to squeeze in beside her.

When he returned, the tune had finished and a hubbub of conversation had taken over momentarily. He waded through the crowd to join his family, gathered in one corner of the room, where he was met by two more familiar faces:

'Billy; Kim – 'ow are yeh, lads?'

'We're grand, 'Enry – 'ow's yerself?'

'Foine, boy, foine. Wher' yeh for?'

'Coal, fer Croxley. Sylv's on the boats wi' littl'un.'

'They h'okay?'

'Oh, ah!' Billy leant forward: 'We've got anoother'n on the way!'

'Well doon, Billy, that's great!' Suey congratulated him; he gave her a carefree grin:

'Aye, ain't it joost?' Michael, Harriet and Ginny sat back smiling, obviously already privy to this information, as he turned to Ginny and Sam: 'So when're yew two gettin' in tow, then?' Though both of them blushed at this, perhaps Sam was the pinker; but it was Harriet who took him to task:

'They're too yoong ter be thinkin' o' that, Billy 'Anney! Yew leave 'em alone.' He just turned his grin on her as Suey asked:

''Ow's li'l Alby?' Harriet relaxed and replied:

''E's doin' joost foine! 'E's fast asleep, in the boat – Carrie 'n Josh're playin' oover ther', 'n they'll listen out fer 'im in case 'e wakes oop.'

'Yeh goin' back empt, Moikey?' Henry asked. Michael nodded:

'We've got another load o' that rolled steel out o' Belgrave Wharf, Wednesd'y.'

'Leicester soomit's bad goin', or so Oi've bin told?' Billy asked.

'Yeah, 'tis. We c'n only tek forty-foive ton, 'n even that's 'ard, it's so bloody shaller oop ther'. Moight even 'ave ter tek less – it'd save toime.'

191

'Still – got ter be better than shovellin' coal!' Ginny interjected; Henry looked at her with sympathy, knowing the reason for their antipathy towards the coal traffic, but he shook his head:

''Bout all we get, goin' South, now. Coal fer Apsley, or Croxley, or Nash Mills.'

'S'roight, 'Enry,' Billy agreed: 'Diff'rent loads coomin' back, metal or tinned stooff or whatever – boot 'alf the toime ther' en't nothin' at all, 'n we coom back empt ter Sutton's.'

'True ennooff, Billy. Yeh're loocky, Moikey, yeh c'n go wher' yeh loike fer loads, 'n wi' Ben lookin' after yeh, yeh c'n tek on whatever jobs yeh fancy.' Michael grinned:

'Yeh think we did the roight thing, then, after all?' Henry laughed:

''Oo knows, boy! Toime'll tell.'

Chapter Thirty-Three

That trip back to Leicester proved, as Harriet had suggested, to be like a holiday for them. The weather remained warm and dry, and with four days to cover ground which, in other circumstances, would take them no more than two, they could relax. A day off spent in Stoke Bruerne followed by another congenial evening in the Boat Inn; a gentle run up to Norton Junction and the New Inn on the Sunday was followed by the slow slog over the twenty-two miles of the Leicester Summit to Foxton; Tuesday saw them once more tied at Belgrave Wharf, ready for the shipment of steel to arrive the next morning.

Back at Stoke, Michael had borrowed Sister Mary's telephone to call Ben Vickers. After a lot of deliberation, he had decided to load only forty tons, and asked Ben to pass this on to the shippers. Vickers had laughed:

'I told you the summit was in a bad way, Mikey!'

'And yeh were roight, Ben. Bloody slow 'n shaller, boot Oi reckon if we tek less in the motor, we'll get along better – we all boot stoock in some o' the bridge-'oles las' toime, 'n Oi don' want ter be lettin' folks down.'

'I think you're right, Mikey. Better to carry less and get there on time!'

So this time they set off for the trip to Brentford with only three rolls of steel, a bare fifteen tons, in the Albert. And the next day, as if to emphasize their return to the pressures of work, an Atlantic depression swept in with the apparent aim of getting them as wet as possible. The countryside around the Leicester Summit is an attractive landscape of rolling hills and farmland, but now it stayed obstinately hidden behind a veil of driving rain.

Michael stood hunched in the hatches of the motor boat, his donkey-jacket drawn tight around his shoulders, his cap lowered over his eyes. His only consolation was the knowledge that his decision had been right – the boats drove along more easily with the lighter load, the Albert no longer ploughing so deeply through the mud and silt at the bottom of the canal. Glancing back, he got a desultory wave from Ginny, at the tiller of the butty – no-one else was in sight.

Passing Winwick Grange, about two-thirds of the way over the summit, Carrie at last took pity on him. She emerged from the cabin, her own coat buttoned tightly about her slim form:

'Moikey! Oi'll tek 'em fer a bit.'

'Oi'm h'okay, Carrie, yew keep droy.' But she shook her head:

'No, yew go 'n get droy. We'll 'ave Watf'd locks soon.' He looked at her, but then gave in gratefully:

'H'okay, loove. Watch out fer Yelvertoff bridge, we nearly got stoock ther' las' toime.' She nodded, and took the tiller from him; he stood clear to let her step into the hatches and made his way around the gunwale to the engine-room and climbed down inside. In there, he stripped off his sodden jacket and hung it around the silencer of the engine's exhaust where it quickly began to give off clouds of steam. He put his cap on top of the engine itself, and its own steam swirled off to mingle with the rest.

Climbing back out, he walked back around the cabin, surprised to see Josh standing on the other gunwale beside his sister:

'Yeh'll catch yer death out 'ere in this rain, boy!' Josh grinned, shrugging his shoulders:

'T'ain't that cold, Moikey 'n Oi don' moind bein' wet.' Michael looked at the youngster askance – he had an old cap crammed

194

on his head but no coat or pullover, only a thin shirt which was already soaked, plastered to his stocky chest. Shaking his head at the vagaries of youth, he stepped down into the cabin as Carrie let him past, where he quickly changed into his dry trousers and shirt. Putting his boots back on, he sat on the sidebed and reached forward to give the range a quick riddling to stir it back into life, threw on a couple of lumps of coal, and leant back with a sigh, glad to be, for a while at least, out of the wind and the rain.

The boats forged on through the downpour, sweeping around the twists and turns of the canal as it followed the contours of the countryside, passing below the narrow road twice as it approached the village of Yelvertoft. Past the abandoned coal wharf with its tumble-down outbuildings and unkempt house; then a tight left-hand bend took the cut back under that same road for a third time.

Carrie took the motor round the turn, easing the throttle down and steering wide out to allow for the laden butty behind her. Then under the bridge, and she looked back, to see the bows of the Rita come into sight around the bend; judging it to a nicety, she wound the throttle open again to pull the butty around the turn. But ill-luck stepped in to thwart her – at the precise moment the tow-line snatched tight, the butty's stem hit something on the bottom of the channel.

In the butty cabin, Harriet grabbed the table-cupboard for support as the boat jerked to the left and then rolled back upright; above her, Ginny gave a yelp as she was thrown sideways in the hatches.

Michael, too, felt the motor lurch under him and jumped to his feet to peer out past Carrie's legs, just in time to see the tow-line part with an audible snap. Carrie's knees bent as she ducked; the line, in fact, hit the water a little behind the boat, but she gave a shout of horror nonetheless. He saw her spin the heavy control wheel to take the engine out of gear as she gave another yell, this time calling her brother's name in a tone of fear:

'JOSH!' Michael touched her leg, signalling her to let him up from the cabin, but she stood fast until she had also throttled the engine back, calling down to him:

'It's Josh! 'E's in the water!' He threw himself up the step as she stood back to give him room, and saw the boy struggling in the canal, near the bank and just clear of the bridge, some yards behind the boat. He shouted as loud as he could, to try and quell the lad's panic:

'JOSH! GET TER THE SOIDE! GET YERSELF TER THE BANK!' But Josh's terror was in control and he didn't respond, gasping for breath as he thrashed around. He spoke to Carrie calmly, putting as much authority as he could into his voice as he could see that she too was scared half to death:

'Carrie – put the starn agenst the soide, roight?' She stared at him for a moment, but then, her hand shaking, wound the engine into forward gear and put the tiller hard over. 'Gently now...' he kept his voice soft, reassuring; as the towpath came within reach, he grabbed the cabin-shaft off the roof and jumped onto the bank. He ran back to where Josh still splashed and hollered, and held the shaft out to him, keeping the hooked end to himself:

'Grab 'old, Josh! JOSH! Grab the end o' the shaft!' The boy finally heard him and groped for the pole, touched it, and held on, the knuckles of his hands white with the strength of his grip. Slowly, Michael drew him to the side; when he was close enough, he reached out with one hand and took one of the boy's, prising it from the shaft to do so. Another hand reached down to take the other, and he looked up gratefully to see Ginny beside him, kneeling in the mud. Between them, they dragged the tearful child out onto the bank, where he stood shivering, his trousers and shirt sodden and caked with the silt from the canal.

'Motor cabin?' Ginny asked. Michael looked around; now, Carrie had brought the Albert in as close as she could to the side, where she stood holding it on the back-end rope. In the turn, the Rita had run on, freed of its tow, to bury its stempost in the edge of the towpath; Ginny had managed to jump off with her own stern line before running up to help. He nodded, and they led the still-shaking youngster along and helped him up onto the counter and then down inside the cabin.

'What 'appened, Josh?' Michael asked quietly. The lad stared at him out of wide eyes, but then he shook himself and took a deep, shuddering breath:

'Oi slipped... When the boat rocked, me foot slipped off 'n... 'n Oi...'

'Don' woorry, yeh're safe now.' Ginny put her arm around him and held him tightly; he looked at her for a moment and then nodded, shakily:

'Yeah... Thank yeh, Moikey...' his eyes sought Michael's, and he essayed a weak smile. Michael, half angry at his carelessness, half amused at his bedraggled state, put his hands on his shoulders:

'When yeh said yeh didn' moind gettin' wet Oi didn' think yeh meant ter throw yerself in the cut!' Ginny burst out laughing at this; Josh looked back at her, his eyes still full of his remembered fear; but then he smiled, and began to chuckle:

'Weren't what Oi meant at all, Moikey!' The funny side of things finally pushed Michael's annoyance aside, and he began to laugh as well:

'We'd better get yew droied out 'n then get on ar way agen! Oi'll foind the spare towloine.'

'Yeh're soaked as well, Moikey,' Ginny observed; he laughed again:

''N these are me spare shirt 'n trousers any' ow! Oi'll 'ave ter do 'til we stop ternoight, now.' He ruffled Josh's wet hair before climbing back out of the cabin and going to retrieve his coat from the engine-room.

With their other eighty-foot towrope retrieved from the fore-end locker, he ran back along the top-planks, blessing Ben Vickers for his foresight in providing the spare when he'd re-equipped the boats. Carrie had already reeled in the broken line, and lain it, coiled, on the cabin roof; now she helped him run the new line back along the towpath as he reversed the motor until she could drop its end eye-splice over the t-stud on the butty's fore-deck. Harriet stood in the stern well, ready to take the tiller; Carrie ran back to join Michael, jumping the narrow gap from towpath to boat as he swung it close.

He gave her a grin:

'Yeh'd better go 'n see if yer broother's h'okay!' She smiled back, and slipped down into the cabin as he stood aside for her.

Left inside while the new tow was being rigged, Ginny had taken their towel from the cupboard over the crossbed and told Josh to get his wet clothes off. But the boy was still in shock, and unresponsive; shaking her head, she quickly stripped him naked and towelled him down. He stood passively, accepting her ministrations, and then sat on the sidebed, wrapped in the towel, when she gently pushed him down onto it. A mug of strong sweet tea was thrust into his hands, and he sipped gratefully, his shoulders hunched in the warmth of the cabin.

''Yew all roight, Josh?' Carrie's voice was full of concern as she sat beside him He looked round at her and nodded:

'Oi'm h'okay. Joost...' He shrugged his shoulders, and his sister giggled as she realised he had nothing on under the towel. The sound of her amusement brought back something of the boy's usual spirit, making him chuckle too: 'All me things're in the butty!'

'Serve yeh roight fer fallin' in! Yeh'll 'ave ter stay loike that 'til we get ter Watf'd!' But she took his wet clothes and climbed out of the cabin again, edged around the gunwale and hung them in the engine-room to dry.

They tied that night at the top of Long Buckby flight, by the New Inn once more. An hour and a half after Josh's involuntary bath, at Watford locks, the rain had eased even if the sky was as grey as ever; he'd quickly dressed in his spare clothes, brought to him by his still-teasing sister, and set to with a will on the paddles in an obvious attempt to redeem himself. Another hour on, and they'd all had enough although the dusk had hardly begun to gather – so far as they could tell, on such a dismal evening.

'Yeh won' do that agen in a 'urry, will yeh, Josh?' They were all gathered around a table in the bar, the baby sitting happily on his mother's knees. The boy smiled sheepishly:

'No, Moikey.'

'When it's wet, yeh 'ang on toight, 'n mek sure yer feet 'ave got a grip. Yeh're loocky yer sister's quick h'off the mark – if she 'adn' got the h'injun out o' gear yeh could' a gone in the blades.'

'Oi thought yeh 'ad...' Carrie was looking at her brother, remembered horror on her face; suddenly, she burst into tears: 'Oi thought yeh 'ad!' He stared at her for a moment, and then flung his arms around her:

'It's h'okay, Carrie! Oi'm foine, nothin' 'appened!' She lifted her head from his shoulder, anger flashing in her eyes now:

'Don' yew dare scare me loike that agen, Joshua! Don' yew *dare!*'

Chapter Thirty-Four

After the delays of Thursday, and knowing that Stan Holland at Brentford didn't expect to see them until Monday morning, Michael allowed them to take the trip in a marginally more relaxed fashion than the last time. They tied up just short of the gauging locks on Sunday night, and he reported their arrival in the office first thing on the Monday. Holland looked up with a smile:

'Good to see you again, Mr Baker! I've got a lighter all ready to take your load; and there's a message for you from your office.' He handed over the usual hand-written note:

> *Michael – you have another load from B&F. They were very pleased with the last one! 40 tons of planked pine from Norway, arriving Monday, should be at Brentford Wednesday. To go to Cartwright & Co at Olton Wharf. How did the steel trip go? Good Luck – Ben.*

'Thank yeh, Mr 'Olland! Wher' d'yeh want the boats?'

'Just run 'em into the basin, Michael, chargehand'll tell you where to go.'

As before, the rolls of steel were quickly craned out of the boats and transferred to the waiting lighter once everything was in place. They turned the empty boats and tied them in a vacant spot on Durham Wharf; Michael and the two children set about sweeping out the holds and mopping down the cabinsides while Harriet fed little Alby. Ginny hauled out the dolly tub preparatory to doing the washing; she looked up to give an ironic wave to their last load as it disappeared towards the tide lock and the River Thames, and then turned with a smile as the traffic manager strolled up:

''Ello Mr 'Olland!'

'Hello, Ginny. How are you all?'

'Pretty good, thank yeh. Got a coopl'a days h'off now 'fore ar next load turns oop.' She carried on sorting the pile of clothes.

'Yes, I know. Good Lord, those trousers are in a state!' Ginny chuckled, holding up Josh's dry but still mud-covered clothes – the boy had been living in his spares until she had a chance to do the washing.

'Yeah – Josh fell in oop on the Leicester soommit.'

'He didn't hurt himself?'

'Nah! Thought we'd got shot of 'im boot 'e got out!' Josh looked up from his broom with a pained expression and exclaimed:

'Yew pulled me out! Yew 'n Moikey!'

''Course we did – Missus 'Anney'd give oos 'Ell if we drownded yeh.'

'Huh! 'N Oi thought yeh loiked me!' Holland's grin was a bit uncertain until they both burst out laughing; Michael had been listening to this repartee with a broad smile on his face:

'Weren't the lad's fault, Mr 'Olland. The butty hit soomat on the bottom in oone o' the turns near Yellertoff, snapped the tow 'n the jerk shot 'im off the gunwale.'

'Well, I'm glad you're okay, Josh.'

The boy gave him a cheeky grin:

'Tek more'n that ter bother me, Mr 'Olland!'

Ginny regarded him with raised eyebrows, remembering the state of him at the time, and his smile became rather shame-faced. Michael laughed:

'Near toime 'e went 'ome now, school'll start agen soon.'

Josh looked around at him. 'Oh, Moikey!'

'Next h'orders'll tek oos oop middle road inter Birnigum – we'll drop yeh at 'ome on the way boy.' The youngster looked rebellious for a moment, but then he dropped his eyes:

'Yes, Moikey.'

'Yeh've h'enjoyed bein' with oos, 'ave yeh?' He just nodded. 'Well, yeh can coom agen, next 'oliday, h'okay?' Now the boy looked up with a sparkle in his eyes:

'Yeah!'

* * *

The train of lighters turned up as predicted on the Wednesday afternoon. 'Wotcher, Cock!' The same blue overalls and flat hat were in charge of their load.

''Ello, Tel – 'ow are yeh?'

'Right as rain, mate! 'Ow's yerself? An' the folks?'

'Foine, Tel. That's ars, is it?'

'Yus, mate. Yeh want ter git started?'

'H'if we can?'

'Don' see why not! I'll git the sheets orf for yeh.'

Michael started the engine and they quickly manoeuvred the pair alongside the flat bulk of the lighter. Biggs untied and removed his sheets, and they all set to with a will, manhandling the long planks of pine out of its deep hold and over into the boats. They'd got maybe a third of the total moved and stowed when Biggs groped inside his overalls and pulled a battered old fob watch from his shirt pocket:

'I'll 'ave ter git the sheets back on in a minute – I'm orf shift at four.'

'Oh, coom on, Tel! Can't yeh let oos carry on shiftin' the stooff?' The lighterman looked horrified:

'Tol' yeh before, mate – yeh can' touch them sheets or the union'll 'ave us all out! 'N it's got ter be covered 'fore I goes 'ome.'

'Oh, h'okay.' Michael gave in with poor grace, knowing he was faced with the utter inflexibility of union rules: 'Joost seems a waste o' toime ter be standin' around doin' nothin' when we could be gettin' on.'

'Yeah, I know. I'll be 'ere at seven, right?'

'We'll be ready for yeh!' The lighterman grinned as he heaved the heavy canvas sheets back over his awkward charge.

* * *

'Welcome 'ome, love!' Josh submitted to one of Vi Hanney's smothering hugs: 'Did yeh 'ave a good toime?' He pushed back out of her embrace:

'Yeah – it was brilliant, bein' on the boats agen!'

'Thank yeh fer tekin' 'im, Moikey!' She looked around at their smiling faces: 'Coom on insoide, Oi'll put the kettle on!'

The Albert and the Rita were tied at the bottom of Knowle locks, and they'd all trooped up to the little house by the maintenance yard to return Josh to his adoptive mum:

'Bill 'n Stevie are out at work, boot they'll be back soon – whoy don' yeh stop wher' yeh are ternoight? 'Ave dinner with oos?' Vi fussed around like an eager mother hen, brewing tea and offering a tin of her home-made biscuits. Michael laughed:

'We saw Bill, oop in the rockin'! They 'ad a tree down 'cross the cut.'

It was late on Monday afternoon. They'd finished loading the timber soon after lunch on the Wednesday, and got away at last after clothing over the boats and mopping them down once again. The trip north had been steady if unspectacular; Sunday night had seen them at The Cape in Warwick, always one of their favourite stops, and they'd set away in good time the next morning. But the day had gone awry for them when they came across a stoppage in the cutting approaching Shrewley Tunnel – a tree had blown down overnight, right across the channel, and the local maintenance crew were engaged on cutting it up with chainsaws and dumping the resultant wreckage into an old butty.

Now, he went on:

'We'd best get on, Vi. Oi want ter be at Olton 'fore they start in the mornin', ter get unloaded.'

'If we roon 'em oop ter the top, Moikey? Then we c'n get off early 'n still be there...' Ginny was trying to be her most persuasive; he hesitated, and the attractions of a talk with Bill, and spending an evening with his old friend, won out:

'Oh – h'okay. Drink yer tea, then we'll get 'em oop the floight.'

'Are yeh sure yeh've got enooff fer all of oos?' Harriet asked; Vi waved her concern away:

'Sure Oi 'ave! The day Oi can' feed moy friends ain't coom yet!' She chuckled: 'Bill's alwes bin good with 'is traps – rabbit stew do yeh?' She smiled around at the chorus of assent: 'Wi veggies from ar garden, 'n all!'

Later, they were all sitting around in the kitchen, feeling replete, glasses of beer in front of the men on the stout scrubbed oak table while Vi and Ginny fussed happily over the washing-up. Harriet, engaged upon feeding Alby, echoed all of their thanks:

'That was loovely, Vi! Thank yeh.'

'Ah – ain't lost 'er tooch, 'as she?' Bill chuckled.

'Can we be h'excused, Mum?' Josh asked.

Vi turned from the sink: ''Course yeh can, lad.'

'Coom on, Carrie!' The two of them scrambled up from the table and dashed out into the back yard to play. Stevie stood up from the table as well:

'Oi promised ter go 'n see Ellie ternoight, she's got a noight off.' He looked apologetically at Michael. The two had spent much of the meal catching up on old times:

'Yew go 'n see yer girl, Stevie! We'll see yeh next toime we're boy.' The young man smiled and reached for his coat as he turned to go. Bill took a swig of his beer and looked across the table at Michael:

'So 'ow's it goin' then, Moikey? What's it loike bein' a noomber oone?' Michael laughed:

'It's grand, Bill! 'Arrie was woorried about it, the h'insecurity o' bein' ar own boss, loike – boot wi' Ben gettin' the h'orders fer oos, it's workin' out real well.'

'Yeh've got plenty o' work, then?'

'So far, yeah. This is the second trip we've 'ad fer this timber coomp'ny, we've bin roonnin' steel from Leicester ter Brentf'd fer the Waterways.'

'Reg'lar contracts, are they?'

'Seems loike it – s'long as we keep ar noses clean!'

'Good fer yew, Moikey!' Vi spoke up from behind him: ''N yer boats look a picture'– we've 'eard oother boaters say 'ow smart they are. Yeh should be proud o' yerselves!'

'Yeh're goin' ter stay on the cut, then?' Michael looked at Bill, puzzled: ''Course! whoy wouldn' we?'

'Ther's them as say it's all finished.'

'Yeh've bin listenin' ter 'Enry!' He glanced apologetically at his wife; Harriet smiled back:

'Dad's alwes bin a prophet o' doom! Alwes looks on the black soide o' things, 'e doos!'

Bill gave her a grin, but he said:

''E could be roight, though. Oh, not yet, mebbe, boot oone day. Coomp'ny's gettin' about doin' soom o' the work what's needed, boot ther's them oop top 'oo want ter see it all stopped. At least so they say. They want everythin' ter go boy lorry, or so we've 'eard.'

''N ther's folks leavin' the cut every day,' Vi chipped in again: 'Jobs on the bank pay better, fer less work – yeh can' blame the men fer goin' fer 'em, 'specially the yoong'uns.'

'Loike Bill, yeh mean?' They all laughed at Michael's quip, but Bill picked up the challenge:

'We coom off mostly fer Stevie, 'n so's Josh could go ter school – boot the reg'lar hours 'n the pay's not ter be sneezed at!'

'A lot of oother folks're thinkin' about their kiddies, Moikey,' Vi added as she and Ginny rejoined them at the table: 'Gettin' 'em a h'education's goin' ter be h'important fer 'em. 'N yeh can' go ter school if yeh're alwes on the move, yew know that.'

'Oi s'pose yeh could be roight...' Michael looked at his baby son as his voice trailed off. But then Bill lightened the mood:

'Oi'm not tellin' yeh ter give it all oop, boy, far from it! Yeh're doin' well, 'n we're all proud o' yeh. 'N yew 'n Ginny can teach the kiddies 'ow ter read 'n wroite – most boater's can' do that. Oi'd 'ate ter see the trade finish, so yew keep it oop! 'N stop boy ter see yer old mates whenever yeh can, eh?'

'Course we will, Bill!' Harriet reached across and gave his hand a squeeze. Ginny spoke up for the first time:

'It's grand about Billy 'n Sylvie, ain't it?' Vi smiled maternally:

'Aye, 'tis. 'Noother grandkid, eh Bill?' Bill smiled back:

'Ah! mebbe she'll 'ave a boy this toime!' Vi looked around their faces:

''E'd loove a gran'son, with 'is name!' Bill laughed now:

'Li'l Jack 'n Gabriel are great, 'n Oi loove 'em ter bits – Boot it'd be good ter see the 'Anney name goin' on!' Ginny grinned:

'Ther's alwes Stevie!'

'Aye – we reckon they'll be gettin' in tow soon, eh Bill?'

'Reck'n so.' He agreed with his wife, sounding satisfied: ''Ow 'bout yew, yoong Ginny?'

The girl blushed and looked down at the table; he laughed again: 'O-ho! Loike that, is it?'

'Sam, is it?' Vi asked gently; Ginny nodded. Vi went on: 'We 'ad 'eard, loove.' Ginny looked up, and now she was smiling that shy smile which Michael had noticed before:

''E's loovely, ain't 'e? Oi've known 'im all this toime, 'n never thought of 'im... loike that!' Vi reached over to pat her shoulder:

'Well, 'e's a real noice boy, 'n we wish yer well, loovey.' Michael slipped an arm around his sister's shoulders:

'Ev'rythin's goin' joost foine fer all of oos, ain't it?'

Chapter Thirty-Five

'Albert! Stop teasin' yer sister!' The four-year-old flashed a cheeky glance across the dinner table at his mother and surreptitiously gave Susie another poke in the ribs.

'Ow!'

'Alby!' This time the little boy's eyes were raised to his father, contrition in them:

'Sorry, Daddy.'

'Say sorry ter yer sister, not me boy!' The dark eyes swung to his left:

'Sorry, Susie.'

'That's better Alby.' He turned back to his mother:

'Yes, Mam.'

Olive Vickers had watched this little scenario with a barely-concealed smile; now she leant over the table towards the two children:

'Would you like some more jelly?'

'Can we, Mam?' Harriet laughed at her son's eager expression:

'Joost this oonce, then!'

Mid-August, 1954. After four years of hard labour, Michael had decided it was high time his boats were docked. They'd performed with little trouble, except for a broken band in the gearbox the year before, but now they were looking tired and rather shabby, the hulls in need of blacking and the paintwork getting dull as well as scractched and knocked from the inevitable wear and tear of a working life.

It was Sunday, August the fifteenth – they'd left the pair at Nurser's dock that morning, as arranged for them by Ben. And the day before had been an occasion for high celebration:

'Yesterday went very well, Mikey.' Vickers sat back in his chair, replete after a satisfying Sunday dinner. Michael nodded, smiling contentedly:

'Certainly did, Ben. She looked loovely, din't she?'

'Beautiful! She's grown into a very pretty girl, Michael. Always was, mind.' Olive agreed as she returned with two full dishes.

'Thank yeh fer lendin' 'er the dress, Olive,' Harriet said.

'Oh, it was our Carole's, love. Fitted her a treat, didn't it?'

'They're staying on with Henry and Suey, are they?' Vickers asked.

'Fer now, any'ow. Gives 'em four on the pair.'

'How is your dad, Harriet?' Olive asked.

'Mooch better, thanks. 'E keeps goin' on about retoirin' boot Oi can' see 'im doin' it.'

'They're headin up to Sutton's?'

'Yeah – goin' back empt as usual,' Michael confirmed: 'Sam 'n Ginny'll join 'em ther' on Thursd'y.'

'Well you tell Henry to take care of that back of his! He's always trying to do too much on his own.' Olive scolded the absent boatman by proxy; Harriet laughed:

'Oi'll tell 'im, Olive. Fat lot o' notice 'e'll tek o' me, though!'

The Sunday morning had seen a number of farewells: Sam and Ginny ('Ginny Caplin! It sounds foonny!' Carrie had commented. 'Sounds wonderful! Ginny had retorted) were first away, on their way for a few days in the same guest-house Michael and Harriet had been to ('Mrs Oldroyd'll look after yeh – she was loovely, weren't she Moikey?'). Then they'd seen Carrie onto a train as well, to go and stay with her brother at the Hanneys for a week while the boats were on the dock. And of course most of the boaters who had attended the wedding had been off early, about their resumed business, many of them with rather thick heads – the Old Plough had seen some riotous fun the day (and night) before.

'It was good to see a lot of the old faces yesterday,' Ben commented: 'I hadn't seen Bill and Vi for years!'

'We get a card from them every Christmas, and send one back of course,' Olive added: 'It was a shame Stevie and Ellie couldn't be there!' Michael laughed:

'Talk about rotten toimin'! We'd both fixed dates 'fore we realoised.'

'They get back from their honeymoon today, don't they?' Olive asked; he nodded:

'Oi 'ope the weather's bin as foine fer them as it's bin 'ere.'

'In Cornwall, weren't they?'

'Aye, tha's roight.'

'Young Josh has become a fine-looking lad, hasn't he?' Harriet chuckled: 'Got all the girls oiyin' 'im oop, 'e 'as!'

'Fifteen – don' seem possible, doos it?' Michael added.

'Billy's still working for the Waterways, is he?' Ben asked.

'Yeah. They're on the wheat roon, down Wellin'boro River – 'e 'n Sylvie managed ter get ther' fer Stevie's weddin' boot they're soomwher' down the river at the moment.'

'How are they all?'

'They're foine! Emmie's foive now, 'n Li'l Bill's three. Did yeh know they'd 'ad anoother'n?'

'No?'

'Yeah – little girl, they're callin' 'er Vi'let. 'Bout two moonths ago.'

'Oh, that's wonderful!' Olive said: 'Give them our love if you see them, won't you?'

'Your nephew's a real live wire, isn't he?' Ben asked Harriet; she laughed:

'Jack, yeh mean? 'E's a little beggar at toimes! Leadin' 'is broother 'n ar Alby astray!'

'How old is he?'

'Noine. Gabriel's foive, 'n little 'Enry'll be three this moonth.'

'Rosie's a sweet kiddie, isn't she?' Olive said.

'Doin' well in school 'n all. So's Jack, coom ter that.' Michael told them.

'How's Joe like working for the Post Office?' Ben asked.

'Pretty mooch, Oi reckon. They're livin' in 'Emel 'Empst'd now – 'e did h'evenin' classes ter learn ter read 'n wroite, 'n Jack still teases 'im about 'elpin' with 'is 'omework!'

Olive's expression became more serious:

'And Carrie – how is she now?'

'Mooch better, thanks.'

'She seemed cheerful enough yesterday, didn't she?' Ben said; Harriet nodded: 'She's gettin' oover it, slowly. A week wi' Bill 'n Vi 'n Josh'll do 'er a lot o' good, bring 'er out of 'erself.'

'It was awful, that poor young lad getting killed like that.' Olive shook her head, remembered horror at the news on her face.

'It's alwes a risk – 'e was only troyin' ter 'elp. Joost went in at the wrong moment, got caught between them two barges.' Michael's own shock echoed in his voice.

'Brentford, wasn't it?' Ben asked quietly.

'Yeah. Poor kid, she was so sweet on 'im.'

'She croied fer days when we 'eard,' Harriet added.

'She'll find someone else, in time. She's a pretty girl, another boy'll come along for her, you wait and see!' Olive's tone was comforting.

A brief silence fell, in unspoken memory of young Charlie Nixon.

It was Olive who finally broke it:

'Are you sure you'll all be comfortable crammed into our spare room?'

'Oi should think so!' Harriet told her: 'We spend ar loives in two boat cabins remember – your spare room'll be loike a palace teh oos!'

'What's it loike ter 'ave stairs, Missus Vickuss?' The four-year-old piped up; Olive laughed:

'You'd better come and see, hadn't you, Alby? I'll show you where you'll be sleeping – you coming to, Susie?'

Chapter Thirty-Six

The week passed quickly enough. Michael, unused to having time on his hands, spent a good part of each day down at the dock – at first, the men there regarded him suspiciously, half-expecting him to interfere with their work on his boats, but they soon realised that he was happy simply to lend a hand wherever he could to keep himself occupied.

Harriet also found herself missing the constant busyness of their usual life, the always-changing scenery that was the background of work on the boats – but she also enjoyed the rest, time to chat with Olive Vickers and her neighbours. And most days she too would stroll down to the canal, taking the children to see how their boats were coming along, exchanging brief greetings with the families on any boats passing through, stopping to talk to those tied along the length.

It was on the Wednesday that Ben Vickers appeared on the dock around mid-day:

'Mikey – how d'you fancy a pint up at the Plough?' Michael looked around from the top of the ladder where he was diligently rubbing down the paintwork of the Rita's cabinside:

'Yeah – whoy not?'

As they walked over the iron bridge at the dock entrance, headed for Butcher's Bridge and the path up to the village, Ben broached the subject he wanted to talk about: 'You've heard about this new carrying company they're setting up?'

'Willer Wren, yeh mean? We saw a pair o' their boats goin' ter Olton wi' timber on, coopl'a moonths ago – seen 'em agen, oonce or twoice.'

'What did you think?' Michael paused to think:

'Look smart enooff – boot Oi wasn' 'appy 'bout them gettin' in on ar timber roons.'

'No – problem is, Mikey, that Barker and Freeman have been taken over by the people Leslie Morton's dealing with. You know Morton?' Michael shook his head:

'Never met 'im. 'Eard of 'im, o' course.'

'He's a real go-getter. He was largely responsible for the build-up of business on the Grand Union before the war, and the building of their new fleet of boats. He's the power behind Willow Wren, even if the money came from elsewhere. I hear he's out to secure new contracts anywhere he can; and not doing badly at it, either.'

'Oh yeah?'

'They're running coal from around the Warwickshire coalfields to Nestle's at Hayes, as well as the timber. And I hear he's on the track of other work.'

'Yeah?'

'It occurred to me that we might talk to him. The feeling I get is that he's likely to end up with more work than his boats can handle – they're buying up boats, setting crews on, all the time.'

'Yeah – Oi know as 'Orne's, 'n Jack 'n Rose Skinner're workin' fer 'em. 'N word is that Alf Best's goin' fer 'em, 'n all. Boot we're doin' h'okay, Ben – Oi ain't sellin' out to 'em.'

'I don't suggest you should, Mikey! We can get other work if the timber runs dry up, I'm sure. But I wondered if it was worth talking to Morton, see if he can use your boats on sub-contract, maybe?'

'Yeah... 'alf of what we're doin' now's subbin' fer Waterways, ain't it? So Oi s'pose it wouldn' 'urt ter talk to 'em. We know the timber business – mebbe we c'n do each oother a turn, eh?'

'That's what I thought, Mikey! You'd be happy for me to contact Morton, then?'

'Yeah, whoy not?'

At the pub, they met Harriet and Olive with the children. Over their drinks, the men discussed the idea of working with the new carriers for while longer, but could reach no real conclusion in advance of Ben calling Leslie Morton in Paddington. Conversation turned again to the family:

'Noice ter 'ear from Carrie this mornin', wasn' it?' Harriet said.

'Aye – she sounds mooch broighter, don' she?'

'You said a few days with her brother would buck her up!' Olive agreed happily.

'Said she's missin' the boats though!' Michael chuckled.

'Well, you'll soon be back on the move, Mikey. Frank says they'll be done by Saturday.'

'It'll be good ter get back ter work. Oh, this week's bin great, boot...' Ben laughed:

'I know! Itchy feet, eh?'

'Ther's no 'oldin' 'im down, Ben!' Harriet agreed; she patted her expanding tummy: 'In more ways than oone!' They all laughed at this as Olive asked:

'Have you decided on names for the baby, Harriet?'

'Not really. Prob'ly do the h'easy thing, call it Moichael or 'Arriet, dependin'!'

'Ah, we'll see.' There was a gleam in Michael's eye: 'Moight be good ter call 'im after granddad Morris.'

'Fred, yeh mean?'

'Yeah – what d'yeh think?'

'Freddie Baker; yeah – granddad'd be h'over the moon, wouldn' 'e?'

'Oh, he'd be delighted!' Olive agreed: 'What if it's her, though?'

'Oh – 'ow 'bout Olive?' Their laughter echoed around the bar-room.

* * *

Sunday lunchtime, and a sharp summer shower chose its moment to give them all a quick drenching as the boats worked through the duplicated locks of Hillmorton. Running the motor into the last of the three, Michael looked across to where the butty was just sliding to a halt as Harriet braked it with the heavy strapping line on the top gate, and felt his heart swell with pride at the way the fresh paintwork shone through the dull day. The legend on the cabinsides had been simplified now to read just: 'Michael Baker, Canal Carrier' – to include son, daughter and unknown bump had seemed a step too far. For a moment, the restored brightness of the boats took him back to the uncertain days of 1950, when they'd struck out on their own with an almost naïve confidence.

Boot it's all worked out foine! He smiled to himself as he raised a bottom paddle and leant against the balance beam to watch the Albert slowly descend into the cavern of the emptying lock. The steel traffic had never been too reliable, and now it had shrunk to the point where the occasional loads were handled by pairs of the national Waterways fleet – they were on their way to Sutton's Stop, the junction at Hawkesbury between the Northern Oxford Canal and the Coventry, ready to load from the Warwickshire coalfields. With little else available in the way of Southbound orders, they'd accepted the need for carrying coal some two years earlier – only Ginny had held to her antipathy for such work, but even she had grown used to it as time went by and the continuing sub-contracted loads had kept them busy.

Ginny – boogger, Oi'm goin' ter miss yew! It felt so strange to be boating without his sister at his side. But he still had a first-rate crew – Carrie was as self-confident, as self-possessed as ever, and the three of them could and would work just as efficiently as they had with four. And hopefully, by the time she left them, as she one day inevitably would, young Albert would be old enough to take a part in the proceedings. The little devil! His smile grew wider at the thought of his son, dark-haired and brown-eyed like his mother, an epitome of mischief who could be so polite and respectful when the mood took him. He had already begun to teach his child the rudiments of reading and writing, and the boy was proving an attentive and eager pupil, which pleased Michael more than he let on.

Life on the cut had settled into a rhythm now. The pressure of the wartime work and the uncertainties of the late 1940s had resolved themselves into a steady flow of orders, enough to keep the remaining pairs of boats working hard and long hours, both the British Transport Commission's fleet and the surviving independent carriers. And now someone was even setting up a new company – if what Ben had said about this fellow Morton was right, maybe they would see a revival of trade on the canals? *Loike Billy alwes said, ther's still a job fer oos!*

But despite that overt optimism, despite the fact that at last some of the overdue maintenance on the system was being done, despite the knowledge that new designs of boat were being developed, Michael still felt an underlying doubt. The speed of road transport would always be a threat to the slow but reliable waterways – and he remembered a comment of Henry Caplin's from years before: 'Anoother big freeze-oop, the boats stopped fer a few weeks, 'n that'll be it...'

The big freeze of 1947 had lost a lot of trade to the lorries when the canals were frozen for almost two months, and if it did happen again... They'd been lucky since, the winters generally more mild, the occasional freeze short-lived enough to cause little disruption.

For now at least, life was good. He stepped across the bottom gates, kicking them open as he did so, and jumped down onto the cabintop. Running the motor out, he swung the stern across and backed towards the other lock; picking up the cross-straps, he wound the engine into forward gear as Carrie joined him, setting off through the returning sunshine on the easy run to Hawkesbury and the Greyhound Inn.

Chapter Thirty-Seven

March 14ᵗʰ 1957

Weller, Winstead and Watson
34 Wickham Terrace
Brisbane
Queensland
Australia

Dear Brett,
With reference to your instructions regarding the Morris case: I regret to inform you that Michael Henry Thompson is deceased, having been reported missing on January 8ᵗʰ 1940.
Knowing that you would want further detail in this matter, I have made some enquiries, with the following result:
Michael disappeared from the family home on the night of January 7ᵗʰ, after an altercation with his father – there was a history of trouble in the family, and the boy seems to have been the major victim. A search over the next few days failed to find him. The weather at the time was very cold, with a severe frost that night and snow lying. He is therefore presumed dead, although his body

was never found; the assumption is that he drowned in the nearby River Great Ouse, either by accident or suicide, and his body was then swept away in the flood stream which followed the subsequent thaw.

I trust this information, though unfortunate, is useful. If I can be of further assistance in this matter, please do not hesitate to contact me again.

Percival Woollard, Partner
For Forman Woollard & Partners

* * *

'Mummy! Daddy! Look!' Michael and Harriet turned to the door of the Greyhound's public bar at their eldest son's excited shout:

'Ginny; Sam – good to see yeh! What'll yeh 'ave?' Ginny embraced her brother and kissed his cheek:

'Babycham fer me, Moikey – 'n Sam'll 'ave a point o' moild oonless 'e's changed 'is ways without tellin' me!' Harriet had been giving her brother a hug; now he nodded with a grin:

'Aye, that'll do, Moikey! 'Ow're yeh doin'?'

'We're foine, Sam. 'Ow 'bout yew?'

'Pretty good, mate. Council found oos a little 'ouse in Longford, joost oop the road from Mam 'n Dad, 'n we're gettin' settled in now.'

'No little Caplins on the way yet?' Harriet asked teasingly; Sam looked down at the little boy still clinging to his hand and smiled:

'Not yet – we're 'opin' ter 'ang on 'til things're a bit more settled. Yew still stickin' at three, are yeh?'

Harriet laughed:

'Yeah – they're enooff trooble! Fer now, any'ow.'

Michael clapped his brother-in-law on the shoulder and led him over to the bar for a fresh round of drinks while their wives sat together in the corner; Albert climbed onto his aunt's lap as his mother asked Ginny:

'Yeh saw Susie outsoide, did yeh?'

'Yeah – she 'n Freddie were playin' wi' soome o' the oother kiddies boy the boats. 'E's gettin' ter be a big lad, isn' 'e?'

'Aye!' Harriet smiled proudly: ''E's goin' ter be tall, loike 'is Daddy.'

'Freddie's not's big as Oi am!' Albert protested; Ginny gave him a hug:

''Course 'e isn't, Alby! Yeh're what, six now?'

'Nearly seven!'

'Roight! 'N yeh're still moy fav'rite nephew – boot don' tell Freddie, eh?' She whispered to the child, who giggled and hugged her back as she asked Harriet:

'Wher's Carrie?' Harriet sighed:

'She's stopped ter clean out the butty cabin, says she'll be 'ere later ter see yeh.'

'Never really got oover losin' er Charlie, 'as she?'

'She ain't so bad, now – it's near on three year, yeh know? Boot she still as 'er quoiet toimes, now 'n then.'

Their men rejoined them, passing glasses around, and pulled up two more chairs.

'Wher're yeh fer, Moikey?' Sam asked.

'West Drayt'n, wi' roadstone out o' Griff Quarry. Loaded terday.'

'Ben Vickuss's still keepin' yeh busy, then?'

'Oh, aye! We've got plenty o' work – 'e usually 'as a back load fer oos, most trips. 'E leaves oos a message at Bulls Bridge or Brentf'd, dependin', then 'ere at Suttons fer h'orders this end. What about yew, Sam?'

'Yeh know Oi got that job in the furniture place? They're teachin' me ter use the wood-turnin' lathes at the moment. Foreman says they'll 'ave me a proper trained-oop joiner in a few more moonths.'

'That's grand, Sam!' Harriet congratulated him; Ginny smiled:

'Aye, we're doin' foine, even if we do miss the cut. Oi'm workin' ther' too, in the canteen, loonchtoimes.'

''Ow's Dad now, Sam?' Harriet asked.

'Oh, 'e en't so bad. Back plays 'im oop a lot, so 'e don' get out mooch now, boot 'e sends 'is loove. Mam too – we said as we were coomin' ter see yeh ternoight.'

'D'yeh get ter see 'Anneys mooch?' Ginny asked; Michael grinned:

'Aye, we stop in ev'ry toime we get oop middle road! Alwes troy 'n mek it so's we stop ther' overnight – Vi's cookin's as good as ever!'

''Ow're Stevie 'n Ellie doin'?'

'Real good, Oi reckon,' Harriet told her: 'They've got a little girl now, called 'er Grace. 'N they've got a 'ouse o' their own, now – Ellie's dad bought it fer 'em when she got pregnant.'

'Josh's got 'imself a 'prenticeship with a firm o' h'engineers, doin' well boy the sound of it.' Michael added.

'What about Joe 'n Gracie 'n the kiddies? D'yeh see anythin' o' them?' Sam asked.

'Now 'n then, when we're down that end o' the Joonction. Yeh know they lost their yoongest kiddie?'

'Oh no! Li'l 'Enry? What 'appened?' Ginny's distress sounded in her voice.

'It were the TB as got 'im. Gabriel 'ad it 'n all, boot 'e pulled through h'okay.'

'Tell 'em 'ow sorry we both are when yeh see 'em next, won' yeh?' Sam commiserated.

'Yeh don' get ter see 'em yerselves?' He shook his head:

'We'd loike teh, boot ther's so mooch ter do at the moment, wi' decoratin' the 'ouse 'n ev'rythin'. 'Aven' seen 'em since Christmas.'

'We should wroite to 'em,' Ginny told him: 'Joey c'n read now, remember, as well as the kiddies!' He grinned at her:

'Yeah, we should! Yew c'n do that, can' yeh?'

''Noother job Oi've got, then!' she complained to the heavens, laughing. The door opened again, and they all looked around. Ginny got up, smiling, as Carrie walked over and gave her a hug; Sam took the girl's free hand in his:

'Carrie, loove, it's good ter see yeh! Let me get yeh a drink.' She smiled at him:

'Yeh're as 'andsome as ever, Sam Caplin! Oi'll 'ave a shandy, if yeh will.'

He chuckled and headed for the bar as she sank into his vacated chair.

'Yeh're lookin' well, Carrie,' Ginny told her; she smiled:

'Oi'm doin' all roight, Gin. It's grand ter see yeh! Oi'll joost stop fer the oone, then Oi'll get the children back ter the boats 'n put 'em ter bed so's yew all c'n catch oop wi' things.'

'Oi'll look after the kiddies, Carrie, yew stay 'n 'ave a drink or two,' Harriet protested, but the girl shook her head:

'No, it's h'okay 'Arrie – Oi'll coom back agen when they're asleep, mebbe.'

Sam returned with her drink, and went to stand behind his wife, slipping his arms around her neck and bending to kiss her as she looked up at him.

The conversation meandered around their lives, their friends and relations; Carrie took the children back, collecting Susie and Freddie on her way, and then returned after a while to rejoin the gathering. A last drink, a last chat, and Sam and Ginny left for the last bus back to Longford as Michael, Harriet and Carrie strolled back to the boats.

'Can yeh see oos ever leavin' the cut, Moikey?' Harriet put the question casually.

'Oi don' think Oi'd ever want teh, loove. Boot that ain't ter say it won' 'appen. Oi've bin thinkin' about Alby, 'n Susie – they could be in school if we was on the bank.'

''Yeh're a good teacher, Moikey – they're doin' all roight wi' yew, ain't they?' Carrie suggested.

'Yeah – boot are we doin' what's roight fer 'em, really? Are the goin' ter be jobs fer 'em on the cut when they're grown oop? If they 'ave ter work on the bank, they'd be mooch better fer a proper h'education.'

'They c'n read 'n wroite – Alby's near as good as me!'

'Oi know, Carrie – boot Oi still woonder what ter do fer the best, soomtoimes.'

Chapter Thirty-Eight

April 11ᵗʰ 1957

Forman Woollard and Partners, Solicitors
Stowe Chambers
West Street
Buckingham
England

   Dear Percy,
   Thank you for your letter of March 14ᵗʰ,
regarding the Morris case. Your information came
as something of a shock to us here in Australia
as our instructions from our client, while
unconventional, seemed quite clear.
   It is apparent from those instructions that
Anthony Morris believed his nephew to be alive
and well. I have since been in touch with the
station manager at Marloo Creek, and he assures
me that Mr Morris had several times spoken of
meeting his nephew, with a wife and children, on
the occasion of his father's funeral, for which
Mr Morris had returned to the UK.
   There is also in our possession a letter
addressed to 'Uncle Tony' and signed 'Michael',

dated late last year, shortly after the funeral of Frederick Morris. It gives no clues as to the whereabouts of this 'Michael', and there is no return address, but it also refers to a 'Harriet', presumably the wife, as well as an unknown number of children. The writing itself is unusual, being somewhat unformed, possibly childlike. We do not have the envelope and therefore no postmark which might assist in tracing the writer.

I appreciate that this is not a lot to go on, but I would be grateful if you can make further enquiries on our behalf to enable us to conclude this business in the best possible way.

    Yours, Brett Watson
    Weller Binstead and Watson

Percival Woollard peered over his glasses at his secretary as he lowered the letter to the desk in front of him:

'Have you read this, Sheila?'

'Yes, Mr Woollard.'

'What does this damned digger want us to do, find a ghost for him? The record is quite clear, Michael Thompson is dead! And I do wish he wouldn't call me Percy!'

'They never found the body, Mr Woollard.'

He looked at her:

'No – I suppose you're right. But suppose he is still alive – where the blazes are we supposed to start looking? And who are we looking for?'

'How old would this lad be now?'

'Oh, I don't know! Let me think – about, oh, twenty-seven or -eight.'

'Old enough to have a wife and maybe a few children?'

'Yes, I suppose so! But where the blue blazes is he? Even if he is still alive?'

'Maybe the abuse was bad enough for him to run away and not come back?'

'So what are you saying? He's gone and joined the circus?' Sheila, well used to Woollard's temperament, smiled patiently:

'Not the circus perhaps – a band of gypsies?' She suggested.

'Oh, in that case we've no hope of finding him!'

'Someone did, though.'

'Eh? What do you mean?'

'He went to his grandfather's funeral – someone must have known how to fmd him.' Woollard stared at her:

'I suppose so... The old man would have known, I imagine. If he hadn't died last year... Damned inconsiderate of him.'

'I don't suppose he did it deliberately, Mr Woollard.'

'There are no other living relatives, not that we know about anyway – I suppose we could start there, try the funeral directors, see if they have a list of the people who turned up...'

* * *

'Whatever 'ave yeh got ther' boy?'

Michael laughed at Bill Hanney's jocular question. A mild spring evening, and they'd run the boats up through Knowle locks and were tying them, still breasted, against the towpath as Bill strolled up to meet them.

''Alf a load o' timber, Bill!'

'Wher's the oother 'alf?' Bill looked around and waved as a dungaree-clad Carrie called a greeting from where she was tying the fore-ends.

'H'aylesb'ry.'

'Oh ah?' Michael straightened up and rubbed his hands together to displace the worst of the mud on them:

'Yer bank's a bit mooddy 'ere, mate! Got a split load this toime – twelve ton o' planked poine fer H'aylesb'ry 'n fourteen o' special 'ardwood fer Olton.'

'Ah – s'bin rainin' most o' the day. Took the H'aylesb'ry stooff in the motor, did yeh?' Bill had been casting a humorously critical eye over the oddly laden boats. The butty lay half-down in the water, with its hold partly full of the hardwood billets, while the motor rode high, its stem almost out of the water, completely empty.

'Aye – we left Carrie wi' the butty at Maffers 'n me 'n 'Arriet 'n the kids took the motor down the h'arm. Thought we'd 'ave dinner wi' you 'n Vi, if yeh're oop fer it? Then on ter Olton in the mornin'.'

'Left me all alone they did!' Carrie pretended distress, and Bill put his arm around her:

'Rotten booggers, en't they loove? 'Course yeh're all roight fer dinner, Vi'd be real oopset if yeh didn' stop in, yeh know that!'

'Good-oh! We'll joost get cleaned oop 'n we'll walk down wi' yeh.'

Bill sat on the gunwale smoking a roll-up while the others quickly washed and changed into their better clothes. In mere moments, an eager voice drew his attention:

''Ello, Ooncle Bill!' He looked around, pinching out his cigarette:

'Alby – 'ow're yeh doin' boy?'

''Oi'm foine, Ooncle Bill!' Albert came up and took his hand, smiling up at him, and Bill ruffled the boy's hair. His other hand was quickly grabbed by Susie, and then Freddie toddled up and put his chubby arms around Bill's knees, chuckling in delight at seeing his honorary uncle.

Bill laughed:

'Tek it easy, yew lot, yeh'll 'ave me in the cut else!'

''Ow are yeh, Bill?' Harriet stepped out onto the bank, and he bent forward as best he could to kiss her cheek:

'We're grand, 'Arriet. Yeh are coomin' fer dinner, eh?'

''S'long as Vi won' moind oos turnin' oop loike this?'

226

'Nah, 'course she won'! We saw yeh go boy, so she's got h'extra on already.' Michael joined them, looking around his almost-gathered crew:

'Waitin' fer Carrie are we?'

'Joost coomin', a voice called from within the butty cabin; then she emerged, in a pretty flowered print dress.

'Oh, yeh look loovely, girl!'

'Thank yeh, Mr 'Anney!'

She treated him to a coquettish grin and did a twirl on the towpath, making them all laugh.

They set off to walk down to the lengthsman's house, Bill still with a child attached to each hand; Freddie had released him, taking his father's hand instead.

'D'yeh get many split loads, Moikey?' Bill asked as they passed the top lock.

'Nah – oonce in a whoile. It's a bit of a nuisance, boot it's better'n no back-load at all. We're 'avin' ter roon back empt 'alf the toime now.'

'Yeh're still doin' all roight, though?'

'Oh, aye. Ben's keepin' oos pretty busy – mostly coal goin' South, wi' the odd load o' stone, 'n timber or metals coomin' back. All soobbin', fer Waterways or Willer Wren – we've doon oone or two trips down the H'Oxford cut ter Banbury, fer Barlows, boot that's bloody 'ard work wi' a butty in them narrer locks. Ther's plenty o' work ter keep oos goin'!'

'Tha's good, Moikey.'

'Yeh sound doubtful, Bill?' Harriet asked; the older ex-boatman shrugged:

'Oi joost get the oidea ther's less 'n less boats passin' oos as toime goes boy.'

'Loike Oi said, Bill, most o' the stooff goin' South's coal now, 'n that's coomin' from 'round Coventry. We only get oop this way if we get a load loike this'n, fer Olton, or soomat fer Sam'son Road.'

'Yeah, Oi guess so. Tell yeh what, though – we're seein' a few pleasure boats nowadays!'

'Pleasure boats, Bill? Yeh mean folks coom on the cut fer foon?' Michael sounded incredulous; Bill laughed:

'Yeah – don' seem sensible, doos it? Boot they do, boy! Most of 'em in little wooden boats, old loifeboats, things loike that. Look fer all the world as if they're 'avin' a good toime 'n all!'

'Coom on, Moikey, we've seen oone or two loike them arselves!' Carrie reminded him.

'Aye – 'n Oi didn' believe it then!'

Chapter Thirty-Nine

May 15th 1957

Weller Binstead and Watson
34 Wickham Terrace
Brisbane
Queensland
Australia

Dear Brett
*With reference to your Morris case: I am
pleased to inform you that we may be making
some progress.*
*I have followed back from Frederick Morris's
funeral, and believe I may have traced the young
man you are seeking. I am trying to arrange a
meeting, at which I will attempt to confirm if he
really is Michael Henry Thompson.*
I will keep you informed of progress.
Percival Woollard, partner
For Forman Woollard and Partners

* * *

Michael's face wore a puzzled expression as he strolled back to
the boats:

> *Michael – There is no back-load available for*
> *you immediately, so I suggest you return to*
> *Sutton's. Can you also stop by at my house on*
> *your way? And let me know when that is likely to*
> *be, as there is someone who wants to meet you.*
> *Love to Harriet and the children,*
> *Ben.*

'Sounds very mysterious, don' 'e?' Michael read the note over
again to Harriet and Carrie.

'Oi don' loike the sound of it,' Carrie commented, but Harriet
reassured her:

'Oh, yeh know Ben – if it'd bin anythin' nasty 'e'd 'ave warned
oos.' Carrie chuckled:

'Yeah – loike when that woman wanted ter tek Ginny, eh?'
They joined in her laughter at what had become a Baker family
legend, often repeated among the boating people.

The boats were tied in the layby at Bulls Bridge, after unloading
fifty tons of coal for the nearby Nestle chocolate factory the day
before. It was still early morning, the sun breaking through a light
mist in the promise of a fine spring day:

'If we get goin' now we c'n be in Braunston day after
tomorrow,' Harriet said.

'Aye. Oi'll go ter the h'office 'n ring Ben, tell 'im we'll be ther'.'
Half an hour later they were on their way:

'Olive's doin' dinner fer oos Wednesd'y noight,' Michael told
his wife as they stood together in the butty's stern well, watching
Carrie steer the motor under the bridge by the Nestle works.

'Did Ben tell yeh what 'is mysterious visitor's about?'

'Oi don' think 'e knows 'imself. 'E did say it was soomthin'
ter do wi' Grandad.'

'Grandad Morris?'

'Aye.'

'Oi thought that was all sorted las' year, after 'is buryin'?' Michael shrugged:

'So did Oi.'

* * *

'Mikey, Harriet, come on in! Carrie – how are you, love?' Ben Vickers met them at the door of the cottage. He ushered them into the living room: 'Mr Woollard has just arrived – Michael Baker, Mr Woollard.'

Michael regarded the portly man in the dark suit suspiciously, but he stepped forward to shake the outstretched hand:

'Mr Woollard.'

'Mr – er – Baker?'

'Moy woife, 'Arriet – 'n moy sister, Carrie.' Woollard shook each hand as it was offered, uncomfortably aware of the doubtful looks in their eyes. Olive Vickers put her head around the door of the room:

'Alby – Susie – Freddie – come in the kitchen with me, you can help with the dinner.' The children followed her eagerly when their mother nodded.

'Why don't we all sit down?' Ben suggested, waving Woollard to one of the armchairs. The man smiled uneasily:

'Thank you, Mr Vickers.'

'Yeh wanted ter see oos, Mr Woollard?' Michael sat with Harriet on the settee while Carrie stood behind them, leaning on its back.

'Yes, Mr... Baker. I am acting on behalf of a firm of solicitors in Brisbane, Australia...'

'What's this all about, then?' Woollard looked even more uncomfortable:

'I'll come to that in a moment, if I may. If you are who I think

you are, Mr Baker, this will be very much to your advantage.'
His tone was defensive; Michael allowed himself to relax:

'I'm sorry if we seem soospicious, Mr Woollard – las' toime soomeoone coom after oos loike this they troied ter tek moy sister away.'

'Oh – I see.' Woollard glanced at Carrie, who told him.

'Not me – ar oother sister.'

'Oh – well...' He turned back to Michael: 'Mr Baker – can you tell me when your birthday is?' Michael frowned in puzzlement, but he answered:

'Twentieth o' March.'

'What year were you born?'

'Noineteen twenty-noine.'

'So you're twenty-eight?'

'S'roight.' Woollard nodded:

'And how long have you been on the canal, working on the barges?' Michael caught Ben's flinch and smiled:

'They're boats, Mr Woollard, not barges. 'N Oi've bin on 'em since Oi was ten year old.'

'Oh – sorry. How did you come to do that, Mr Baker? Join the boats?'

We're gettin' ter the nitty-gritty o' this, Michael thought:

'Oi ran 'way from 'ome. Mr Woollard – Ben said this is soomat ter do wi' moy granddad, Fred Morris?'

'Indirectly, yes, it is.'

'Will it 'elp if Oi tell yeh that moy name then was Thompson – Moichael 'Enry Thompson?'

Woollard sat back and smiled:

'That is exactly what I am trying to establish, Mr... Baker?' Michael laughed now:

'Oi've bin Moichael Baker fer seventeen year now, Mr Woollard! Alby Baker took me in 'n brought me oop, yeh see.'

'I understand. Do you have any proof of your original identity? Papers, anything like that?'

'No. Oi thought that was all finished, see.' Carrie interrupted from behind him:

'Oi think Ginny's got yer birth sustificates soomwher' – she tol' me oonce Grandad'd given 'em to 'er.'

'That would be most helpful! Ginny is your other sister, is she?'

'Aye – she's married, lives in Coventry. We c'n get in tooch with 'er if yeh loike?'

'You can call her from here later, Mikey,' Ben told him.

'So – what is this all 'bout, Mr Woollard?' But the man answered him with a question:

'You met your uncle, Anthony Morris, at your grandfather's funeral, I understand?'

'Aye, we did.'

'I'm afraid I have some bad news for you all. Your uncle and his wife are both dead – they were caught in a fire at their home in Queensland, several months ago. As you may know, they had no children, so you, and your sisters of course, are their only surviving relatives.'

'What doos that mean?' Michael had visions of being presented with a bill for a funeral; Woollard saw his expression and smiled reassuringly:

'Anthony Morris was still alive when the station manager got him out of the house, but he died before the Flying Doctor service could reach him. He was able to tell O'Brien, the manager, that the estate should go to you if he died. That statement was witnessed by several of the hands, so it has force in law. His solicitors in Brisbane have been trying to trace you ever since – and now we've found you.'

Michael was still suspicious:

'Joost what doos that mean, Mr Woollard?' The man smiled:

'You are now the owner of Marloo Creek Station in central Queensland, Mr Baker. It is a substantial property, with a good income from its herds of beef cattle, and some wool production.'

'Soobstantial?'

'Around four thousand square miles.'

A stunned silence descended on the room, only broken by Carrie's disbelieving whisper:

'That's 'bout 'alf of H'England!'

Woollard paused to let it sink in before saying:

'However you look at it, Mr Baker, you are now a considerably wealthy man.'

* * *

'Well, now you've got a real decision to make, Michael.' The meal had been passed in near-silence, only the chattering of the children interrupting the thoughtful atmosphere; now Ben brought them back to thoughts of the future.

'We 'ave, ain't we? Should we go 'n troy ter roon this place arselves? Or sell it 'n tek the moony?'

'What did Ginny say when yeh called 'er?' Carrie asked; he laughed:

'Oi don' think she believed me! It's oop ter them as well, o' course – 'alf of it belongs ter 'er, boy roights.'

'What do yew think, Ben?' Harriet asked; Vickers sat back in his chair:

'It's your decision, you three, and Sam and Ginny. I don't want to influence you – but I will say this: I'm nearly seventy, and I won't mind retiring properly, if you don't need my help any more. So don't think you're letting me down if you decide to emigrate. If you stay, and stay on the cut, you'll have to be getting your own orders sometime soon anyway.'

'We could have a nice holiday,' Olive suggested: 'We'll come and visit you in Australia once you're settled!'

Their laughter echoed around the cottage kitchen.

Epilogue

Steven Hanney turned away from the window with a sigh and glanced at the calendar on his office wall: The twelfth of September, 1987: The season would be slowing down to its close over the next month, with just a surge of demand over the October school half-term holiday to round things off.

Saturday, and turn-around day for the fleet of hire-boats. The scene outside his window had been one of efficient, controlled chaos, as the teams of cleaners scurried from boat to boat and the yard men filled water and diesel tanks and pumped out toilets. The first of the week's new customers would be arriving at any moment – in fact, the murmur of voices through his partly-open office door suggested that they already had. But he had other things on his mind – two new boats to be built during the quiet winter months, the plans for them on his desk awaiting his approval – and the end-of-year accounts to be gone through with their accountant.

In the outer office, Grace Hanney looked up with a smile as another customer approached her desk:

'Good morning – can I help you?'

The tall, well-built man in the expensive-looking raincoat with a broad-brimmed hat on his greying sandy hair gave her a cheerful smile; behind him, she quickly took in the others of his party – a lady who had to be his wife, and another couple, perhaps slightly younger, the woman probably his sister from her looks.

He addressed her in a clearly southern-hemisphere accent:

'G'day – yeh've got a boat booked fer us today.' He looked at the nameplate on her desk: 'You're Grace Hanney, are yeh?'

'I am – do I know you, Mr...?' The man laughed:

'Yeh wouldn' remember me – but yer Dad will!' Grace smiled uncertainly at him as she got to her feet:

'He's in the office – shall I call him?'

'In there?' The man pointed to the door behind her.

'That's right, sir.'

The man chuckled again:

'Then fergive me, Grace...'

He stepped past her and paused by the partly-open door where he could not be seen from its far side, and raised his voice:

'Yew turn that lock round, Stevie 'Anney, 'n yeh'll be learnin' ter swim in it!'

If you've enjoyed this book, you'll be pleased to know that there are other books available from the same author. See overleaf...

'Northamptonshire's own answer to Inspector Morse'
Image Magazine

'Impossible to put down'
ChoiceMagazine

'Plots brimming with unexpected twists'
What's On Magazine

These four D.I. David Russell novels may be ordered from any good bookshop. Just ask for:

Flashback by Geoffrey Lewis   ISBN 978-0-9545624-0-3
Strangers by Geoffrey Lewis   ISBN 978-0-9545624-1-0
Winter's Tale by Geoffrey Lewis   ISBN 978-0-9545624-2-7
Cycle by Geoffrey Lewis   ISBN 978-0-9545624-3-4

published by SGM Publishing.

SGM Publishing
35 Stacey Avenue, Wolverton, Milton Keynes, Bucks MK12 5DN
info@sgmpublishing.co.uk
www.sgmpublishing.co.uk

Departing from the detective novels for which he is known, in *Starlight* Geoffrey Lewis tells a tale of schoolboy friendship set against the backdrop of the Oxford Canal in the days when the commercial trade was in decline; the canal itself threatened with closure. In a story where the mood ranges from heartwarming humour to unbearable poignancy, he conjures up the world of the 1950s; factual events and real characters flit past in the background as he leads the reader through the long heat-wave of the summer of 1955, as it was seen by an eleven-year-old boy living in a little North Oxfordshire village.

Starlight was published in 2005 - for more information, please check our website at www.sgmpublishing.co.uk or telephone 07792 497116. ISBN 978-0-9545624-5-8. Cover price £6.99.

The first two titles in the Michael Baker trilogy which finishes with this title, *The New Number One*.

It all started when ten-year-old Michael Thompson had had enough. Mentally and physically abused by his drunken father, treated like a skivvy by his mother, he had taken all that his miserable life could throw at him; but then the final blow came when his dog was taken away as well: On a bitter cold night in January, 1940, he set out to commit suicide – but all does not go according to plan…

The three books tell a story of England's canals through the Second World War and beyond. The pressure and the pain, the humour and resilience of the boating people. Tragic and heart-warming, this trilogy charts the progress of a job becoming ever more difficult, against the broader panorama of worldwide events.